HEADLESS BEINGS

Headless Beings

BY MARGARET MALCOLM

PUBLISHED FOR THE CRIME CLUB BY

DOUBLEDAY & COMPANY, INC.

GARDEN CITY, NEW YORK, 1973

HEADLESS BEINGS is a work of fiction
based on certain observed incidents in
Great Britain. The characters and situations
are all fictitious.

Margaret Malcolm

ISBN: 0-385-03802-X
Library of Congress Catalog Card Number 73-79693
Copyright © 1973 by Doubleday & Company, Inc.
All Rights Reserved
Printed in the United States of America
First Edition

I

For some strange reason I couldn't stop thinking about Culloden, and suddenly I said, "Gilbert, there were several young chaps in the thatched hut, weren't there? You saw them, too . . . didn't you?"

He glanced at me quickly and back to the road. "Oh. So you're still there?" He was having trouble with the car, which seemed to be holding a series of small jousts inside the engine, galloping ahead furiously and colliding with something.

I held my breath. "I thought you had the car checked yesterday."

He moved defensively. "I did." His voice was controlled, and it made me hesitate to say anything more, but I didn't like the way the car acted.

Then it settled down and I asked, "Hadn't something changed, after we walked around the hut? When we came back, something was gone . . . wasn't it?"

He laughed. "Aunt Hortense, you're out of your mind."

"I'm beginning to think so, too. What is it about this land? I see, and then I don't. I blink and the glimpse is gone." I rubbed my eyes. All the color! And the land swelled, almost seemed to move. I decided to have my glasses checked.

"Say it out loud, Auntie. You know it helps you to think if you hear it."

"I don't want to be a bore, really . . . but something keeps me thinking about it."

"Out with it."

"That's just it . . . I don't know! I went outside, and I thought how terribly small, how terribly low. I'd hate to live there all my life, that close roof,—like a hat pulled down around your ears."

"Continue. More stream of consciousness."

"All those people. That couple by the door. Knapsacks. Not very young. The man with them kept his back to us. I couldn't hear. And a bunch of young men, chaps with their hands in their back pockets and their elbows sticking out, just moving around."

"Aunt Hortense, you see the darndest things!"

"But Gil"—I drew in my breath—"I know they were there! I kept looking for the fellow in charge, and none of them moved toward me with that look. Then we went back and I wanted to get some of those queer pamphlets from the rack, and everyone was gone. The funny pamphlets, too. Only tourist information."

"Well, you'd better forget it or you'll go balmy. Here, look at this! Here's something to think about! Here's a real sight!"

He jerked the car into a lay-by and snapped off the engine.

"Just look at that! Just look at that, will you!" His voice high with excitement, he shoved open the door, jumped out and ran toward a high spot on the other side of the road and stood there moving his head from side to side. The door banged shut.

I opened my door and listened. There was complete silence. Long sweeping rolls of land folded sheets of layered water in the distance, water spread like beaten silver between folds of deepest green. The land undulated up from the water, higher and higher to the horizon as far as I could see. There was something curious about it, some strangeness. Lochs, they called them here.

I turned my head and looked at the lochs sidewise. Sure enough— there were several levels to the water. Land rose up, rounded and in gentle slopes, with spines on their summits. The bens. So many, grouped like huge carcasses of prehistoric beasts, green, their heads buried under water. In a moment they would rise, their backs would hump and the heads emerge. They'd fling off the ooze from their huge nostrils and bellow. I waited.

But nothing changed except the mist, which lightened. In the far distance the clouds opened and shafts of sun poured gold streaks across purple back clouds, speckling the wide landscape. There was no sound.

Gilbert got back into the car, and neither of us spoke. He turned the key, and for a long time the engine churned. Then with a cough, the spark caught. We drove rapidly along twisted roads and slowed down on the climbs through the narrow gorges. The bens bent their summits forward like solicitous old men leaning over us. I could visualize our small car creeping between them, looking like a child's tiny toy. The Scots even gave them human names: Ben Nevis, Ben Drummond, Ben Lomond. They thought of them as old men, turned to stone.

Darkness increased and rain streaked the windscreen, and the bens were hidden in heavy clouds. I welcomed this change, for the sight was moving; it had awed and frightened; it was almost too much.

My thoughts came back to small affairs. I might use this time to put the address on Gretchen's letter. I had the address book now. I reached into the back seat and pulled my brief case up and rummaged inside it.

"Gilbert, I've lost my brief case!" I wailed, pulling out typed papers, scientific lists of numbers and symbols, pages of them. I flicked them to the floor and pulled out notebooks of scientific jargon, lines of neat typing.

The car had been running smoothly, and Gilbert held the gas steady, only glancing at me. I might have said that I'd seen a bug. He looked unconcerned.

"Gilbert, we've got to stop! This isn't my brief case!" I pulled out other notebooks and more pages of typed lines. "All that genealogical work I did—gone!" I could not believe that he would not slow down. We were moving as fast as before.

"We've got to go back! Turn around! I have to go back!"

Indecision, beginning with a queer look at his chin that swept upward and involved his eyes, finally swept into his mind. He slowed the car slightly.

"Hortense, be sure! You had it this morning when we left. I picked it up with your bags and put them all in."

He was looking at the brief case as if I had lost my senses.

"Yes, yes. But this isn't mine!"

He lessened the pressure on the gas pedal and peered at me, then at the brief case, which was nearly under his nose in the cramped little car. The motor coughed. He made a gesture of exasperation. He was irritated with both me and the car.

"But it looks like yours." His tone was reasonable.

"I know it does, but it's not! It even has the same scratches, but it's not mine! We've got to stop!"

He kept on driving slowly, his eyes moving from my face to the road, clearly doubting my sanity. I tensed. Someone had taken mine, and had made a substitute. I began to get frightened. I needed that research I had done! Somebody had stolen it; not only that, but had gone to a lot of trouble to see that I had a bag which looked just like my own. Anger and fear mixed.

I made an attempt to check my rising emotions. "Look, the road's narrow, but you *can* turn, Gilbert," I pleaded. Who would have taken my papers? Who had concealed it long enough to get us out of Inverness? Suspicion is completely foreign to me; it was unnerving. I was coming unwound.

Gilbert coasted to a lay-by and stopped. He seemed to be having as much trouble with his feelings as I was; there was exasperation, doubt, and suspicion of me showing there in his face. Just as he reached for the ignition key, the motor coughed out.

I sat in silence and watched him fuss with the engine. Then, forcing his lips shut over the word that barely escaped, he bent and began a deliberate examination of the papers, each one separately. My exasperation and irritation grew. I now hated Gilbert.

"You're right," he stated flatly, after looking at everything thoroughly.

"It's real good of you to say so," I snapped.

While he had been poking through the contents of the brief case, I had been examining myself: you are cockeyed, Hortense, but you aren't insane. You do not wear a flowerpot instead of a hat. You do not eye other people with suspicion to see if they're about to stab you. You do not touch the doorjamb every time you go through to make sure it's still there. You are batty, but you're sane.

I said, loftily, "Perhaps you agree that we have to go back?" I was as high in my tone as the Salisbury cathedral spire.

At his quick glance up, I continued, "Oh, Gilbert, I know I act balmy. It just keeps off those terrible bores. Really, I know. Don't you understand? Now please turn around." I had calmed down a little; now I felt sorry for him.

He moved his hand toward the ignition and let it hover. "I just don't like the way the car's acting. Something's wrong with it. It acts as if someone threw trash in the fuel line—a handful of sand. Something like that. I don't think it'll make it back, not as far as Inverness. No way!"

"Gilbert! Don't think of the car! It doesn't matter; I don't care! Throw it away afterward. Please!"

He was staring ahead in silence. I bit my lip. After a long time he shook his head. "We can't. Not like this. Not now. It's dark. Here, get out of the way—" And he half pushed me to one side and opened the glove compartment, extracted a map and spread it over our knees.

I sat and stewed. I hated his deliberate ways. Of course he'd had to develop them, all those years of scientific research. He didn't need to use them now! What if we only chugged back? The pony express, the United States Mail—they could have done it! If the car broke down, never ran again, if the rain turned to sleet, a new Ice Age began, and darkness became eternal night—it made no difference. I had to get back to that hotel. Or the records room.

Gilbert thought so long that I wanted to poke him with my corsage pin. Finally I snapped, "Oh, come on! Let's move!"

"Now think, Hortense! Think back to where you last had your own case."

"So you agree this isn't mine? How nice." I drew into my coat collar and regarded him gloomily.

For a long time he looked straight ahead. Then again he asked about the last time I'd been sure the brief case was my own. It was too much.

"I will scream if you don't start the car at once. I will scream very high and loud, and make you wish you'd never been born to your mother, my dear sister, and that you—"

"Oh, stop it!"

We glared at each other like a couple of fools. Suddenly I started to laugh. Gilbert's face took on a long-suffering look, and then the tears started and I fished out a handkerchief and mopped my eyes and sobbed for a while. Later I blew my nose.

"All right. I'm okay. I don't try to make you mad, Gilbert, but I've got to get that brief case. Don't you see? All those records—all that stuff I found out about that famous Scot for those Bruces down in North Carolina—all that stuff I copied yesterday and the day before? I wish I'd never heard of Stewart Bruce!"

"Just take it easy, will you, Aunt Hortense? And let me explain: this damned car isn't up to going much of anywhere. Now don't get all excited, we'll make it down this bunch of hills—bens—and coast into the nearest petrol station. I promise to help you get your own brief case. Okay?"

He was sweetly reasonable. The mist washed the windscreen gently, like a mother cat washing her kittens. The world was still turning. What had been lost, really? He was very young, and he was very dear. And I *had* been acting like a bitch.

I took a deep breath. "I took it with me when I went up to that old castle. Where the records room is, in Inverness." I closed the brief case I'd been clutching, aware that it was heavy and that I held it as if I were drowning, and it was a life jacket. After I'd tossed it into the back seat I said, "I've already been all through this in my own mind, you know."

"Never mind the snide stuff. I think slowly. And then what?"

"I read through the lists of names again. Stewart Bruce's had been initialed." He was making small motions of his hands in front of his face. "It doesn't matter. It meant that Alan Bruce verified his brother's—Stewart's—death at Culloden. I copied out some facts from a book of local history. Old Scottish clans began again in America; some of the names, things like that. Then I had to go to the rest room."

"The rest room?" He was shaking his head.

"As a matter of fact, I did. It was a long morning. And when I washed my hands I thought how odd about those two fellows out there."

"What two fellows?" He was starting to look interested.

"Those two fellows with the beards. In the stacks. The records room. They seemed to know me. They were awfully quiet."

"Aunt Hortense, you have the average American's dislike of—"

"I do not! I like beards! Anyway, it wasn't the beards. It was something else." I frowned.

"Good God! I'll never understand women!" He was shaking his head.

"That's it!" I sat up straight.

"What? Women?"

"No. The rest room!"

Gilbert rubbed a hand over his forehead. "The rest room?" His voice sounded tired. "What in the hell happened in there? My God, Aunt Hortense!"

"Don't swear, Gilbert. It was after the rest room. During it, too. I'm sure it was! It had to be!"

"Do let me in on the little secret of what you saw in there." He regarded me in patient hostility, the headlights' reflection showing two small furrows between his eyebrows.

"Oh, for heaven's sake! Turn around, Gilbert! It happened while I was in there. Somebody took my brief case! Don't you understand!"

"Who in the name of all that's holy would want *your* stuff?"

"That's not the point! Somebody did. I don't know! Gilbert, stop acting like that. Somebody wanted it, and somebody took it!"

Gilbert exhaled and thought. I saw him go through all the motions that said he was deciding. I got more and more restless. These blasted bens! That terrible mist! It was raining now, and it was just plain spooky to sit here in the dark and think about someone stealing my brief case. For all I knew, they were sneaking up on us now from behind, a claymore in their hands. Or whatever it was modern Scots carry.

"They're called dirks," I said aloud, shivering.

"Huh?" But it had brought him out of his reverie.

"Please try the engine again," I begged. "Maybe it'll start now. This rain—you always say moisture inside the carburetor—" I stopped at his look, but began again. "I've got to *do* something, Gilbert. I'll find a telephone. I'll call Mrs. MacIver at the Glen Mhora and tell her to please call the police, and to expect us back tomorrow."

His hand went back to the ignition. It was no go. Nothing happened.

The thought of police gave a different focus to my thoughts. I sat stunned. What was happening? Gilbert kept trying the ignition. Then he finally got out and walked to the back of the little car and fussed around. He came back, stood looking up and down the deserted road as if he might conjure up a passing car. He got inside finally, pushed me back into my corner and opened up the glove compartment again. He swore.

"What a damned mess! Should've known there wouldn't be a flashlight!"

He got out and headed to the rear. I got out, too, wobbling a bit. "I'll start walking down that way." I pointed ahead. "You keep fussing with the car. I'll find someone. A telephone. Something; maybe even a garage."

He came to stand next to me. "I don't like it. We were in good shape. Something's been bollixed. How in hell do you know what you'll find?" He batted a fist into his open palm gently, his eyebrows drawn together.

He put a hand on my arm. "Look, Aunt Hortense, you start off if you want to; maybe you'll find something. But I doubt it. Looks as if we're right between everything. It's miles of this stuff. It's all deserted."

"This isn't America!" I snorted. "There can't be miles of nothing! It's not Kansas, Gilbert. Great Britain has one of the highest population densities—" But he stopped me.

"Okay." His tone was flat. "See what you can find. But we're a long way from anywhere. I'll give you fifteen minutes. If you don't find a telephone or something by then, come back. D'you hear?"

He looked young and very anxious. I opened my handbag and gave him a couple of the packs of matches I always pick up in restaurants, and he promised to see if he could find the difficulty quickly. I promised that I'd come back in fifteen minutes. We checked our watches and I started out.

He never would have let me go off down that road if he had

known how long it would be before we saw each other again. I walked as fast as I could, hoping he'd pull up beside me at any minute. I descended and turned a curve; now the headlights faded away. I probed at the road with my cane, listening for the throb of the little engine. Maybe he'd be here in another minute, the door held open.

In the darkness the distance seemed immense. Everything was farther than it had seemed when I was inside the car. Mountains, dark and forbidding, loomed on each side. I wished that I could rail at Gilbert. It would be a comfort. There was no one.

You have me.

Hmph. You're part of *me!* If I bid you, you'll disappear; you're a figment, a pure figment. Listen to Gilbert and he'll tell you. Science has proved that man is a group of tissues, largely water, bounded on one side by—I mean surrounded by another kind of tissues which we call "skin." When the skin is unbroken, disease germs are prevented from—

The road was hard to see. I stubbornly put one foot after the other. Surely there must be someone in this vast landscape! A road means men; men made it and men move along it. Men in cars. Man, embracing woman. Generic term: Mankind. Someone will come along.

But there were no cars. Seldom have so few lived apart from so many. I pushed my cane carefully with each step and went on. Fifteen minutes isn't a long time, I said to myself. I dared the two streaks of Gilbert's headlights to appear, any car's headlights to appear. I kept on descending the road, cautiously. The darkness and mist deepened.

What a land to live in! What a place to be marooned! Far from everybody human, every trace of humankind. Man embracing woman—a warm thought; a far possibility! So they fought over this land, began things they couldn't finish for this bleak ground! Big deal! Didn't have sense enough to finish.

This was their land. Their home.

Stop it, will you? I'm not playing games. Yes, they *fought!* Lost half their men, doing it! I'd give a couple of pounds sterling now to see one fighting, warm-blooded Scotsman. Maybe he'd stop fighting for one damn minute and help an old woman. I need it.

You and your disguises! Think you've got a good one, eh? Baggy coat, saggy handbag, glasses. Smart, too, aren't you? Go on—use your big brain!

My mind's perfectly all right! I need light.

No need to be so testy. Restrain yourself.

Restrain myself? I'm so restrained I feel strapped down! I'll burst into little pieces if anyone comes up behind in this dark and says, "Boo." Small pieces, that'll fly all over this blasted landscape like a Salvador Dali painting. Drooping over tree limbs—if they've got any trees here. Probably not.

Be calm. Be quiet. Stop being angry and afraid. Stop trying to prove yourself. You have a good deal of sense. You need more before you understand.

Understand what? I put my faith in feet. Right now they're doing fairly well; one after the other. This cane helps a bit, too. What can *you* do?

I can guide you.

Fine. Provide light.

There was a long quiet time. I sloshed along the wet road and wished that I didn't feel so alone. I had rather liked that silly conversation with myself. Or it had seemed to be myself. It gave me something to think about besides the wet and cold; I could match wits with it, at least. I hoped that I hadn't done away with it; I *had* been just a bit irreligious.

You're coming to a bend in the road. You can't see it yet; it's just a few more steps. Keep on with one foot after the other. Fine. Now, down below, around the bend, there is a place. Keep on; left, right. That's it.

I can do that alone. In fact I have been for years, except when I broke that hip. I'm also watching my watch. I've got just two minutes to discover that place you promise. I'll keep going until the big hand reaches this place on the dial. How about that light?

I had been going downhill steadily. At the bottom the land opened up wider. There was more sky to be seen, and at the far north was a bit of lighter cloud. The slight illumination helped considerably. I navigated a slight curve in the road.

My golly! My golly! Sure enough, a light shone down there.

I moved faster, feet pounding against the narrow macadam. With a half minute left, I had made it.

The building to one side looked small from the road, but I hadn't yet learned to reckon distances in these parts. It was surprising to find that the narrow lane up to the building was so long. I tried to increase my speed. I had made it!

Nearer, the place loomed huge. It was apparently a ski lodge, some kind of hotel. Its size, so far from any town and so near the mountains, suggested the plausibility of a winter resort. It was very new: the ground near the building, seen in the bright light which poured from the windows, had not yet healed. No new grass had taken over yet close to the walls, and no planting of shrubbery broke the abrupt rise of walls from the earth.

Through wide french doors and windows the yellow light poured across rough green hummocks. Everything showed the need for a good landscape gardener. New though it unmistakably was, there seemed to be a great many people inside. It struck me as odd for only a moment that we were in midsummer. This was civilization. Telephones. And help.

From the porch I saw many very young people; young men with beards and girls with long hair. They were moving about, some others coming into the lobby of the place from what seemed to be a dining room, darkened, just to one side. I pushed open the door. I wondered why so many here, in this deserted spot of earth.

The room paused in a sudden tableau. Faces stared. I had a strong urge to duck out into the night and run back up the hill to Gilbert. But just beyond the registration desk was a wall telephone. I took a deep breath and pushed back the strange impression, marched toward the telephone as if it were an island in a hurricane. I took off my glasses and wiped off the mist.

So there are young people here; so they stare. Bad manners, and they'll learn. As you did, a long time ago.

I found the telephone book and riffled the pages, hearing a subdued murmur, knowing that some of the kids had passed down the long hall behind me toward the back part of the building.

Let's see—Inverness. Two shillings. Dial oo and wait for operator.

I rummaged inside my purse. Paper notes were crumpled and pushed down on top of the coins. I finally found two shillings and thankfully turned to the instrument, shielded by a curved clear-plastic screen over its top, open to the room otherwise. I would have preferred a closed booth, but what good luck to find a telephone! I stood just a bit off the lobby in the end of the hallway which ran down into darkness at its end. A bit of light down there, a red-glowing WAY OUT sign at the turn.

So many impressions: glasses smudged; hope I remember right. Coins, double zero. Strange, something odd about this place. New. Smells of paint and linseed oil, varnish. It was well furnished. The lounge, when I turned just a bit to my right, had big throw rugs of dark colors against polished wood floor. Very nice. A good change from those red carpets and big gold medallions in English hotels. Good for the Scots! Nice subdued taste.

The telephone system was rotten. So long, always you wait so long. There were quite a lot of armchairs; tables with lamps on them, lit. A wide fireplace across the back of the lounge, across the hall opening, almost in front of me. Most of the kids had left. Nice fire—good! Good—no potted palms.

The line whined; a distant voice said, "Operator?" That twang—they did it here, too. A hand came down on the receiver fork. Silence.

"Good evening, madam. Perhaps we can help?"

I gasped, turned and looked into the face of the woman I had seen in the graveyard in Chipping Cranford.

I was leaning on my cane, considering why the curious black weathering on the Norman carving over the east portico arch, when the cane tip caught between the cobblestones. I yanked it out, and it showered a spray of pebbles into the heavy shrubbery by the dark stone wall. At that moment a streak of white flew out and scrambled into the sepulcher to my left; startled, I reeled, upset with myself for being put off by a cat. Gilbert had gone around the church to try the doors, and the wind had risen. I could hear him coming back on the little path bounding the church building. It was good to know he'd soon be at my side.

But from around the corner appeared a woman in her late thirties. She wore dark red slacks and a matching coat, the collar turned up coachman fashion. Her brown hair hung straight to her shoulders, where she'd had it cut bluntly. Just as she came abreast of me the wind snatched her hair upright, sent it streaming out around her face, and then straight up. Suddenly it dropped back onto her shoulders as if she had combed it. She stared at me as she passed, her hands in her pockets and her shoulders hunched, not breaking a slow stride.

I might have dismissed her from my mind without further thought, except that she wore a pair of huge, circular glasses of a deep pink color, which covered half her brow and extended halfway over her cheeks. In the fading light under the giant yews and oaks, she had a strange, compelling appearance. She was followed at a slight distance by a younger woman of quite unremarkable looks.

I stood braced on the cane for several moments after they disappeared through the churchyard gate, and it was annoying that when I tried to call to Gilbert, my voice came muffled by a frog in my throat. I had to clear it several times before I made a clear sound.

He appeared immediately, almost close enough to have seen the women. His hearty voice saying that the church was locked all around, and his strong hand under my elbow guiding me toward the street were comfortable. "You'll just have to come back in the morn-

ing, old thing. Do you think the Sloans'll mind waiting another day
for a message from the dead? Let's make for the pub at the Queen's
Arms. You look cold, scared to death, too. How about a glass of Harp
and bed?" He shivered. "This is called summer?"

I would have known her anyway, even without the glasses, so
strongly etched into my mind from that night in Chipping Cranford.
Now it seemed strangely good to see someone I had seen before,
and the offer of help was a godsend.

"Is there some kind of trouble?"

I waved an arm. "We're stuck up there on the road. My nephew.
I thought I'd call Inverness." So good to talk to another human! So
good to see the nod of comprehension, feel the hand on my arm
guiding me to a chair.

"Do sit down, madam. You look all in. Would you like something
to drink? A bit of whiskey? Of course." She held out a hand and one
of the young men came forward with a tray holding the liquor,
glass and soda. When she had fixed the drink and handed it to me,
she asked for directions to the car. By now she had summoned a
second chap, who stood listening. All of these fellows were bearded.

In a moment the chap went out into the night. I sipped my drink,
wondering about these young people. The girls wore their hair long
and the men were bearded; they looked like almost any bunch of
hippies, but with one difference: the men's hair was cropped; not too
short, no burr haircuts, but cut. They did look clean. They were milling about the room, some of them going up the stairs behind the
reception desk, others into the darkened room which I assumed was
the dining room. Several who had been sitting in the lounge arose
when I glanced their way, and moved off. So many young people!

As if she knew my thoughts, the woman said, "We're getting the
place ready for the winter trade. These young people are university
students, working during their long holiday. A good way to get experience, don't you agree?"

I nodded. The drink felt good. "You have a garage?" I asked.

"Not yet, although we're planning one."

I struggled to my feet. "I've got to call Inverness."

She put a hand on my arm. "My dear lady, won't you let one of the young women take care of that? Here, just give Frances your number. She can stand there and keep trying. Sometimes it takes a good bit of time; we are away from things just a bit."

The girl was already at our side. I gave her the coins and the number and sipped again at the drink, already warming the miles of tubing and inner passageways.

Rose Glasses stood. "I'm sure you'd like dinner. You haven't eaten, have you? Please don't protest: it's no trouble. There's plenty."

The girl was staying there at the telephone, occasionally jiggling the fork. Rose Glasses came back with a tray. Roast beef, Yorkshire pudding in its red juices, new little boiled potatoes and cabbage. "You just eat and relax. When your nephew comes, we'll fix him another." She disappeared into the dining room again.

I ate and felt the tensions slipping away. Several times I glanced at my watch. It was taking much longer for that chap to help Gilbert than it should. The little car should be able to coast downhill if they couldn't fix the motor.

Perhaps they had decided to work on it up there: a silly plan in this dark and rain. But men often seem to choose difficult ways, I appeased myself. I wiggled around for another look at the door. Maybe Gilbert would walk in at any moment. The kids had gone from the lounge. The room seemed unnaturally empty; it looked deserted.

But the kids weren't paying guests, I reminded myself. Probably they were upstairs in their rooms catching up on all kinds of things, perhaps including sleep. They were here to work, not to lounge. They had just finished dinner when I entered, probably.

Things were too quiet, too deserted. Nobody manned the reception desk. Explainable, Hortense; nobody is expected. The place really isn't open.

But beyond the desk the girl had left the telephone. She had been stationed there. Why hadn't she stayed? I got up and went to the telephone, remembering that first call I'd tried to make, when the fork had been pulled down. It had given me a jolt. Why hadn't I reacted more strongly to the peculiar act of having a call cut off? Rose Glasses had been so immediately helpful, had then reinforced her offer to help with food and drink. So helpful; so comforting. That chap with the whiskey—he'd materialized very quickly, too. Almost too quickly. Almost as if they'd known what I needed. And the chap who'd gone up to help.

I got out the coins, studied the phone book, dropped the coins and listened. Dead.

I jiggled the fork and waited. I held back growing dismay. In the hinterlands telephone service is discontinued after ten at night. A glance at the time proved that it was only nine-thirty. I glanced around, wishing for someone to come through. Perhaps they'd had trouble with the telephone before. I wanted to ask many questions.

No one came. It was so quiet!

After a while I went back to the chair. I must not let my nervousness grow. Many things work out; fear and apprehension only increase strain on the nervous system. There had been enough of that. Sit and wait; don't push the panic button. Anyway, waiting always seems long.

But something was needed to fill the time. I decided to go over the events of the past two days. If I was quiet and studied each thing, step by step, I might find the answer to the mystery of my filched brief case. Surely Gilbert would come before I had finished!

Some chemist's notebooks and papers had gotten into my hands; his brief case looked just like mine on the outside; inside, a small zippered pocket was missing. Which proved that it was not mine. Maybe the man was looking for his things, as upset as I was.

If I had picked it up by mistake—but if I had, when?

Perhaps I had been confused with somebody else, possibly someone under surveillance, someone suspicious and being watched. But a chemist? A new and deeper mystery. How could it have happened? Taken from the Glen Mhora room while we were at dinner? Why?

Had someone been suspicious of me? Someone had substituted a brief case sometime. In the records room at Inverness? I had only been trying to learn the ancestral line of an American family, who claimed the notable Stewart Bruce as its distinguished forebear, and who had asked me to verify the legend that had come down word of mouth. Those chaps in the records room—they, too, had had beards.

Why would anyone want to interfere with me, a genealogist? They *had* been different; the man in the room on the first day I'd gone there was not young, or bearded.

Beards! No, I *do not* dislike beards! Oh, surely Gilbert will walk in now, red-faced and wet and angry! He'll be furious at the car and the delay; probably at me, too. That was his way; his anger spread out for a short time and encompassed anything near. Where was he? I'd be glad to have him come in now, anger and all. Where was everyone?

I shifted around to see the door again. The night was as dark as before. The windows reflected the bright lights of the lounge, good-looking chandeliers of a rustic type that held many light bulbs. The dim red WAY OUT light at the end of the hall beyond the reception desk was even reflected. It was very dim, that hallway beyond the desk. I turned and stared into the dark at its end until my eyes watered. Did I only think that someone stood in the darkness and watched? I blinked back the flow of tears from eyestrain. Impossible to see. My eyes were playing tricks. Someone seemed to be down there in the dark, watching, but I could not see well enough to tell.

I realized that I had for some time been shifting around and turning my head. I was letting myself get worked up into a state of nerves; yet Gilbert should surely have come by now! The quiet of the place was unnatural, yet I didn't feel alone. It was eerie.

I determined to allow fifteen minutes for the situation to change, and if nothing happened by then I would leave. I looked at my watch.

Waiting without something to do is hard for most people, harder for me, for if a bus is late I'm inclined to walk a few blocks. I looked around the lounge for books or a magazine. There were none. To fill in the time, I fished up a small file from my handbag and smiled rather self-consciously at my glance around the room to see if anyone might take offense. Of course there was no one.

That took only a few minutes. The intense silence and absence of people was preying on my nerves. I had had enough. I decided to leave, whether the time I had set was up or not, and put a small bill on the tray which would more than pay for the dinner and drink, pulled on my coat and went toward the door. I half expected to find

Gilbert coming up the narrow roadway, and if he was hungry or not, we'd find some other place for him to eat. I wanted no more of this odd crowd.

My few steps across the room seemed heavy and weighted with importance, as if watched. I tried to shake off the feeling as I twisted the handle. It turned easily, on the opposite side the outdoor handle moved with it, but the door was stuck. I pushed, then pulled, and finally threw my body's weight against it, only gradually understanding that it was locked.

I felt my scalp prick, and in a flow of panic, I turned and scanned the room, my eyes flicking back and forth in search of anyone alive. I had stumbled into a queer place, was among depraved people who had made sure that the door was locked and then had disappeared. Yet there was a certainty that they were all here.

I crept to the telephone, fearful of making any sound, jumping when the coins clacked into the metal box. I could hear my own breathing on the line, and constantly kept my eyes moving across the room. The line was dead.

Stealthily, I pulled the fork down. The money came into the return box with a rackety-clack. I jumped and retrieved the coins with shaking fingers, holding my breath at their silvery slither in among the other coins in the purse, then turned very slowly to peer again down the dark hall, where the red glow of the WAY OUT sign seemed to mock. There seemed to be a hallway going off to the left, but it was quite dim, and now I feared my own senses.

I went back to the lounge, hoping to find something in the reception desk that would give the name of the place, or a newspaper or a letterhead bearing the lodge name. Surely I was having a bad dream! Not all of those young people had fallen asleep. Had they deserted the place?

The desk was clean, the drawers beneath clean, the cubbyholes on the wall at the back empty, and as I searched, my fear became overlaid with a new emotion of guilt, to be now searching through a desk not belonging to me. The strange sensation of dreaming persisted, yet on the small table next to the chair I had occupied was the dinner tray, the fat now congealed on the plate.

That sight helped to restore a little balance, and I moved finally to the center of the lounge to scan the balcony that surrounded it on three sides. Could anyone be up there, above my head? Its heavy, dark railings seemed to conceal no one, the many lights of the chandeliers allowing for no dark spots. I called loudly, "Hallo! Anybody here?" Then called again. The call echoed in the high rafters, but there was no answer and no one came.

Completely nonplussed, I moved slowly around the room, trying to scan the balcony and to see down the hallway beyond the desk. How could they have not heard?

I must find someone! I must get out! I would have to look around this place, find a way out or find a living, breathing person who would explain what was happening. I forced myself toward the dining room in quiet so intense that I could hear my spine clicking with each step. At the door I paused for a long time, afraid to open it and go on.

Then I made myself push it open. It went in slowly, and I stood still and watched the shaft of light broaden across the floor, hearing myself breathe in short gasps, angry at myself for my fears, angry at the situation, only half believing it and yet knowing that I was not asleep and dreaming. The light shaft revealed many small tables covered with white cloths, the room very dark on either side. What if someone waited there? I hesitated, then lifted my cane up over my head and jumped into the room and beside the door. I lashed out with the cane.

It hit the wall with a resounding bang, and I snorted at the sound and my own audacity. For a long time I clung there, my back pressed tightly to the wall in the dark beside the door.

As my eyes became accustomed to the dark and nothing happened, I began to think once more. The sound had been enough to start the advance of troops. Had everyone actually left? I couldn't think of anything else to do but to go on and explore, and there seemed to be a terrible need to do it quietly and with caution.

Staying to one side of the light shaft, I peered low under the tables. If people were hiding here—quite a lot of people—where were they? I brought the cane up overhead, hoping that if someone jumped, it would break his blow. If he attacked me from a distance, perhaps I could give him a good swat with it.

I scurried across the light shaft and panted into the dimness on the far side, stooping and still trying to see beneath the tables. A dark object at the side cut a black oblong across a door which was dimly outlined in the wall. That must be the door to the kitchen, and the dark which cut across it could be a service stand. It seemed to be in the right place for that, but was anyone lurking behind it?

I inched forward, stopped and listened. If someone waited there, he was too quiet to hear him breathing. Then I darted behind it in a rush, one hand out. There was the cool, smooth surface, the back, the wide bare floor. No soft body.

I stayed crouched there for a long time, until my breathing became more normal. I welcomed this chance to crouch. I felt trapped. Yet I was doing the hunting. Nothing in my life before had prepared me for this. I wanted to stay in this safe corner until daylight came, yet I knew that I must get up and go on. My knees were stiffening.

Finally I stood and waited, trying to get a good course of action in mind. I might go back to the lounge and sit and wait, or I might try to find another way out of this place. Perhaps I would find someone. I hoped there would be no sudden blow. Yet the most frightening thing was of feeling alone.

I could not go back and sit where I could be watched. I reached out and lightly touched the kitchen door. It flapped weakly back for an instant, revealing that a light had been left burning. My dizziness from crouching had gone, and I decided to dash inside the kitchen. If anyone was in there, I'd try to take him by surprise.

I whisked in, the cane high in one hand. A round rack of spoons and equipment hung over the stove in the middle of the room, the implements swaying gently. I held tightly to a heavy table just inside the door. New. New smells. But had someone darted out when I had come in?

My pulse steadied amid familiar kitchen equipment, and I was grateful for this odd sense of comfort from homespun things. As I looked around at the utensils for preparing food, I was flooded with

a sense of the ludicrous—as when on the stage I had risen above myself, and had been able to assess the part I played. I saw myself galloping in, an arm upraised with the cane like a banner, head held high
and eyes flashing. I wanted to laugh. If anyone had witnessed that
performance—any normal person—he would have been amused at
that entrance.

Then I stopped smiling. This place wasn't inhabited by normal
people. Something was wrong. The door had been locked. I had
called and received no answer, had made enough noise whacking at
the dining room wall to have brought someone to inquire why I was
wrecking the place. If the situation were normal, someone would
have come. Gilbert would be here by now. But normal things were
not happening.

I got the shakes. This was no play, no dream. I had not gone mad,
either. There had been people; I had sat in the lounge, thinking how
the chaps resembled those lads in the records room in Inverness. I
had eaten and had a drink. The kids were near. They had not gone
out. I had seen them going upstairs, and down the hall to the back.

A click. I jumped, knees suddenly filled with jelly. A purring sound
followed. I slowly turned and, following its source, saw the refrigera-
tor. The cane came back down, and after a moment I began to
breathe more naturally.

I had taken all the comfort to be gained from the kitchen. I moved
toward that other door now, past the small night light, feeling again
as if this were a play, and only I had not read the script. Everyone
else knew what it was.

This fantasy feeling persisted. I opened the door and looked down
a narrow hallway, and directly across from this door, at a service entrance. Above it a WAY OUT sign gave enough light to make
out many doors opening at regular intervals down the length of the
hall. I tried the service door. It was locked, and there was no crash
bar, as in America. At the far end of the hall was the WAY OUT sign
I had seen earlier from the lounge.

I took a deep breath, now that I had found the second possible
exit locked. I would try to open the doors on the rooms along this

hallway, probably servants' quarters, and I advanced without being able to open any, yet wondering at the same time if one might not open onto a sleeping person, or perhaps onto a group of the kids, who would look up quickly at me. By this time I was almost fearful that I would find them.

At the end of the hall, I tried the other exit, only to have the same result. I was securely locked in, and now I knew it. I stood at the mouth of the wide hallway that led back to the reception desk and pondered. The lounge looked as empty as before, and there was the telephone, highlights bouncing off its polished plastic shield. I decided to try to call once more. If I could only reach the Edinburgh police, or the Inverness police. I would dial the two zeros and whisper to the operator for help.

Now I moved steadily along the gleaming floor. I was nearly up to the telephone when the lounge was plunged into darkness.

My mind felt slithery, full of eels, and my scalp pricked up and then constricted into a knot at the back of my head. I stopped moving abruptly and moved close to the wall, stifling a gasp. There seemed to be no one in the lounge ahead, and I could hear no sound coming from it. Yet surely as I felt the cold wall at my back, I felt a sense of someone being inside that room.

For a long time I pressed my back to the wall, until it gradually came to me that the room was not quite dark. Out of the line of vision to one side there was a small light. Probably it came from one of the lamps, on a corner table. I had to go in and face whoever was there. I could see the backs of the chairs near the doorway, and a few of the tables, and the edge of the reception desk.

I moved like an invalid who is just learning to walk again, sliding my feet slowly, one in front of the other along the floor. At the entrance, my foot caught the edge of a thick rug, and I fell forward, flailing out with both hands. The cane hit a low table. I pulled myself up.

"Mrs. Sutherland."

I jumped and turned. A woman was getting out of a chair in the far corner and moving toward me. I screamed.

"Don't do that. It won't help." It was Rose Glasses.

"Don't move one more inch," I said, my voice croaking like a frog. "I intend to hit you if you come any nearer!"

She stopped, and for a few seconds we faced one another. There were yet a few chairs between us, and finally she decided to sit down, indicating with a motion that I should sit, too. I stayed on my feet, wary, the cane still held high.

"Oh, do sit down. You'll feel better, and we have to talk."

She didn't make any attempt to come closer, and as I gradually calmed down, I lowered the cane. It felt good to have the chair beneath me, for my knees had gone weak again.

"That's better," she said. She nodded at the cane. "Why don't you stop gripping that? You don't plan to hit me, you know. You don't really want to." Her voice was soothing, the kind of voice nurses use, or caretakers of the elderly.

And then I got my cue. There was protection in helplessness. If I could act the part of an old dodderer, I could conceal my real feelings. Something so strange was happening, so unlike anything I had ever known before, that I needed protection. Now that I faced Rose Glasses, I felt much better. She was a human, with her own fears, and she was better than the darkness and my fearful imaginings. She was watching me, trying to find out what I would do. I determined to play my part as well as I could.

We eyed each other warily until I found my voice again, a surprise to hear that it had risen in pitch an octave, and wobbled remarkably. If I had tried, I couldn't have gotten a more desired effect, but the thought flew past instantaneously. "Why am I locked in here? Why am I being held?" I quavered.

She kept her hands lightly clasped in her lap as if she instructed an unruly child. After a lengthy silence, she replied. "You might be a bit upset, I suppose."

I trembled with frustration and suppressed rage. "Upset?" I echoed. "I'm so upset that I may faint . . ." I pushed up my glasses and shook. When I looked up, she had leaned forward, a tiny line between her eyebrows; otherwise, she looked as impassive as when she had walked through the graveyard.

"Who *are* you? Who are these people?" I asked, my voice helpless with anger.

She continued to watch as if studying a specimen.

I tried again, hoping perhaps to frighten her. "I want to call the police," I insisted, wishing that it came through sturdily, and hearing only a weak and ineffectual sound.

Finally she decided to speak. "Now, Mrs. Sutherland, you've no need to feel as you do! I'm just not able to explain a great amount. My name is Anabel MacPherson. You have frightened yourself this evening, you must realize."

"I'm not in the habit of frightening myself," I said, taking off my glasses and wiping my eyes, waiting for her to continue. When she did not, I asked, "And where's my nephew? Where's Gilbert?"

She took a deep breath, as if long forebearing. "Now, please do try to understand, madam. I can't tell you where your nephew is. And do try to pull yourself together. You really have put on quite a bad performance, when there's no need to carry on so!" Her tone was demanding, slightly angry.

I might push her hard now, perhaps break her reserve. But if I did, would she realize that I was not quite so helpless as I wished to be thought? I said, "Why *can't* you tell me about Gilbert? Oh, where *is* he?" The last sentence ascended like a banshee in a high wail.

She leaned forward and put out both hands. "Your nephew is quite all right, madam. Really, he is! You'll have to take my word for that. And so are you. Really, you know that you are! You must remember that you asked for help, that we gave it, that we gave you dinner?"

She seemed put a little off course, for she made an involuntary motion, her fingers slightly trembling, and took off her huge glasses. The light shone full into her face. I saw that one of her eyes was blue, the other brown.

Now that she seemed off balance, I pushed a bit harder. "I insist on calling the American embassy," I began, starting up from the chair.

Her hand was tight on my wrist. "And I insist that you do nothing of the sort! When you are quieter, I shall see you to your room, Mrs. Sutherland. You are upset. You will soon feel better." She sounded as if she had been asked to conjugate a verb, and her dark eye glittered while the pale one faded back in her face.

"My room? But the car—" I waved a shaking hand in the air, then saw it and brought it back to push the hair off my forehead. There was no need to act the part of a perplexed old woman now. I slumped back into the chair, and the cane, which had been against my legs, rattled off onto the floor.

So I was to be kept here; a room was ready for me. I did not have to try to act. This was real.

"Now, please try to understand. I don't like this any more than you do. You'll just have to stay here for some time. I think you'll be comfortable. This is really quite a nice place." Her voice was placed high in the masque of her face, a cultivated English voice. She watched as I absorbed the knowledge that I could not leave, and seemed ready to show me upstairs.

"Wait!" I took out a handkerchief and blew my nose. I suddenly wanted to cry like a child. When I had quieted down a bit I asked again where she had been, why she had let me roam the building. My voice trembled from fatigue and frustration. Anger, too, was rising. I pushed it down; it would likely steady me. I would have to stay for an indefinite time, and if I stayed, I wanted as much freedom as I could have. Only if she felt me completely incompetent would that be possible.

"While you walked about here, I was upstairs trying to figure out the best way to say this. And I told the young people to leave you alone. They are very fine, you know. There's absolutely nothing to fear from them, Mrs. Sutherland."

That tone again. Soothing. Nursing homes. Hospital nurses. I was projecting. She went on: "You can trust me. You're not in any danger at all. We'll make you quite comfortable. I'm afraid that I can't tell you any more. Now, if you're ready—" She stood and waited.

I got up, too. I walked unsteadily toward the stairs. She followed. At the foot of the steps I paused. "So you're not fixing this place up for winter?" My voice was trembling. I had very nearly come apart.

"Oh, yes; we *are* fixing up the lodge for winter. There's a lot yet to do. We're here to work."

I pulled myself up by the handrail. I would watch and listen. Best thing to say little; listen much. When I could, I'd get away. I'd get to an embassy somehow. Or to the police. If I acted too keen now, they might cart me off into the night. Swaddled up. Perhaps the kids were fine; peaceful, too. I'd see.

II

I awoke tired from a restless sleep, a distressing habit that has always plagued me, for whenever in need of sleep I am particularly restless. It seemed early, although the morning was dark. I could see high clouds rolling in the dark sky outside the small window of my room. My watch had stopped; I had forgotten to wind it. The lodge was quiet; it must be too early for the others to be up. But even though I lay still, sleep would not return. My mind jumped like a mountain goat from crag to crag, seeking a foothold.

When I had climbed the stairs up here last night I had seen the lounge from between the railings of the balcony that surrounded it on three sides. It had occurred to me that Rose might have stood there to watch, for everything was visible except the door to the dining room and the fireplace at the back. I shivered. It was an excellent vantage point.

In spite of her words, I did not trust Rose. It was only partly true that I had frightened myself. If she had told me early that I was not to leave, I might have protested, but it would have spared me a harrowing time. They had me outnumbered. The surrealistic silence had compelled my solitary jaunt around the place. Rose had demonstrated callous indifference, even cruelty. What was the reason I was kept here? I could not imagine, and I shivered again. That frightening exploration had at least given me an idea of the layout of the building, I reasoned, which might come in handy when I tried to make an escape. I would lie low and try to plan.

The room I had been given was comfortable, with a single bed, new bedding, a tiny private bathroom with one of those heated chrome towel racks. The view from the window was of moors, now dismal in the early light, undulating to the distance, with not a build-

ing in sight. The furniture was minimal: one straight chair and
a bed table with a small lamp gave the impression that the room was
designed only for sleeping and changing, not for any social life. After
Rose left I had searched it: if there was a "bug" I couldn't find it,
and if there was a peephole, I couldn't find that, either.

But the key was gone from the door. I shivered, remembering the
way Rose had watched me as I walked unsteadily to the bed and
eased down on it. She looked as if she studied a specimen of fossil-
ized life from a previous age. "Don't come down for breakfast—we'll
send up a tray," she had finally said, and while I developed my
dodderer part, smoothing my hair with a shaking hand, she lingered
and seemed undecided for a moment about my condition. It was
the only time she had seemed warm and human. Then she went to
the door, turned and said, "You'll feel better in the morning,"
opened it and went out, shutting it firmly behind her.

I heard no sound of her leaving, and after a moment I tried the
door. It was unlocked. Rose had disappeared from the hallway without making a sound. When I tried to lock the door I found that the
key had been taken. This disturbed me. I wanted to lock myself away
from them. I smiled to myself ruefully, thinking how I had tried all
of the antique keys that I carried in my overloaded purse, frantically searching for the many that I had accumulated in the antique
shops Gilbert and I had earlier visited, when I had allowed myself
the luxury of buying them instead of the breakfront secretary I had
really wanted and had no place for. Of course they had not fitted
the lock, and I had tried even the smallest of them in the vain attempt to barricade myself for the night. I smiled again, remembering how Gilbert had protested at my buying the keys. "Why do you
buy that junk? Your bag looks like a magpie's nest," he had said, his
smile only partly concealing his disdain.

He was right: my bag was a mess. But it was pleasant to handle
the old keys, and they gave me a feeling of possession, deprived of
home and handling only papers and my clothing and suitcases. I
half pretended that I would have the keys mounted for a wall decoration if I took up permanent residence in London or one of the
Cotswold towns, but the real reason was that I liked them. There

were many by now—we had toured the antique shops as an after-lunch recreation all the way up from London—and they ranged from huge to tiny. The old lockmakers had taken pride in their craft and had made their keys as beautiful as they made their locks intricate. I could hold them and dwell in my imagination in the times of lords and ladies, of political intrigues and sword-wielding, a rich storehouse of thought that pleased me, even if Gilbert was too young to share backward looks.

I had propped the chair against the door, and it was at the same angle that I had left it. No one had bothered me.

What had happened to Gilbert? I was frightened for him, and baffled. The chap who had gone to help him had not come back through the lounge while I sat there. Did they hold him captive in another part of the lodge? I planned to try to find out. If he had gotten away, he would send help.

Gretchen would help me, too, I thought, and then suddenly realized that the letter to her had been left in the brief case, was gone with the other papers. Another source of help crossed out, for if she had answered and gotten no reply, she was enough of a friend to ask questions in the right places.

I shivered again and my legs cramped. I was not cold, but growing aware of the riskiness of my situation. This might be the biggest role of my career—a leading lady who didn't know the script, in a company of amateurs. A shaky proposition. That strange Scot in the Queen's Arms kept popping to mind; he had appeared again in Edinburgh, too, at our hotel; he'd seemed to know me. I remembered now that he and Rose had been in a room there at the Queen's Arms, and had decided some time ago that had been a dream. Perhaps it was not. Did he have any connection with this crowd?

The muscle cramps increased. It was foolish to stay in bed. I decided on a hot bath. Steam rolled up in moist clouds as the yellow water splashed into the tub, and I thankfully lowered myself into it and felt the muscles relax. As I bathed, my mind felt more relaxed, also. I would watch for a chance to get away, keep up my character with intuition and luck, and perhaps find out what this bunch was up to.

I dressed in the clothing I had worn, feeling less than elegant. As I did, I thought of the resemblance between these young men here and the chaps in the thatched hut at Culloden. What was it—was there any connection between them? All of them were bearded, but they wore their hair clipped fairly short. Could the beards be a symbol, a sign of a unity that I hadn't learned? It seemed foolish to give the thought any credence, and yet in an inexplicable way it hung together, made an illogical logic. The resemblance between these men, and with the chaps in the records room in Inverness, as well, might be a link of some kind.

The morning at the thatched hut had left a firm impression, and the reason escaped me. It had been unsettling, nebulous, a fragment of something not understood. With no effort at all I could still visualize the look of the sky as we drove upward into it from the low bowl in which was Inverness to the high ground of Culloden—a mackerel sky, the clouds small, flecked, high and even against pale blue. It was blotted out momentarily by trees at our turn onto the narrow road that led to the battlefield, and emerging, appeared deeply overcast in only seconds. Mist fell heavily.

We had driven only a short distance when we caught sight of a handboard, a small hand-lettered sign propped against the wall of the thatched hut. Gilbert had to brake unexpectedly and back up, his face showing consternation at my near command to stop there, rather than to go on at once to the battlefield.

"It says 'Open,' Gilbert: it's an information office," I explained, trying to mollify him, hoping he'd leap to sudden understanding, not meaning to sound curt. There were several cars parked at the fence.

A larger sign near the road was partly concealed by two men, who half leaned on it and kept up a low-toned conversation, completely absorbed in what they said and not noticing us. I wondered crossly why they stood and talked in the rain, annoyed at not being able to read the information written on the marker. We hurried past them toward the hut, with no thought of anything strange about the situation. I recalled feeling out of sorts, of planning to read the sign later.

The hut was small, the low door appearing even lower under a heavy thatch of heather. I had to duck my head to enter, and forgot it and the two men in front immediately. Directly across on the facing wall was a rack of unusual pamphlets which claimed my attention, not at all like the pamphlets usually found in government information kiosks.

Official government guidebooks had blue backgrounds, white letters. These were made of slick white paper printed with a single bold symbol, a strange device: a simple black line curved down and returning up. It was like the early Christian symbol of a fish, except that the head pointed down. The two top lines, its tail, were open. It looked like a child's drawing of a purse, but it was done very well, creating and holding its tension in that sweeping line, lowered and upthrust. There were a lot of pamphlets, all seeming a bit different, and all with that strange symbol, which I had never seen anywhere else. I wanted very much to get a few of them to examine.

However, I could not. For directly in front of the rack a man and a woman wearing knapsacks and rugged clothing talked with another man. They had to move slightly to let me come inside the small building, but the space was filled; it was impossible to touch the rack behind them, unless I asked them to move. They talked loudly, as if in argument, and they stayed right where they were, without a show of courtesy. The woman was especially angry. She spoke in English, and suddenly it was another language. There came a quiet, inaudible answer from the man in a dark business suit, and then her loud voice was joined by her companion, a rough-looking camper in heavy boots, and his language was also foreign. I thought—Good heavens, Women's Lib here, too? The most admirable qualities of women—their balance and quiet management—all that is lost here, too?

I tried to move toward the side of the room, divided in the center by a stone fireplace, but this part of the hut was filled by a group of young men with beards who seemed aimless, their hands stuck in their back trouser pockets, their arms akimbo, their eyes vacant of expression. They milled about aimlessly, and they took up all the space except the tiny spot just inside the doorway where I now stood.

Gilbert could not come inside, but getting a glimpse, muttered something about going around to the back for a look down the hill. It was raining quite hard now, and the wind was cold. I was put out about such discourtesy, instinctively contrasting these young people with those at the bar in the Queen's Arms, who had made way for Gilbert while not seeming to notice him. Really! Such people! I had thought.

I tried not to hear the argument, but it was impossible. Part of the time the language was unintelligible, then again there were English words. The young men moved back and forth, drifting like clouds. Their elbows blocked me from the pamphlets, where a sign across the top said KEEP GAELIC ALIVE.

A chap nearest me turned, and I reached toward the rack and was able to pick up a couple of pamphlets. He turned back quickly, his elbow struck my hand and all but one slithered across the floor. I bent to help pick them up, tucking the one I had retained into my bag, and several other chaps moved close to me. There was no place to go but out.

"Hmpf!" I said, emerging to the rain, where Gilbert stood. "That crowd in there needs to learn some good manners!"

"Well, come on, Aunt. There's a stone down the hill; marks the place where Bonnie Prince Charlie's stable used to be." He took my arm and guided me down a narrow walkway beside the hut. "We'll wait a bit, they won't be there forever. Just look at this roof—it's heather."

"Yes. Held on with chicken wire."

"Keeps birds out. Holds it on. Wind."

We peered across a sloping grainfield, flattened in places by recent high winds. If a stone stood on the slope, the grain was all which could be seen. I was getting wet and awfully cold.

"I give up. You may stay and look for the stone if you like, I'm going inside. If those people are still there, they'll just have to move over." I clutched the collar of my coat against the wind and moved back to the door as rapidly as I could.

It was only a few steps from the back to the front of the tiny hut, and I wondered how people could have endured to live inside such a small place, only one window, and long winter nights and rain and chill. Animals were usually bedded on the other side of the fireplace. Many Scottish wives had lived their lives out in places not so good as this, I reflected, my head lowered against the chill wind and rain.

It had been only a few minutes, yet when I got to the front of the hut the cars had disappeared—all except ours. No one stood at the sign. Inside the small room the people had disappeared; one chap stood at a counter which I had been unable to see previously, where souvenirs were for sale. He was clean-shaven. I would be willing to swear that he had not been here before. We had heard no one leave or arrive. I think that my mouth dropped open.

I turned, reaching for the rack of pamphlets. They were gone. Only the usual blue-covered government-issue information sheets were lined up. The young man came out from behind the counter and asked if he might assist me. I stood there feeling stupid. None of this material had been here only moments ago. What had happened to the white papers with their strange mark?

The strangeness, the mystery, had begun at the thatched hut, I reflected as I combed my hair. I had been unable to stop thinking about it, had pestered Gilbert and had been put off by his matter-of-fact answers. He saw factual things; I saw other things. But what had I seen? Many times I had thought that I had started the downhill slide.

There was a tap at the door. I took away the chair, and a good-looking young girl with her long hair bound back by a red ribbon held a tray. She set it on the table and was leaving, but I stopped her.

"Good morning. Will you tell me your name? I'm Hortense Sutherland, but I expect you know."

"I'm Mary, ma'am. I'm glad to meet you." She made a small curtsy and started for the door.

"Don't go, please," I begged, one hand outstretched.

"I'm sorry, ma'am. I have to." She bobbed again and was gone.

The food was good. I ate and realized that there would not be much chance of involving any of the kids in conversation; they'd been given instructions, that seemed clear. I was to live isolated. But I had to try to get away.

Old habit patterns reasserted themselves when breakfast was finished. Always there had been a place to go, something to do. If I went out to search a client's forebears, there were people to watch: women with children, perhaps someone getting tangled up in an umbrella. It had been useful in my work. I liked to read, but there were no books here. I could not stay completely alone for an indefinite time. But how could I leave?

I cursed my luck for breaking my hip a year ago, for the agony it often gave when I walked, for my vertigo. I knew that it was impossible for me to walk far, even if I could get out of the lodge. Motorists sometimes passed; I could hear the sound of an occasional motor fading away, out of sight of my window. Perhaps I might be able to hail a car. I had no idea what kind of a story I would give, even if one might be persuaded to stop on this bleak highway by the sight of a forlorn figure begging for a ride. Gilbert and I had seen lots of young people backpacking in England, holding out their hands, their long hair blown out by the wind. I wondered what kind of figure I would cut doing that. It made me laugh to imagine it. And yet I must try.

I could not stay long inside this tiny room, where the only things I had to think about were my wonders and doubts and fears. I dreaded a slack mind and a slack body. I must set about doing what I could. If I went at it easily, even limited activity might bear a reward.

I decided to test my freedom. It would be good to see the lodge by daylight, relieved of terrors I faced last night—the solitude, my fear, even, perhaps, my own hallucinations. I decided to return the tray. Perhaps there was another telephone, or a car might have been left near the place with its keys in the ignition. I wasn't above car theft. In spite of ignorance of British laws, I'd let my story stand on its merits: any court would uphold car theft over kidnapping, I felt sure.

On the way down to the lounge, things looked pretty good, even normal. It was hard to understand the terror I had felt last night. Several of the kids were dusting the tables, and one ran a vacuum sweeper. They looked up as I went past, and though I expected to be told rather like a small child to go up to my room, nobody said anything. As soon as they realized who it was, they glanced back at their work.

I made my way past the desk and telephone, knowing better than to try to use it, and advanced toward the narrower hall, on my way to the kitchen. Nobody stopped me, so it seemed that I had been given a certain amount of clearance in the place.

Under the WAY OUT sign I stood and surveyed the hall, remembering how I had gone along it trying the doors last night. One seemed wider than the others, which I hadn't noticed before. I tried it. It opened onto basement stairs.

I hesitated. Dim sounds came of the kids at work in the kitchen, and I stepped quickly inside the doorway just as the kitchen door opened. I pulled the door shut and stood in the gloom in momentary panic, hearing steps coming down the hall.

They passed, and panic was followed by anger as I realized an apology had formed in my mind, ready to give if I had been caught. I was clutching the tray in both hands as if it were the passkey to redemption, and I rationalized my emotional reaction as I went gingerly down the stairs, the dim light below now seeming normal. Surely I must fight my own fears, must establish some kind of stabilizing influence within myself if I were to survive here. For how long was a question that threatened to unsettle me again, but it seemed good luck to have a look at this undercroft of the building. I set the tray on the floor at the foot of the stairs and turned. From down here not a sound could be heard.

It was a large cavern of a basement. At a far side was a door which was padlocked; I surmised that it opened into a garage behind the main part of the lodge, and I hoped to explore it later. The workmen had left a small pile of rubble, swept neatly into a corner. The marks of cement finishers were new on the walls, and the smell was moist and aromatic of lime.

A corner had been enclosed by raw pine lumber; a door to this fruit cellar, I took it to be, was closed and locked with a padlock. On the floor outside this room many large boxes lay rather at random; they were boxes such as furniture-moving companies use, and had been apparently set down here and left. Most were sealed with broad sticky tape, but I moved around them and studied them, and finally found one which had a corner loose. I stuck a hand in and felt the smooth, slick finish of paper, and pulled out a pamphlet with that strange sign I had seen at the thatched hut at Culloden. I had just started to examine it when I heard the door at the head of the stairs open, and I put it back quickly and moved off.

Someone's feet were visible from where I stood, almost under the stairs, and as yet I had not been seen. I stepped quickly to one side; there was a small pile of dirty workmen's clothing. I picked up a pair of streaked white overalls on top and I bent over, absorbed in what lay beneath. Just in time.

Rose Glasses stood at the foot of the stairs. She was studying me.

I straightened and looked up, pushed back my glasses with the back of my hand and smiled vacuously, holding up a pair of men's huge gum boots, streaked with white cement and plaster. I waved them and the overalls just slightly in the air and continued my inane smile.

"Mrs. Sutherland," Rose said in a cold voice, "we want you to have some chance to move about. We don't think the cellar is the place for it. You're not supposed to spy."

I grasped the galoshes firmly, and brushed back wisps of hair with the other hand—a gesture that old women use—and moved slowly away from the little pile of clothing. The boots were indeed a lifesaver. I smiled an old lady's smile.

"Spy? I'm not spying. I want to go outside, and I don't want to get my feet wet."

She watched, suspicion and indecision battling on her face. I moved ahead, more sure of the ground, to the bottom of the steps, where I grasped the handrail to pull myself up laboriously, grunting a little, as if I might not make it without help. She followed, and we went slowly. I was playing my part to the hilt in a benefit performance for her, but she didn't know it yet.

At the top of the steps I fumbled at the knob, making fussy sounds at my inability to open the door, drawing in my breath with small exasperated gasps and rattling the knob a little. As I hoped, she reached around me to turn it—a feat, for the stairway was not wide, and I acted oblivious to what she was trying to do.

In the hallway I began too effusive thanks, seeing the uncertainty grow in Rose's expression. She was wondering if her first impression —of spying—was correct, or if I was really near senility, and I hoped to keep her wondering. Limping, smiling and nodding, I went back to the lounge. She followed until I had reached the wide stairway, then seemed to make up her mind. The kids had finished their work, and we were alone.

"Wait, Mrs. Sutherland! Just a moment, if you please."

One foot was already on the step, and I brought it back down carefully, humoring obviously my old hip break. I knew that I must be careful, that the part must not be overdone, for she was sharp. I didn't want her to get onto the fact that I would spy if I could.

"Yes?" I stood watching her and wetting my lips, sucking them in a little, as I'd seen old people do. The kids were in the dining room. From the sounds coming from there, they were having some kind of class. I heard a low voice which sounded like it was lecturing, though I couldn't hear what was said, and a spatter of talk followed by a high, girlish voice. Then the sound of a deeper one.

"We want you to have complete freedom. Within the confines of the area, of course. But that doesn't include the basement. You should move about; it would be cruel if we confined you to your room. However, unless you co-operate with us, we'll have to lock your door."

I put one hand to my chest and gasped. She might be uncertain about me, but she was dead certain of what she said.

I held out the boots, allowing them to slip a little and fumbling for one which started to fall to the floor. I bent over and braced myself on the cane and grunted. I let Rose Glasses pick it up and give it back.

"I hope it's all right if I take these? I mean—you don't think it's stealing, do you? I didn't think they belonged to anyone." I first clasped the boots and then held them out to her with a gesture of resignation. She made a quick motion of denial, and I kept talking.

"If it was stealing to take them, I don't want to do that. I went down there to see if I could find something for my feet; you know, it's wet out there, and I've got to do something, walk a little bit each day. And I'm afraid I'll catch cold."

She bought it. The whole thick slice. She began to look very sorry for me, and came forward and put her hand on my shoulder and patted it.

I gulped, for a laugh had started. The gulp was such a good cue that I continued it for a little while. She helped me up the stairs, and at the top she patted me again and said that I might keep the boots.

I plodded an invalid way back to my room and collapsed on the bed, congratulating myself on the performance. I had learned to sense audience, its sympathy, the moment it began. My character was a success, and I had a freer hand.

I got my coat and cane and started for the outdoors. I half expected the lodge door to be locked, but it wasn't. Nobody seemed interested that I went out, or followed, though I expected that, too. I stood at the foot of the porch steps for a moment, considering which way to go. I remembered quite well the road from Ballachulish through the bens; I had scant idea of what lay in the opposite direction; I wanted more than anything to find a trace of Gilbert. If I could find the car, or marks of a struggle, it might be a better thing than to wonder as I had been doing. So I turned off from the lodge driveway onto the macadam highway in the direction we had come.

The morning had improved. High clouds opened in the distance, and sunlight streaked colors of chartreuse, gold and emerald on the distant land; it changed constantly and blended with the purples and blues of the shadows, so that the landscape itself seemed gently undulating, like a living thing. In the low area near the lodge the ground was soggy, and I was glad for the gum boots, even though their size and awkwardness made it an effort to lift them from the clinging peat and brought into play some new muscles I had forgotten about. On the macadam the boots were a nuisance.

I soon knew, too, that I was in bad shape to walk far. From high ground I saw no other building in sight; if I planned to walk for help, I would have to go rather far. There simply seemed to be nothing except the lodge hereabouts—no manor, house or croft where people might live. I considered flagging down a motorist, but it was as yet too early in the day, at this hour tourists still at breakfast. I would stay several hours, or try to come later, and I would try to stop any moving vehicle, even a truck.

When I reached the top of the long slope I had descended in darkness last night, I looked back and saw the lodge looking small and not particularly noticeable, its brown shingled walls almost blending with the exposed brown earth around it. Anyone passing would think it was waiting for winter trade. Snow would make its dark color show up to good advantage.

I went on toward the place where the car had been, climbing and feeling the pull in leg muscles, yet feeling happy and light, like a girl off on a college holiday. I was extremely proud of myself for having gotten away so well. From the vantage point I had reached, the boulders hid the building from sight. I was free! If I could find the car—or if I could hail a passing motorist—it seemed that perhaps I was making a clean getaway.

The road mounted steeply and twisted far ahead into the dark bens, then disappeared. The road glistened with early wetness; the bens were purple and shrouded in night clouds. I scanned the road. The car was nowhere to be seen.

A curlew flew up suddenly from the gorse close beside me, crying its high, piercing whistle, and the wind blew my hair and sang a calm whirring sound past my ears. Sunlight suddenly bathed me, its warmth a delight. It was a beautiful morning in a primeval world.

Then from behind the boulders down below the turn, where the road went off to the lodge, I saw a young chap emerge and stride rapidly toward me, his hair lifting up and back with each step, in a kind of lifted bounce. I went as quickly as I could toward the place I imagined I had left the car, the boots a real handicap to speed, and the chap gaining. I must get a look at the spot, for signs of a struggle or a bit of clothing, anything that might reveal what had happened to Gilbert. I didn't expect to stop a car this time, for the last humans we had seen were at Ballachulish yesterday, and then those miles of deserted glens and bens. There was nobody near except for that fellow, and I had to find out for myself what had happened.

There were no marks of tires in the chippings at the side, no flattened grass or disrupted peat beyond, no signs of a struggle. There was nothing to show that we had been there. It was as if it had not happened at all.

"It's no' so good to wander afar-r." The voice of my tail was deep and rich. He put a gentle hand under my elbow and turned me around, his clear eyes showing a slight, tolerant smile. He looked businesslike, on an assignment.

I let myself be turned. I had found what I sought. It was disconcerting to have found nothing. I felt empty.

I walked a plodding way beside him, not talking. Questions pushed inside my lips, and I denied myself the luxury of asking them. It would be unwise to appear capable; better to do as old people do —comply silently. I judged from his manner that Rose had talked with the kids, and the "tolerant" mood had been set. I pretended that my feet filled my thoughts. The limp, the cane, the absurd boots were good character props.

When I spoke, it was feeble, in keeping. I stopped and partly turned toward the place I had looked for the car. "I came to find my nephew. Have you seen Gilbert? Gilbert is my nephew. I only wanted to see him—" And I waved toward the place and managed a sudden loss of balance that brought his hand quickly under my elbow again.

"Careful, there. Mind the step." He said it gently, in exactly the tone used with the elderly and I smiled up at him in gratitude. I must watch my characterization in order not to get too obvious. Flashes of lucidity are common in senility, too.

When we got back to the lodge he helped me off with my coat and boots and saw me all the way up to the room. After he had left I smiled ruefully to myself; I wanted not to come in, but to see what lay in the opposite direction. At least I had found no blood on the highway. Had Gilbert gotten away unharmed? And I knew now that I was watched. I would go out again as soon as I could.

I could not sit at the bedroom window long and watch the clouds change. By the time one of the girls came with the lunch tray I had had enough. She was Isabel, she said. She bobbed and left. She gave me no chance to talk with her. I felt like the woman in the case in Chipping Cranford—made of marble, something to see and shake the head about, worth a smile. But not alive, not human.

As I ate I remembered that time; I had seen the marble effigies the day after I'd seen Rose in the graveyard, when Gilbert came and we walked down a narrow, cobbled street past a high stone wall of yellowish gray, behind which a derelict manor house was set far back. The ruin beckoned to me. It appeared cold and gray against the evening sky, seeming to try to attract attention with its four pierced stone flues high atop its chimneys. In spite of the walls, the old mansion was not concealed, and its unusual chimney flues seemed to be held up almost jauntily over the ruin. They were cut into shapes like flowers—lotus buds, I thought. I had wanted to learn when the place was built, and by whom, and why it had been allowed to fall into a state of awful neglect. When we had left the higher ground of the graveyard we had passed its entrance gateways—three curious arches grouped over a roadway and two side paths. The arches looked oriental, Saracen, possibly. They were asymmetrical, pointed at the top, each slightly off level, tilted. They didn't belong in England.

I had called Gilbert's attention. I had just seen Rose when I had expected to see him, and now there were these curious gate arches, and that queer ruin with the fluted stone chimney pots.

"Aunt Hortense," he had said, "you see the darndest things! Come on, let's get to the pub. That old place may beckon you, but the pub beckons me. How about a pint of Harp before bed?"

The evening had gotten dim. Wind was blowing, and there were chills on my spine. We walked down the sloping street beside those dark walls toward a streetlight, the memory of the strange woman persisting. I felt odd, in a surrealist world, out of place, lopsided and off balance like the arches, and obsessed by curious things like imps and grinning gargoyles.

After perhaps a hundred feet we passed a newer house, its upper-story windows looming and staring black over the wall. It seemed to have crept away as if it feared the ruin; or else it tried to guard it.

"You're grabbing your head scarf as if you're afraid your head might fall off," Gilbert said with a grin.

I had shivered and let go of the scarf, and tried to grin back at him as if I had felt no sinister nudges. We walked toward the light at the corner beside the peering black windows over the wall. And then, with one tiny change, all the pieces slipped together differently, and the aspect became ordinary, usual: a bobby appeared from around a corner under the streetlight ahead, the light outlining his helmet. He stopped briefly to inspect an unfinished house, and resumed his leisurely stroll in our direction. When he got close he stopped and bowed.

"Good evening. Lovely night, isn't it?" His voice was mellifluous, light; he clasped his nightstick behind in both hands, and rocked back and forth, inspecting us. "Off on a holiday, eh?"

I waited until the courtesies were out of the way to ask my questions.

"Oh, I really don't know much about this town yet, madam. I've only just come on to this town two weeks ago. I was for several years in Lower Slaughter. You really must go there. It's a charming place. It's hilly, you know. It rolls, and you can see for miles around."

I was disappointed. "Oh, you really don't know about that old mansion?"

"I'm afraid not, madam. But let me urge you, before you simply turn and go back to the hotel, do walk around this corner and up a half a block. It's not very far, really. I always come by for a look this time of evening. If you go right along, you'll get to see the roses. They're all ready to nod their heads to you. They're really quite beautiful now, and there's just enough daylight left for you to see them." His voice was high, a tenor's, and placed forward in his face. He smiled and bowed good night. I gave up. We walked up the street for a look at the roses.

The pub was warm. Around the bar stood a dozen or more young people, the young men, with Prince Valiant haircuts, were dressed in well-pressed suits, and the girls who stood there with them looked a good deal like them, except that they wore dresses. Neatly tailored dresses in dark colors.

Unisex, I thought. Too bad, too. It seemed such a pity, to waste all those elegant hormones they were producing, when the differences between the sexes is such fun. As in the punch line of some old, long-forgotten joke, "*Vive la différence!*"

But of course, I told myself, they didn't really. Who knows what went on beneath their neat, ordinary clothes? When they were away from others? They talked together in quiet tones, now and again breaking out into melodious laughter which dropped down almost at once.

I found a seat on the padded bench along the outer wall and loosened my coat while Gilbert went to the bar. The young people made way for him as if by some kind of instinct, not really looking at him, but letting him up to the bar. I surveyed the scene, and then I remembered the roses. Yes, they had been quite worth the long walk around the corner and down another block, and it had made me sleepy.

Gilbert returned with two nob-glasses of beer. I quaffed mine deeply and felt its warmth seep over me; the warmth of the room, enhanced by a fire at one end, crept over my cold bones. I'm well padded, but inclined to chill quickly.

An animal lay asleep before the fire. At first I had thought it was some kind of fur rug, but now I could see that it was a boxer. In addition to the dog, there were a couple of small round tables and an assortment of armchairs with leather-padded backs and arms—the kind one sees in all British pubs. They were filled with people, and others stood nearby, around the fire, with the dog lying quietly in their midst. The dog at that moment got up slowly and moved from the room. She was a huge boxer, as large as a lion, with the largest skull I've ever seen on that breed, and huge black nipples. Motherhood was long behind her.

At the many small round tables toward the side were an assortment of people, some American tourists, but most were natives, I felt sure. My eyes roamed across a group of six or seven at the table next to ours. I jumped just slightly when I recognized the woman in red; even here in the dim pub she wore those rose glasses. She listened to someone in the group, and if she saw me, she gave no sign. She looked so ordinary now that I wondered what had gotten hold of me, why I reacted so strongly in the graveyard. I shivered, and then felt the warmth of the alcohol.

An uncomfortable feeling persisted. These people weren't beer parlor loungers. I had pulled off my head scarf when we entered; now I smoothed back my hair with my hands and wished that I had brought along a well-fitted afternoon dress. "I'm rather a mess, I'm afraid," I apologized to Gilbert. Why hadn't I put a girdle and some dressy shoes into the suitcase?

He inspected, his head slightly lifted and an analytical look on his face. He took a good deal of time with it. I slipped out my powder compact and tried to take the shine off my nose unobtrusively. Gilbert was turning and looking over the others in the room.

He looked back, his face showing a lopsided grin. "Hortense, dear, you've no need to worry; you're better looking in your 'natural state,' as we biologists say, than most of 'em here. Pubescent girls excepted." He laughed, then slowly turned again to regard the girls at the bar.

He was really a very satisfactory young fellow. I smiled, thinking that we two had developed a good working relationship, even though there were times when I would have liked to swat him with my handbag. But this wasn't one of them.

He began to study me again with the detachment of a scientist. I wiggled and turned my head to one side. At the small table between ours and the corner sat a Scotsman wearing a kilt.

I pulled my eyes back to Gilbert, who said, "Your complexion is perfect. Very healthy specimen. And the way you hold yourself—just the way you're sitting there, now—your posture. Maybe I should call it 'style.' To use your language, I think it's called 'presence.'"

I was feeling much better. Gilbert always spoke honestly, the source of some uncomfortable moments for me occasionally, when I wished that he didn't. I suppose that I had developed a too critical eye about myself, taking into account physical flaws more than most people. My profession as an actress had compelled it, and I may have become oversensitive. Especially since that fall. The cane constantly reminded me that I grew older. I tried not to limp, but I knew that I still did. I tried not to dwell on it.

The decision to go into genealogical work had helped, I thought, deeply drinking the slightly bitter beer. New work after retirement from the stage made my life become meaningful. It occupied my restless mind and gave opportunity to travel around this beautiful country. Much freedom. Now, too, I could be myself without having to worry about living up to an image.

If I became dizzy and tottered a bit, no one whispered that I was losing my grip, and the fear that had hounded during the last years was dissipating. I smiled at Gilbert over the rim of the glass and said, "This is the best of many worlds." His eyes met mine, and he nodded understandingly.

The Scot leaned against the back of the bench, his hands playing idly with a package of matches. His eyes roamed alertly across the room. He was getting slightly bald, and wore his reddish-sandy hair smoothed across the spot. Because of his beard, I sensed rather than saw a slight smile, and I felt that he had heard our little remarks to each other, though he looked quite uninvolved with it.

From his fine grooming and easy posture came a quiet assurance. He was very still, except for his eyes and hands, turning over the matches. I had an impression that he knew who was in this pub, knew who we were and accepted us, and a good feeling came very quietly. He had good vibrations.

The warmth of the room and the drink suddenly hit, and I pulled my coat open and drew out my arms. Gilbert again had his eyes on the young people standing at the bar. I glanced back at the woman in red.

But she was not there. Sometime, perhaps while I had been considering the Scotsman, she must have left. Her crowd was picking up their belongings and moving away.

The crowd by the fireplace had drawn closer together, now that the boxer was gone, and were conversing in low tones. In the room there was an easy kind of sound, a hushed sibilance, of many voices speaking softly, like prayers being whispered. The dim lights picked out shields and coats of arms hung on the rafters, and I made out the Osborne crest up there.

A motion on my left caused me to half turn. The Scot was getting up for another glass. As he returned, our eyes met briefly; again there came the feeling of complete acceptance. As he seated himself he brushed against my large handbag, which I had carelessly left open beside me on the bench. It turned over slowly and completely emptied itself out onto the floor, pouring out comb, lipsticks, compact, keys, scraps of paper and the small pencils and notebooks which I always carry.

It took considerable time to pick it all up and to stuff it back, and the Scot helped, our heads brushing as we bent into the tiny space, with Gilbert, too, pushed forward into the cramped quarters.

It was only after we'd gotten it all in and had sat back that the Scot said, "I'm sorry, madam." He said it with tremendous dignity, with a slight burr on the word sorry, and an inflection of deference on madam. I liked him very much.

"My fault for having left it there, open," I said. "I'm afraid my handbag is rather like my mind: a large receptacle crammed with bits and pieces, a tremendous amount of information scrawled on untidy scraps."

He laughed. "Not at all. I like your picture, but I don't believe it. You're on some sort of mission?"

I nodded. "I trace lineage. Genealogy. I like finding out things."

"A lucrative field, I hope?"

"Yes. I enjoy being paid well for the kind of thing I would do, anyway."

"Aye. That's the best kind of work. And is the young man your son?"

Gilbert had gone back to the bar after helping to retrieve my things, and he lingered there chatting with the barman. I explained that my nephew was in graduate school, biology, at Berkeley, and was now between semesters. The Scot raised an eyebrow. "So you're Americans? Odd, I took you for British."

"Half. My father. We left after he was killed in the first war."

He nodded. "I see. Your mother felt safer there. But you got into it later, didn't you, so you might say that it did you no good."

I looked at him closely, but there was a whimsical quality about his face that bespoke kindness, even though his words were cynical.

"Well, I'm back here now. I like it here. I enjoy the involved antiquity of Europe. The sense of history."

He nodded. "And do you plan to travel north at all?"

"As a matter of fact, I got a new commission just yesterday. We'll be going to Edinburgh, I believe. It should be interesting; I love that city."

"Edinburgh, eh?" He eyed me speculatively. After a long moment he said, "If you plan to do some shopping there, perhaps I might suggest a good place for woolens—less expensive than the ones on Princes Street, and they have a good selection. That is, if you're thinking of that sort of thing at all—" He looked slightly disparaging at his temerity, and I hurried to set him at ease.

"I'd be delighted to know about it. There's no sense in spending more than one has to—" and I listened while he gave directions to a small place off the tourist paths.

Then he became very quiet. I decided that he hadn't meant to talk, and had only done so because I had been a bit forward. I enjoy people so much that I often encourage them to talk; but from training I've also learned to shut up. If he now wished to think his own thoughts, the choice was his. I wondered what he had seen of war. He was just the right age for the last one.

Then with a small sigh he seemed to acknowledge my thoughts, and he began to speak from his ruminations.

"Aye," he said, finally, letting his voice linger long on that one syllable, so that it was almost a long-drawn-out groan. "I served in the Royal Navy. Had my ship sunk under me three times." He shook his head. "They always found me and got me onto another one."

He was smiling slightly, miles away, in a world of cold and damp, wide expanses of silver water and sky.

"Aye! I recollect one time when we were patrolling off the Outer Hebrides. Have you ever been there? You have to go. It's the wildest country, the most faraway place left in the world."

His voice picked up speed, and his words became more emphatic. "You know, people were moved off the islands by the government. It said the land couldn't support them. There's nothing there now, only islands—most of them uninhabited." The thought seemed to snag in his mind. He drank his beer and waited. After a little he continued.

"We had maps of the islands, as we had the maps of all the countries. We were off this uninhabited land, very close, and the men were restless; it'd been weeks since they were ashore. Every now and then, whenever we could, it was customary to put a small whaler ashore so that the chaps could get the feel of land again, and to get a bit of exercise.

"This day the captain assigned me to command the whaler with ten men in it, to row to one of these deserted islands and walk about for an hour or so. After our exercise we were to go back to the ship. This was the first time for me; I'd never gone ashore there before.

"After we got on the island this particular time, my men were walking about and cutting up, turning cartwheels, boxing, springing about on the turf at the water's edge. The land rose farther back, in a kind of little hillock. Not very high, but high enough so you couldn't see beyond it from the shore, where we were.

"The men got to talking about how good beer would taste right then. Of course we didn't have any with us, and they chided the fellow who'd spoken about it, rather roughly, but a bit wistfully, too. Pretty soon they were all grumbling, saying they wished they had beer."

He stopped for a long time and looked, unseeing, at the bar.

"I will never know how I knew it," he continued after the long silence, as if he hadn't stopped. "In fact, I shouldn't have known anything at all about that island. As I said, I'd never been there before, and we knew that it was deserted. Intelligence had given that information, and had cleared our exercise. I heard myself telling the chaps that we'd get some beer, and to follow me. And I began to walk over that hillock, with the men following.

"From the top of it we could see quite a distance. There was a narrow, rutted roadway down at the bottom, a roadway that hadn't been traveled for many years. We could see a small group of houses, or some sort of small buildings clustered below, rather nestled, you could say, in the curve of the road. Very small.

"We walked down, and the men followed me inside one of those little huts. Thatched roof. Inside, it was small, and a rude room. But there was a bar, and some rough shelves behind it, with some of those pottery mugs. Very old. A couple of men sat at a table; regular country people. Not very fancy. They touched their caps when we came in, and then looked down at the table again. Didn't pay much attention to us.

"I asked if we could buy beer, and one of them got up and got it. Everybody had a couple. Then I decided we'd have to get back to the ship, and so I ordered the march back. The beer had tasted good. The men were happy.

"We piled into the whaler, and as we began to row out we could see that the captain had a lookout watching for us with a spyglass. I guess they were worried when we disappeared, but when they saw us coming, the spyglass came down, and when we climbed up the rope ladder, almost every hand was on deck to watch us.

"One of the young boys—he was only about sixteen—wasn't used to drinking. He'd had two beers, and he had trouble getting up the rope ladder. It kept swaying from side to side, and he flopped about a bit. His hat fell into the water. I can still see him trying to reach it, but it floated away."

The Scot stopped for a long time, and I waited, smiling, for I could see the youth, too. I wondered just why this man had chosen to tell this story to me; surely not to extol the joys of drinking. He wasn't quite that sort.

"When I got on deck, the captain was furious. He wanted to know where we'd been; we were quite a bit late. I explained that I'd led the men over the hillock and we'd found a pub.

"We were in the captain's cabin by then, and I can still see him pulling out his maps and shouting at me: 'You *couldn't* have found a pub! You couldn't have gotten beer! That island is deserted!' He was jabbing with his finger at the map, and sure enough, it showed that island was uninhabited. But there was beer on my breath."

I had listened with interest. It seemed now that his story was done. And yet it wasn't. It was puzzling.

"You found people? You did have beer?"

"Aye! We had beer. Aye! We found people."

"But how do you explain it?"

"Sometimes there are no explanations." He shrugged and glanced past.

"But I don't understand. I'm sorry I must be so literal."

He looked at me without expression. Finally he said, "The captain said the next time he put a boat ashore there, he'd go himself, and see. But our orders came to move out before he could."

"Perhaps there were some old, forgotten recluses?" I watched his head shake. "Well, you're Scottish—are you sure you hadn't been there, sometime in the past? Maybe you forgot about it?"

He shook his head. "No. I didn't know until I got there. I still don't know how I knew. I had never been there, madam. Yet it looked just as I knew it would look, the little thatched houses, and all."

The bartender was ringing his bell, and I gave Gilbert my empty glass. It was only after I'd gotten up to my room and was getting ready for bed that I realized the Scot hadn't told us his name. Nor had I told him mine.

It was an abrupt change for me to sit alone with my thoughts. I did not like it much, but it had been interesting to remember that story. How it stood clear in my mind! The pub and the people had been interesting; and the fanciful ruin with its topsy-turvy entrance-way, even the way I'd seen Rose appear at first, her hair standing up straight as she strode past me in the graveyard. I longed to see people, to be among them. I wanted to watch them, people intent on their own interests, pushing each other out of the way, jumping onto busses, scrambling for a seat on the tube. Such things had been useful as techniques for me in past days, and the habit of watching died hard.

I missed the challenge of getting myself up and out, even a small one such as finding the right bus. I felt comparatively free of fear now, for the kids seemed quiet, and I was not molested or abused.

Now a new fear crept up, that identity might disappear. Like a patient in a nursing home, I might become a nobody, fade away into nothing with no one to talk with, no books to read, nothing to do. There was a lot to remember, but that was what old people did, wasn't it? I had tried to fight that lately, to keep busy, to find work and interest myself in many things, and had succeeded until now.

What were the reasons for keeping me? How long? Why?

Thoughts snickered and twisted. I felt muscles stiffen against it. I must do something!

I took the lunch tray to the kitchen with the thought to help the girls clean up, hoping to learn what they did here, what the operation was about.

The girls at work were attractive, but as soon as I appeared their talk ceased. I began to put away the clean dishes, and they pushed me out gently. Even an old fool would get the message. I departed, no information gotten.

Returning through the lounge I made an attempt to speak with one of the young chaps who sat in front of the fire. He had a wide, open face with the superlative ruddy complexion of the British, and he smiled and nodded at my remarks about the weather, then excused himself and left.

No such thing had ever happened in previous experience. I sat down at the fire and soon found myself in an island of silence. The kids had faded again.

I had to go outside. I could not sit among them, I could not sit in my room alone. I could not stand the unfreedom, the isolation.

I got my coat and cane and carried the boots as far as the lounge, to put them on near the door, purposely taking as long as I could. I wanted them to see me going and coming many times until it was accepted and commonplace, the thing I did. If I came back often enough, perhaps they would stop putting a tail on me.

I had managed the short morning walk fairly well, but already felt its effect on my legs. But since time was not important, I would take it slowly. If I got far away without being watched, I would stop a passing car, or find someone—a native—and ask for help. Some of them must live nearby, perhaps in huts covered with thatch, camouflaged by the heather so that I had not seen them in the morning.

I went in the opposite direction, toward the wide moor. After only a short distance I was wondering how far I could go. The leg muscles pained, and worse, the pin which had been put into my hip felt as if its sharp point had protruded into my gluteus maximus. But it was not yet unendurable, and I plodded along the highway.

I looked back after a little time. Nobody followed. Then I heard a car coming from the direction of the lodge. I would try my scheme. When the car was closer, I held out a hand in the usual signal. The car whisked past, sending some gravel flying up.

It brought on a feeling of sharp chagrin. I hoped the next driver would be more chivalrous, and began to realize how difficult my plan might prove to be. In addition, there were no small houses along the road for the distance I had come, nor any as far as I could see. My best hope was to flag down a car. I could still see the lodge clearly, and I began to understand the reason nobody followed: if I could see the lodge this clearly, they could see me. Possibly someone watched from a window with binoculars.

Yet if I were picked up, I would be whisked away in only seconds. What would I say? I did not look like the other hostelers, and surely a driver would have immediate questions. I had already decided that the truth was out.

A group of three cars came from the direction of the lodge, passed, and the result was a lot of wind in the face. There followed a long dry spell.

It seemed incredible that tourists passed so seldom, but Scotland is a country that attracts a certain kind of tourist—those who love nature and open space, clouds and water and rugged terrain; not the kind who seek pleasure palaces and exciting crowds, human types of entertainment. I had loved Scotland for this, but now I longed for human types. I walked for an hour without being passed again, and I wondered at how this small country swallowed cars and people. At Ballachulish we had waited in line for the ferry, and the moment we had driven off, every car had disappeared, dissipated like the mists in the vastness of the land. It was never like this in America, where in the summer cars travel the highways even during the night.

If a midwestern American couple stopped, I would pose as an aged visiting aunt who had wandered away from the family's holiday retreat too far on her afternoon walk, and needed help to get back. Where would I tell them to take me? I had no idea; I would play that one by ear.

If I told the truth, I feared that any down-to-earth Americans might drive to the nearest place—the lodge—to telephone to the nearest loony farm. I saw the subsequent events all too painfully, the gestures of sympathy, apologies to my kind hosts. It would mean the loss of the help I needed.

The problem was to get a car to stop. None slowed, and a long time passed between cars.

Or I might be a crofter on the way to visit a relative, with American rescuers. I would be vague about where I was going, and point ahead. Then keep my eyes open for a likely looking place. That would work.

I wished that I had an old, broken-down car to stand beside. It would be a good prop, but it was nonexistent. I dismissed the pure burlesque of lifting my skirt and showing a shapely knee, though I had heard women tell of good results from doing it.

If rescued by a Scot, I'd admit being American, no point trying to fool them about it. My story would go that I had come out to the moors with my nephew, who was a botanist, that he had driven off a little distance for a choice specimen, that I had grown tired of waiting for his return, and wanted to go home. It seemed damn foolish, but people do foolish things. But where was "home"? I would have to wave ahead and watch for a good place to claim as my own, hoping that he didn't know the people who lived there. Or I would ask him to telephone the Inverness police, or the American embassy, or the Edinburgh police.

And if I didn't get a lift soon I had to turn back. The exertion for this distance was about all that I could manage. The afternoon was growing old, and to get to food and rest would soon be my only concern.

A motor approached from the direction I walked toward. As it came closer it proved to be a meat-delivery lorry. It stopped. The driver, a big, simple-looking man, touched his cap and I climbed into the high seat beside him and told my nephew-specimen story. He nodded and started up.

I said no more, not wanting to put him off with anything. Very soon, with a deprecating jerk of his shoulder, he said, "Just a wee moment, ma'am, then I'll turn about an' have ye back t' your people. I've one last delivery. It will take a wee amount of time."

I bit my lip between my teeth as he turned in at the lodge, and a short exclamation must have escaped, for he apologized. "I promise not t'be long. It'll be only a short matter of time, until it's all put off. You just wait here. Where did ye say ye was stayin'?"

We were pulled up at the service entrance at the back of the building. I waved a weak hand in the moor direction and managed a weaker smile, slumping down into the seat, and was relieved when he disappeared and didn't wait for my answer. I could see my window from here, nobody looking down from any of them. Perhaps we could make it, after all, I consoled myself.

A chap came outside to help with the unloading. He didn't glance into the seat, but disappeared with the driver at the back of the lorry. They reappeared carrying half sides of beef into the doorway. A considerable amount of time passed after that, and I began to feel uneasy.

Rose came out and made directly for the lorry, to open my door. "Mrs. Sutherland! You should know better!" Her voice sounded grieved, as if she scolded a child. "Come along. Come, now. The poor man's worked up enough. Let's get out. That's right. Come along."

I drew back, but Rose took my arm. "But I only wanted a ride," I protested, trying to retrieve what I could of the situation. The driver had come out and stood in the doorway with the young chap, watching and shaking their heads together and smiling gently. I saw how it was. The aged-senile-guest bad dream had come true.

I climbed down and followed Rose inside, right back at the beginning. But her attitude was some consolation: she apparently thought I acted in senility. As much as I feared it, to have been believed acting it was now a help.

I expected Rose to follow me to my room, but she didn't. I was afraid to see her until I had pulled myself together, and at the delay I felt relieved. I had done a stupid thing and it had backfired. Now my intentions were clear. Yet if the driver had taken the other way, the picture would have changed completely. My single trump card was my aged condition, which I hoped Rose still believed. It had been hard to re-establish in such a short time, my emotions in a turmoil.

She took revenge, but not until the next morning did I discover it. Someone came with the breakfast tray and rattled the door without being able to get it open. When I went to help, I found it locked. I had not heard when it was done, and the discovery was as upsetting as the fact.

Mary came back a few minutes later, apologizing to bother me twice. "Mrs. MacPherson forgot to tell us. I'm sorry, ma'am, that I had to go back for the key." She looked ashamed and flustered, and I sensed sympathy from the kids.

I could not eat, and only drank the tea. I blamed myself for going too fast, and with nothing to divert them, my emotions blended and became fear again. I shook and the tea slopped into the saucer. The room was a narrow prison; its walls closed. When I got a tissue to put under the cup, I found that I was weeping frantically, and needed it to dry my eyes. When my door was unlocked, the situation had been at least bearable; now it was intolerable.

Was Gilbert, too, locked away? Perhaps at the bottom of a dungeon? There were plenty of them in this wild country, deep holes under castles with only a small opening at the top, dark and wet, where a man could scream his lungs out with no one hearing. If only I could telephone Sarah! She would set heaven and earth ablaze to get us out.

We had met her soon after we left Chipping Cranford. To remember her and the way we met was comforting, and I let my mind roam over that time, the morning when we left England, Gilbert sitting in the sunlight that streaked across the white cloth in the Queen's Arms at breakfast. I thought longingly of the freedom I had enjoyed then, not enough aware of it to savor it fully. I had gotten up early and had waited for a long time to get into the bathroom, had gone skulking up the twisted hallway and several steps and back to my room again. Whoever was in the bathroom must have died in the tub, I remember thinking.

I clutched my wrapper and scurried up and back, noticing that some of the guests were up and about—open doors and tossed bed-clothing inside a few of the rooms. Yes, and the Scot I had seen, too, and Rose inside a door slightly ajar. I was sure of it now.

Finally I had been able to bathe and dress. Gilbert must have needed extra sleep, for his door was shut and he didn't respond to my light tap. I went up to the church and got my information, and was back in the lobby when he came down for breakfast.

The dining room was full of tourists, many of them Americans, and the waiters were overburdened, doing their best but getting orders mixed up. Gilbert's kippers were placed before a middle-aged English gentleman who sat at the next table, and his sausages were served to Gilbert. He waved his hands at the waiters, and puffed out his lips when they failed to notice. He looked rather absurd, and he seemed to feel that way. I smiled at the memory. He always did exactly what was needed without extra motions, and the effort he was making was distasteful to him. I could see that he considered reaching across the small space which separated our tables and rejected the thought, put off by the awfully good manners of the English.

We did have toast, and I waited for porridge. I buttered the dry, cold toast and spread on marmalade and watched what Gilbert did, and the middle-aged man at the next table. It was a little cameo, curious and fun.

Apparently the man waited for the rest of his family, for his wife and a little boy of about five years came. She looked at the un-touched kippers and lifted her eyebrows, seated the child and then herself. The man pointed to his plate and made a gesture of denial, and the little boy began to squirm.

The waiters continued to ignore Gilbert. I spread another piece of toast.

"The Sloans aren't going to be happy over what I learned today," I said.

The waiter discovered him at that moment, and he didn't answer me right off. After the sausages had been removed, he answered, his mouth full of toast. "You got up to the church before breakfast?"

"Well, you know how it is, these midsummer days. I woke up. The warden had the doors open. Really, you wouldn't believe what they've got in there. It's a sight. A marble case twice the size of a man with a white marble couple inside, holding hands and peering out as if they see the Promised Land. They're wearing little crowns, but the inscription—it's in gold leaf all over the outside of the doors—says they were 'wool merchants, servants of God.' "

Gilbert ate a kipper and chuckled. "Great!"

"It says she had the case and the figures carved after her husband was killed in the Civil War, and that she was eternally faithful to her husband, and the case must not be opened until after her death. They look all ready to step out."

"Sloan?"

I nodded. "There go their dreams of nobility—right up in marble."

My porridge came and I poured on cream and salted it. At the next table a young couple with a little girl had joined the middle-aged man and woman, and the boy of five was squirming around and making querulous noises. The grandfather clucked at him several times, but the boy kept on. Finally the grandfather said, his voice clear, yet very quiet, "Look here, old man—if you don't stop that squirming and grumbling, I'll have to throw you out of the window."

I shook more salt on the porridge, trying not to seem watchful, yet taking immense delight in the child's reaction to this absurd statement. He sat very still and seemed lost in thought. I smiled, wanting to laugh aloud.

The young mother had her hands full with the little girl. She had been put into a high chair close beside the table, and she crawled out of it and onto her mother again and again. Without a word the mother placed her into it again. The tableau was full of motion from that one spot; the child emerged from the chair the moment that she had been put into it, almost oozing out as if she were a kitten. There was no sound from either the mother or the child, and the crawling out and putting back went on and on. It was fascinating to see. It was impossible to not see. I marveled at the mother's patience.

We finished our breakfast, the porridge warming my stomach like a flannel heating pad. The food had arrived at the next table and the children were busy; the little show was over for the moment.

"Come on, and bring your binoculars," I said to Gilbert. "I've got to have a better look at those chimney flues before we leave, and you've got to see the marbles."

"And then we'll be off to Scotland, Aunt?"

"Aye! That we will!"

There came a knock at the door, and then it opened. I sighed. The memory of that time had been a good respite. Now I had to come back to bleak reality.

"I'm sorry, ma'am." Mary's face, as she bent to pick up the tray, was sympathetic.

"I understand. Mary, is Mrs. MacPherson here?"

"Yes, ma'am."

"When you get downstairs, will you tell her I want to talk with her?"

"Aye." She bobbed her curtsy and went.

But I waited a long time. It put ice into my heart. Whenever Rose was near, she looked at me as if the back of my head had come off, and I'd forgotten to put it on. She was in some way connected with the Scot, and I had vaguely known it in Edinburgh, but had discredited my recognition of the fact.

There was nothing better to do, so I let my mind follow that trip northward from Chipping Cranford, across undulating moors that were like beautifully manicured, empty landscapes of far horizons. It raised my spirit to think of the look of the sunshine across the views of rolling land, which had been planted and cultivated in huge acreage squares, not a soul to be seen.

The day had turned gloomy, the clouds so heavy that it seemed to be nearly night by four, only about ten feet of the road ahead visible. Rain finally fell heavily, and Gilbert had to hold a slow pace. He grew increasingly curt as the windscreen became opaque with water, and the few cars which we passed threw up more. I was disappointed not to be able to see anything—it was as if we flew, except for the water flung from beneath; we were actually inside a cloud.

He stopped trying to talk. We rode in a silvery-black semidarkness, and I forgave Gilbert's curt silence from nerves. I was bored. I let my mind idle among the events of the past day. Short episodic images projected on the screen in my mind, flicking on for a few seconds and changing. It was as if I watched an illustrated lecture, minus the talk.

There was the Queen's Arms dining room; the mother smoothing down the little girl. Then the bobby pointing up the street toward the roses. Then the ruin behind the wall.

I grew tired of it, and cold. When Gilbert turned on the heater at my request the windows fogged. I swabbed them off until he abruptly said to stop. I sat back and eyed him and wondered how long this trip would take; it seemed endless.

The pictures began again. This time I saw corridors of English hotels. One after another—hallways. All were essentially alike: red carpets, or red background with big gold medallions, or red carpets with flowers. Walls painted in levels of different bright colors; walls papered in flower prints; dadoes painted a different color. Ceilings painted bright colors. Many colors, many decorations. Hallways with turns, steps up, steps down, corners to turn; steps up. Colors and decorations, twists and steps.

"So the English love bright colors and pretty things. They love to decorate. What is it you keep trying to tell me?" I stared blankly at the road, hardly visible in the dark rain. The wipers clicked a steady metronomic beat. It was tiresome. It was good to see Edinburgh looming ahead.

We drove through its wet streets in twilight between gray granite walls slick with rain. The color matched Gilbert's mood, and our hotel did not look attractive, its entrance an extended walk between a windowless high wall on one hand and a black iron railing overlooking the railroad yards on the other. Gilbert parked the car and struggled with the bags. It was all I could manage to move against a high wind and get inside the building.

But the foyer's warmth was a surprise after that fiercely contested entrance, dark-paneled, softly lit and warm; the staff courteous and helpful. Our rooms were large and clean, the walls a soft wheat color, the woodwork white. No carving, no dadoes. A pale gold carpet, a white bedspread.

Gilbert muttered something about taking a hot bath and closed the connecting door. I sank down on the bed with a happy sigh, and pulled the eiderdown over myself.

Perhaps I fell asleep. I remember thinking of the good fortune we had in getting rooms with their own baths, so that there was no necessity to skulk down hallways to test doorknobs and wait. Languor flowed upwards, my muscles relaxed and I smiled contentedly, contrasting this pleasant feeling with the tension of the trip, and the tension I'd felt in the Queen's Arms when I had scurried up and down the hallway clutching my wrapper and hoping for a chance at the bathroom.

Perhaps I fell asleep. Or, muscles relieved of tension, the subconscious crept out and began to register. I was back in the long corridor and trying the bathroom door, then hurrying back to my room. It was early morning. Many doors along the hall, some of them open, the bedclothing tumbled aside. From a room the low voices of two people talking, a man and a woman, the woman's voice saying, "She mustn't know," quite distinctly, quickly followed by a hushing, as if someone placed a sudden hand upright and the voice dropped, and then the door closing softly. Two faces seen but quickly in passing, not really seen. One was the Scot, the other Rose.

The elongated midsummer twilight was still seeping in around the window draperies when I got up and dressed for dinner. Had I been asleep?

Flames of a table burner soared over a trolley beside our table, the waiter preparing beef stroganoff while Gilbert selected wine, his face pink and cheerful once more. I clucked appreciatively at the plate of hot soup that was served—mushroom, mustily fresh and delicious. I smiled at Gilbert over the white damask and wine glasses. Life was improving. He had done everything right again.

When we had finished eating, feeling jolly and ebullient and the waiter's suggestion of coffee served in the lounge appealing, we moved toward the foyer. There was a slight difference here from the people we had so recently been among—the sounds were subdued, but here we heard a tweedy texture in the speech, a burr in the sound and jocularity in sudden laughter and hearty good feelings. They looked shorter and wider, and they moved muscularly and more quickly.

A group of German tourists occupied tables in the center of the dining room, and talked together loudly as if alone, inspecting the menu cards with haughty expressions and ignoring everyone except themselves. They looked ponderously self-important, stocky, and the women were particularly homely and wore clothes which were extremely unattractive.

We were passing between tables; the eye sees and the mind registers—of no importance, no significance—strangers sitting at tables, eating, laughing, speaking together.

Almost at the lobby door my eyes were caught and pulled back again to a familiar figure. The Scot sat there, examining the bill of fare. If he had seen us, he gave no sign, and we went out without signaling. The low table in the lounge beyond already held a silver coffee pot and two cups, and the waiter was ready to pour.

There came a sharp, businesslike rap at the door, then the sound of the key. The door opened and Rose came in, shutting it and leaning against the jamb, her position supercilious, yet inquiring. I had seen that same facial expression on the Dean of Women years ago, when I had stayed out too late on a date.

My room was nearly dark. The long afternoon had passed while I sat reminiscing. The skies were filled with thick clouds, black and heavy with moisture. I had remembered well, and I knew it had not been a dream, but that I had seen Rose with the Scot at the Queen's Arms, and they did not want me to know something.

"Mary said you asked to see me?" Rose's opening gambit was intended to prod me into a disclosure; her manner had a quick-lance, aggressive thrust, as if she had scant time for games and was annoyed.

I hoped to say the right thing. At the lengthening silence, she moved slightly toward me, bending a little. I sensed a beginning of doubt in her, and worked from there. She had expected anger, perhaps, or self-justification, or defiance, so they were out. I took a little time to feel myself back into character. It was a good course.

It surprised her; she changed subtly, her body language betraying her first attitude and words. As she came forward I sensed that there was some reason to protect me; for some purpose I did not know, I had importance to her and the group, and I suddenly knew that she acted under orders, that she was not the principal in the strange sequence of events I found myself embroiled in.

When I did speak, my voice was unusually low, thoughtful, old, with a tone of unhappiness. I spoke of my fear of closed places, of the need for exercise, of muscles getting lax, of solitude and the aberrations which follow. I made the little speech purposely wandering and only partly cohesive. What I said was true, but its truth must emerge clouded, as if from a wandering mind. I ended by asking that the door be unlocked, and promised not to try again to leave until she was ready to release me. "I'm sorry to be a problem, I didn't mean to be. I wanted to ride, again. I like riding in cars, and my legs got awfully tired."

Something must have recalled her purpose to mind, for after a short silence, she nodded thoughtfully. "You promise?"

I nodded, childlike. "I promise."

"You may walk on the moor, but no rides. You must not go near the road. You can walk until you drop, Mrs. Sutherland, and you won't find a house near enough to reach by foot in this area. You must not go near the road, and you must stay on the moor! Is that understood?"

I nodded.

She studied me in silence for a time. Then she said, "I'll leave your door unlocked. You get one more chance. If you make any more trouble, you'll be locked in again. Do you understand?"

She had raised her voice on the question as if I had gone deaf. I nodded, my hands clasped together in my lap, looking up at her in the way a child looks when he knows he has escaped punishment.

When she went out, it was good not to hear the click of the lock.

It was too late to go outside, and raining, to boot. I would go in the morning. How I would leave now was a problem, for I must avoid suspicion, but I was still determined to get away.

In the morning I went out early. I came back, flushed with the cold air and exercise, to find the kids doing their yoga. They looked up as I limped toward the stairs, and I sensed a feeling among them of slight sympathy, but I may have been mistaken about it. They seemed to half smile, and I climbed to my room for a rest period with a good, comfortable mood enveloping me from the atmosphere in the lobby. I lay on the bed and eased the painful hip. The morning walk had given the muscles a workout, and my hip was acutely painful. I had nearly dropped to sleep when sounds made me alert. Something was happening in the lobby. I got up and crept to the balcony.

Two men in dark overcoats stood at the reception desk. The young people were moving around and scattering, the yoga broken up by the visitors. Rose was coming from the dining room toward the men. I knew that they were police.

I went quickly toward the stairs, and had gone down three steps when someone suddenly grabbed me. I managed only a sharp intake of breath, and his hand was over my mouth. I was lifted and carried down the hallway to the back of the building. He grabbed my coat from my room and threw it over my head before I regained the sense of what was occurring, then continued his race down the hall. I thrashed with arms and legs, which he did not seem to notice; it didn't slow him down.

I heard a door open and felt him running down flights of steps. He carried me as if I were a struggling pet. I sensed the basement, then passing through it and the slight change of feeling of outside air, and the gentle sound of a motor purring, of many strong hands pushing my body into a car, of being dumped, the door shut hastily and the car's gentle forward motion.

I pawed my way up out of the coat. We had reached the highway almost without sound. A black police car was parked at the entrance steps. We drove past and turned quickly onto the highway, and picked up immense speed at once.

Curves flashed toward us, boulders flew past. The chap who drove kept his face rigidly forward, his hands tense on the wheel. I remembered that they called him Malcolm. I turned to look in the back. Another chap was there, and both were tense. The chap in the back watched me; Malcolm watched the road.

He needed his expertise for the speed he took. I could not open the door and drop out, and I sat dumb-struck at having managed to do so little to stop them, or to call attention to myself. Yet I had done what I could. I thought of it with chagrin, for I had many times planned my actions if a mugger attacked in the narrow alleyways to stage entrances and deserted streets at night which my work imposed. I was aghast at the ease with which I had been abducted.

I had screamed a gasp, had kicked with no difference. Now I saw why: Malcolm was as huge as a grizzly bear. I was almost certain that they had managed without the two men knowing it was being done.

Curves and twists in the road flew toward us and disappeared behind, boulders flashed past. I clung to the side and was thrown from left to right, and my previous fears faded in fear of sudden death on the highway. The road flew forward in zigzag turns, and Malcolm took it without lessening our pace.

A lay-by was ahead. He swerved into it and drove through, toward a mass of boulders at the back. They were immense, and I held my breath as it seemed we were about to crash into them. Malcolm slowed and braked, then turned suddenly between two large boulders and turned off the engine. We were wedged between two huge rocks that towered over the small car. The space had just admitted its width.

There was abrupt silence. Since I had first seen the men it could not have been more than five or eight minutes. I sat gaping, waiting for my mind to catch up with events.

Lines of strain showed on Malcolm's face. He stared straight ahead, listening, his hands in exactly the same position on the wheel as when he had been driving, and now still tense. The chap in the back took a deep breath and began a gentle smile. Presently Malcolm relaxed. They remained quietly listening.

We were trapped between the boulders, so close that the door could open no more than an inch. It was a place no one would ever drive a car into. I was sure that it had been selected in advance, and the whole plan carefully drawn.

The situation explained itself. I realized how carefully watched I was. Every eventuality had been worked out: certain people had been appointed to do certain things. I almost admired them. I wondered whose planning it was. Perhaps it was Rose, but for some reason I didn't think so.

We sat cramped in the little car. I seemed to doze, a habit that the elderly fall into when they sit for long periods. When I opened my eyes there was nothing to see except those erupting gray-black boulders, looking hurled by giants at each other in combat. There was no chance to escape here or anywhere.

Who was Rose acting for? Why was I wanted by them? Who were they, what did they do? I did not believe Rose's story, but the truth eluded.

At last the chaps talked in low, terse sentences in Gaelic. I didn't expect to understand, so it was like being shocked by electricity to hear Gilbert's name jump out from their words. I know that my head jerked up, and I pretended that I had dropped off to sleep and smiled a gentle old lady's smile of apology at Malcolm, who nodded back in understanding.

Was Gilbert in on this? It did seem strange, now, that we had coughed our way in that little car through the bens to have broken down so near the lodge. Gilbert had taken the car in for gas and a checkup; he might have arranged something to put it out of commission. He hadn't faked it, anyway—he had been as upset as I was, in his more guarded, less screaming-explosive manner than mine. But why did they speak of him? What were they saying?

I felt the sweat prickle out, and made an effort to sit quietly, pretending that I slept, and keeping my breathing steady and even. Had Gilbert sent the police? If he had, why hadn't he come, himself, to make sure that I was all right?

Why would he have done it? Did he want to get rid of me? I couldn't believe it. Why? In only a few days he would have been in California; he had spoken eagerly of getting down to London when he packed the car in Inverness. He had come to drive me around until I had gotten my feet wet in this new business; I couldn't have made it without him. I was ready to go on my own now, to kiss him good-by and drive for myself. Surely I had made it clear to him how much I valued his help, and he had benefited, as well—he had gotten a wonderful look at this old world from which our new one had come, enjoying it immensely.

If he sometimes got uptight with me, his reaction was not conspiratorial; rather, he'd spoken out, lashing verbally without fear, once he'd gone through his typical period of black gloom. He'd always cleared the air, to go on in his usual curt, buoyant way, completely open to the point of being rude at times. He could say what he liked; I never repressed him. Oh no! Gilbert couldn't be in on this —whatever this was!

Normal breathing restored by these thoughts, I began to wonder if he *had* sent the police. If he had, he was alive. Or were the men at the lodge there for some other reason than to search for me?

The tension inside the car grew thick and palpable. After a long time we heard the sound of a car passing. From the corners of my eyes I saw Malcolm's shoulders slope downward almost imperceptibly in relaxation, but the sweat poured out in the palms of my hands as we continued to sit.

I groaned in inward relief when Malcolm started the car, backed expertly out of our cul-de-sac and turned toward the lodge. I had not thought that I wanted to see that lodge again, but it was comfort to go up to my room, again to be alone.

Moor hopping was my only outlet. On the moors there are puddles and hummocks and small sullen streams that do not seem to go anywhere, and which move very slowly. It was quiet, a good place to think. I splashed ahead time after time and tried to fit the puzzle together. The kids knew something of Gilbert; it didn't seem to be just that he had disappeared after I had appeared, but more and different. I had no idea what. I was a captive, yet there was some freedom to move about. And if the kids were as sympathetic to me as I had judged, maybe I could learn something if I talked with them. I must try, and keep my dodderer part when Rose was around; with them I might try honesty.

The next time the tray came, I tried out my new theory, feeling as fluttery in anticipation as years long ago when I was a girl in search of a part and had walked onto an empty stage to read lines alone to a yawning opening with two men lolling halfway back in the dim vastness.

"Wait a moment, would you please, Frances?" I begged as she set down the tray.

She turned, her face showing surprise, her fingers already clasped on the doorknob. "Yes, ma'am?"

"Listen, Frances . . . do you have to go right back? Can you wait just a bit? I'd so much like to talk with you."

She looked puzzled and a good bit frightened, but she did wait, a flush creeping up from her throat and coloring her face to the hair-line. I wanted terribly much to find the right words, not to frighten her more than she seemed to be already. It was dismaying that she was so afraid.

Dear God, what do I say? That I need friends, need to know something? I cast about in my mind, wondering how to approach her. She was becoming more upset the longer I delayed, and so I finally took a chance.

"Frances—I come from people such as you all are, here . . . 'way back in my lineage I think there's some Scottish blood, probably. My mother's ancestors left your country in search of freedom . . . perhaps I understand you a little. I know that I like you all very much." I smiled, hoping it would help, that she could leap across to an understanding of more than was actually said. And I also hoped that this wouldn't destroy any benefits accruing to me from my aged-lady status with the kids. It was a risk I had to take.

"Yes, ma'am?" She curtsied. She had clear pink skin and reddish hair which curled a little at the ends and very heavily around her temples, and her blue eyes widened. She appeared undecided whether to leave immediately, or to stay longer, embarrassed by her own courtesy, uncertain of how to reply, whether to remain a servant or to become a friend and take part in a discussion.

I did not dare at this moment to ask what they did, didn't dare to ask anything at all, but held off all remarks until she could gain enough strength to speak. I would follow her lead, whatever she might say. She was so uncomfortable that I wanted greatly to reassure her, if I might have, to put a hand on her shoulder—to mother her, I suppose. At that moment I greatly loved her.

From long habit in courteous treatment of her elders, she waited and finally said, "Ma'am, would you be knowing if they were Scots, or English?" She pronounced the last word carefully, as if ejecting it from her mouth in a discreet, quick, well-mannered way.

Surprised by the question, I again groped for words. "Why . . . of course, you know that my husband's name is Scottish—Sutherland— you know that's Scottish better than I do." She was nodding, withdrawn as a fawn, and as ready to move quickly off. She was so vulnerable, so *guarded*. I felt her feelings, and had a small agony of sympathy.

"I'm a mixture, Frances . . . just about everything, I guess. But the people my mother came from left England. Quite early, as soon as America was opened."

"I see." She held fast to the knob, looking more embarrassed, unable to move one way or the other, unable to think of more to say.

I now felt very bad about my idea of talking with the kids. At this juncture I seemed to be opening a wound, just the opposite of what I'd intended. There was tremendous sensitivity in this young girl. I didn't want to hurt her.

In a flow of compassion, I realized that only everyday things would salvage the child. I looked at the tray and exclaimed over the food, picking up a piece of bread and seeming to be suddenly hungry. "Thanks for the tray, my dear." I waved a hand broadly into the air, not looking up, relieved that from the corner of my eyes I saw her slip out.

Where was this getting me? I didn't want to entrap this girl, who had stood captive to her good upbringing. I didn't know if she would report me downstairs; it seemed doubtful, but if she did, there was really nothing to report. Perhaps I had seemed again in my dotage; if so, that was all right. And I would be more selective next time, and find someone with more personal strengths to try to talk with. One of the lads, perhaps.

I shuddered a little over the rebuff I might expect, yet I felt worse about the girl. I had grown used to unkindnesses; no one in the public eye escapes, and I had taken my share of severe criticism, some of it in print. I guessed that I could once more summon the strength to accept pain.

I hobbled ahead, sorting out the information I had, my fear changed by the unlocked door to curiosity again. What was it the kids did? They kept the lodge clean, and the food was appetizing, although plain—the kind that is called "good, simple fare." They had classes regularly, which I only surmised from the sounds emanating from the dining room as I went through, a sound of a low voice seeming to be lecturing, and replies, like questions asked, and the lecture resuming. I had lingered at the doorway several times to putter with the boots, and today had caught sight of the fellow I'd first seen in the records room in Inverness. The kids called him Robert. They had been talking in Gaelic, and only the name leapt out.

I disturbed a nest of plovers, and the female flew upward with a feathery whisk of wings and a purring sound. I skirted it, hoping she'd return, remembering other names that had come through the language. They had spoken of Malcolm Cromarty. Sarah had said that name.

I had kept up my slow gait through the lounge, stopping to retie my head scarf, when the name Stewart Bruce was spoken. Why would they talk about the clan chief I had researched? I had learned nothing, and had written to Gretchen to investigate on the Continent. That letter was somewhere in limbo.

I set myself a goal at a good distance. I would reach it, a small hummock which projected above the others, even if I had to crawl on my hands and knees to return. Sarah had mentioned Malcolm Cromarty, puzzled about his identity. It was when we had dinner with her and Duncan, that evening when her unreserved friendship had been liberally given to us, when we learned of the Scottish warmth and candor.

I saw little warmth here. Rose was cold and demanding, punishing, the only one to whom I could speak, the kids under orders not to talk. But Duncan and Sarah were human, genuine. It seemed long ago, and in my thoughts they had become dear, old friends.

III

We had set off after breakfast to the Museum of Antiquities. The exhibits were fascinating, but told nothing unknown about Stewart Bruce. We emerged at noon to a flashing, sudden rain.

"Gilbert, we're going to have to go to Inverness, I think. I have a feeling it's there—the source."

"If that's the source, then it's Inverness. But what about lunch?"

"I forget how hungry young people get," I apologized. "But first, let's run in for a quick errand. I want a warm head scarf. And I'd like to send your mother some of that wonderful wool. I promised," I added, seeing his quick look of doubt.

I went to the shop which the Scot had spoken about, rather than the elegant ones in Princes Street. As the door opened it set in motion a set of tiny bells. The pleasant jingle faded, and we looked into a shop, which seemed deserted. We passed counters of tourist-type souvenirs and went toward the back, curious to see nobody behind the counters.

A din of voices came from a room at the back, where in the middle of the wall a doorway was hung with twisted portieres of a nondescript color. The sound was almost a roar, and sticking out from the portieres were shoulders, arms and even the caps of blue-clad policemen. Apparently they had not heard the sound of the bells or noticed us, the racket they made so great in the tiny office, which was literally crammed to overflowing with them.

We drew back uncertainly. Here, too? Trouble and police had filled whole editions of our newspapers in America lately. Should we leave? The shop was in a state of mild disarray, but showed no sign of violence, yet the loud argument back there, all those police—

We must have made some motion that caught their attention,

for the altercation abruptly stopped. Ten or twelve big men filed out, touching their caps respectfully as they passed us, and the shop became quiet and deserted. As the last man disappeared, the shop owner stuck his head out from the portieres.

"Come in! Come in!" His voice rang heartily, loud but not rough. He saw our indecision and came forward, both his hands outstretched; his feet struck the bare floorboards firmly, and when I gave my request he moved at once to the counter, swept the piled merchandise to one side in a quick stroke of his bare forearm. He wore a kilt and a short-sleeved shirt, and his necktie matched the kilt's tartan. His decisive, swift motions had bolts of brightly colored fabrics on the counter before there was time to see any one of them, and he moved away and back, bringing still more.

If Duncan Ferguson had lived in the days of great clan chieftains, he would have fitted the mind's-eye version of Great Chief. If he had worn a wild animal skin and carried a club, it would have fitted him, for his vitality was overwhelming. Although he was short by English standards—not over five feet eight—he was a massive man. He turned with an inquiring look, and his shoulders swung around like a castle gate opening. His black hair, clipped short at the neck, sprang up from his forehead in a wild fury, and moved up and down when he walked.

He brought so many different fabrics that I was confused. He came to the front of the counter, pushed away what he'd already placed, crossed the room for more, and his kilt flounced, the tassels of his kilt hose flounced, his hair flounced. His calves, as thick as the head of a chieftain's club, pulled wide the purling of his hose; they were so snug that they almost seemed to squeak and groan with his steps. The tassel ties on his ghillies flounced, the long strings around his legs creaked. His muscles were huge. He looked made for combat.

When he had everything on the counter, he turned with another look of inquiry, and began to push and pull at the mass of fabric, inviting comment. They were all exciting, all beautiful. There were too many to see any of them. The pigments jumbled and tossed in a confusing beat of vibrations, pulsing and throbbing. I had been a long time studying the objects in the museum, and realized now that

I should first have eaten lunch. I felt dizzy, and hated to disappoint this man, but I could not choose anything from that mass of colors and tartans. I put a hand to my head, trying to close my eyes against the confusion, needing to rest.

I felt as I had felt years ago when I had first known that dizziness —just off stage, on the top of a flight of rough backstage stairs, waiting to hear my cue with one hand feeling the splintery rail beneath my fingers. I was to make a sweeping, imperious descent onstage, and the character and her entering words were firm in mind. The actions on the set were moving toward the moment, coming dimly through the flat.

A flash of vertigo had made me tremble. I was frightened, thrown off, and I fought it, trying to hold my character and her feeling and words in my mind. For the first time my body came between me and the part, and I gripped the railing and felt my hand quiver. I had lost the pace of the action.

When the cue came I moved onstage, and managed to get through until the curtain. Perhaps the others didn't know that technique was what they saw, but through the act, to me they appeared as if I looked through the wrong end of opera glasses—terribly small and far away.

Afterward I had seen the doctor. His warning had made me take stock, and though the decision was put off for a few years, I knew that this life was drawing to its end. But I must have something else to take its place, and I didn't know what I might do. I did not want to crash down in full view, and this fear had finally made the idea of retirement more acceptable. The plan to live in Britain and to do genealogical research had helped, too.

Duncan looked suddenly at me with concern. His benign expression changed, and he pushed away the bolt of cloth that he held and moved toward me with his hands held out, grasped mine and helped me around the counter and inside his little office. The strength of his hands was tremendous.

Gilbert waited in the doorway, his head cocked between the portieres. Duncan swept boxes and books from chairs and invited us to sit, then he pushed ledgers and piles of papers back on his desk, reached into a drawer and brought up a bottle of whiskey. He dug out three glasses and splashed liquor into them and waved a muscled arm at the room with a wide gesture.

"Ar-r-gh! What a mess! I've only just come from thr-ree days in Inverness! We should clear out the whole blasted mess and star-rt over! Inverness—th' pipe contests—*what* a disappointment, what a *thing!* This year-r we didn't win!"

I sipped the drink, a picture flashing of Duncan blowing panpipes, so ridiculous that I had to smile. He meant bagpipes; that fitted him. The whine, snarl, swarming sound fitted Duncan perfectly.

He lifted his glass and said, "*Slainte mháth!*" It sounded like "*Slangah va,*" the first two consonants lovingly touched off by the tongue, the *g* soft.

The whiskey burned, but I began to revive.

Duncan went on: "Aye! An' we got only thir-rd place this year-r! What a comedown!" He hit his forehead with his open palm. "Those're the lads ye saw when ye came in—the Edinburgh Piper-rs —all of 'em piper-rs, an' good ones, too! An' last year-r th' Wor-rld Champions!"

"How many bands competed?" Gilbert asked.

"Fifty, lad, Fifty! It's not good enough! We'll not let that happen again!"

Between the twisted portieres appeared the face of a young man. Duncan looked up and jumped from his seat.

"Come in! Come in, Angus! I was just tellin' these good people about the pipin' contest. Her-re, let's have another glass, Angus," and he disappeared around a corner and emerged in a second rubbing a glass with a wrinkled towel, literally scrubbing with the linen until the glass must have grown hot. Satisfied, he placed it on a tiny space he had made on the desk, threw the towel into a corner, poured a large splash of whiskey into the glass, scooped it up and gave it to Angus all in one swift, uninterrupted motion.

Angus, leather-tanned, starting to wrinkle around the eyes, had a full beard of deep chestnut color; it was slightly darker than his hair. He was about thirty-five, I decided, and he was exceedingly handsome. The two began a heated discussion of the contest, and

I listened, feeling like Alice at the tea party because of the unfamil-
iarity of the terms they used. Feeling the liquor take effect, still daz-
zled by the impressions that swarmed, I heard these hearty men ar-
guing, groaning, imprecating, probing. Their voices were sometimes
raised in whimsical tones, inquiring and analyzing their musical
performance.

I have listened to Americans analyze football games, and that is
the nearest thing I can think of to express how it was. They made
statements of what they had done, and their declarative sentences
would taper up into a question: what had gone wrong? Sure, they'd
not let it happen again, but what was it? Their puzzlement was not
querulous, nor did it complain. They were in many ways like small
children who had suffered punishment without learning why. They
were angry, but not at anybody; their anger, which was deep and hon-
est, was not against persons, but against a situation they did not understand. They had done well. They had felt satisfied. What, then,
had happened?

"Oh, the pipes!" Duncan groaned, his head in his hands. "The
pipes! I have fought with 'em, have squeezed the bloody bag and
fought, until the sweat ran down my face! I've tr-ried t' make 'em
play, and they won't play! And I hold the danglin' mess o' pipes and
shake 'em and screech at 'em. And then I shake my head and I say:
Well, all right! So you are the winner! I cannot play you, and you
cannot be played by any man. All right. Now you have won! You are
the victor! I have admitted it; now, come! I entreat you, I ask you—
let us see what we can do together. I will try t' do as you want, as
you like. I will coax you, coax the sounds out of you. Come, now. Let
us try again."

As he spoke, the anguished fervor of his voice dropped until when
he reached the end, his tones were gentle, soft, beguiling, almost like
a woman imploring. His head had dropped and hung from his
shoulders over his chest. He rested his forearms on the desk, his
hands extended and open, as if he held the pipes between them,
and he looked at his hands and shook his head slowly, as if trying to
understand some loved and unruly child.

Suddenly he threw his head back. His eyes instantly lost their puzzled look, and took on sparkle. "Then I put the blasted r-reed into my mouth, and blow it again, easy. And it comes! It comes! It does what I want! We make music together!"

He paused for a moment, his lips opened and his tongue caught between his teeth for a second, while his eyes flashed on the ceiling between several points, not seeing. Then he lowered his head and looked directly at me. "And do you know," he said, his voice low and confidential, "when I co-operate with the pipes, they play! It's not me who's playin' them, it's *us*, playin' together!"

We all broke into laughter. Duncan was an actor, and though he wasn't acting, his performance had been true, a recreation of his feelings. We felt it, too. We all understood.

We left late in the afternoon, reluctantly, and before we did, Duncan had invited us to his home for dinner that night. Not that he invited every one of his customers, he said, but there was something about us which appealed to him. We were to come back around six. He'd be closing by then, and he'd guide us to his house, following him in his truck.

We staggered to the hotel and took a nap.

We got back before Duncan had shut up shop and had to wait for a straggle of customers to finger through souvenir trifles. Then Duncan brought the two flags at the door inside, removed the wire frame of postcards from a nail on the doorjamb, brought inside the mat and an Inverness cape of tartan, and closed and locked the door.

His small pickup truck was parked at the curb, now that the traffic flow had ceased, and he guided us toward it, suddenly stopping with one hand on the door handle and striking his head with an open palm. "Aach-h-h! I don't know what I was thinkin' of, tellin' you t' drive, too! I can just as well take the both of you, if you don't mind bein' cooped up in the back, Gilbert."

"No sense in your coming back later," Gilbert said. "You lead the way; we'll follow."

"Gilbert, d'you mind? I mean, what would you say if your aunt rode with me?" Turning to me, he asked, "That is, if you don't mind ridin' in a truck?"

"I'd love to go with you," I said, climbing in and folding my knees up under my chin. Duncan slammed my door, made his way around the truck and came inside with another hearty bang. "Would you believe—I bought this truck for only ninety pounds? Ninety pounds! I told the fellow, 'That's all I've got: you take it; I'll take the truck.' He did!" He swatted his knee and roared in glee, and swung the truck out into the road as if it were propelled by a jet engine.

"I really wanted to talk with you, Hortense, m'dear. You're goin' to be meetin' Sarah. And I do so much want t' let you know how greatly she's changed my life. Why, since Sarah came, there's no comparison with what it was, before."

He drew to a stop at a traffic light and waited. When we moved ahead he began to talk once more. "Hortense, d'ye know, before Sarah, I'd be drinkin' myself half dazed, all the time. Not just some of the time! *All* of the time!

"She's a smart one, that Sarah! Do you know, she started drinkin', too? Doin' just what I did, glass for glass. One day it dawned on me what she was up to. So I asked her if she wasn't drinkin' rather more than she was used to doin'. She said she was tryin' t' show me what I was like. Oh, it was a revelation! She gave me an awful shock, drinkin' like that! She told me that when I cut down, she'd cut down!" He looked at me rather anxiously, as if trying to feel how I would take this.

"She was better than a lecture, eh? Yes, she's smart," I admitted.

"She made me see it better than anything else would have done. Oh, she's a smart, wonderful gir-rl!

"And that's not all of it, Hortense. This gir-rl, Sarah, she'd had a hell of a life before we found each other. Her husband was mean. He *was* a drunkard. She and her boy, Philip, were livin' in fear with that rascal. She kept tryin' t' make him sober up, and then something happened that made her realize he'd get no better, and she moved out with the boy."

Duncan's voice got lower. "I tell you, Hortense: if I had t' live now without her, I couldn't do it. I couldn't!" He shook his head slowly from side to side, his gaze fixed on the road. Slowly he inhaled through his nostrils, and continued in a deeper tone, very softly. "If there's a God, the kind of a God they teach you about in the churches —and if that God is love—"

His voice had trailed off and stopped. I realized that he was trying to tell me something more than that he loved Sarah; he was also telling me that they were not married. It was a wonder to me, that he cared for my opinion. Did he feel that I might snub Sarah? I couldn't do that. No, I realized quietly. He was trying to prepare me, in case I should find out. A sense of joy flooded my veins; joy for his subtlety, his feeling for nuances, his wish to have things out in the open, to obviate the unexpected. For a man of Duncan's size, muscularity, extreme egotism, also to possess such a fine sensitivity was a remarkable thing. I don't know if I said anything; if I did, it was only a tone or a murmur. There are no words for this kind of revelation.

He began again, quietly. "If that God is *love*, then surely He approves of the way Sarah and I are livin' now! He wouldn't want either of us t' go back the way we lived before! She, havin' such a hard time, with that young boy t' think of, and a husband who beat 'em if he bothered to notice 'em at all. And I—drunk in my cups, not havin' anything to live for! I couldn't live without her!"

"I hope you won't have to, Duncan."

He pulled off to one side. "I'm goin' t' stop here, my gir-rl, and show you my own pub, and Ernest, my personal bartender. D'you suppose Gilbert'll follow us? Can you kind of watch out for him from the back window?"

Duncan signaled elaborately and long, made the turn off the road, parked behind a building and climbed out and peered anxiously down the driveway. Gilbert soon pulled in and parked, explaining that he'd gotten caught in traffic, but he had seen us, and he looked at the back entrance of the pub, a bit perplexed.

Duncan took his elbow. "This isn't my house; it's my pub—my club. I want ye to know how fine a fine whiskey can be, and there's no other way o' findin' out than the way I'm going to show you now."

He ceremoniously ushered us inside, and introduced us to the bartender. "All right, Ernest. Set up thr-ree glasses: one with ice, one str-raight, one with water." Then carefully, the drinks prepared, Duncan lifted a glass in the traditional Scottish toast. We responded. That done, he insisted that we sip a bit from each glass, to learn how the whiskey changed flavor. He was right; it did.

"A Scotsman's whiskey's his friend," Duncan explained. "Here, we'll each have another one. Doesn't that strike you odd, the way the taste changes? Whiskey's like a person; different, yet the same. Then off to Sarah, and her fine dinner. She ought t' be just about ready for us, now."

We climbed back into the truck and car, made a short jog around a corner and down another block or so, and pulled up before a row of small homes. Sarah did have everything ready: the table set with a white cloth and wine glasses, the plates piled up before Duncan's place, a rich smell of pot roast in the house. As soon as we were introduced, she begged us to come to eat.

Sarah was in her middle life, about forty, I'd say. She had lost the supple slenderness of youth, her figure a bit thickened around the middle, and her neck and chin were well padded with fat. But her legs and ankles had kept a youthful shapeliness which her pointed-toed shoes and high heels set off very well. She wore her brown hair simply, and no makeup. The way she moved, her quick repartee as she brought in the pot roast and a bowl of potatoes and one of cabbage, and her assured sparkle when she passed Duncan and he brought his hand down in a chopping motion across her buttocks, told of her happiness.

We ate and talked as if long-time friends, which her son Philip, a very thin blond youth of fifteen, watched, at ease and seeming well contented. As I thought about what Duncan had told me in the truck, I marveled that the two of them had been able to reach Philip and to include him in their love; for they had done that, it was plain to see. He was as confident and in better control of himself and his feelings than many boys of that age I had known. Did the key lie in Duncan's candor and delicacy, which I'd observed so well? Probably. His attitude was warm, personal, singular.

The food was passed again, and Duncan served the meat a second time, spearing thick slices on the end of his carving knife and holding it out, leaning across his plate. The talk was of the pipers, and then turned to Sarah, who in her early days had been a musical comedy singer.

"I've done 'em all. Everything. *Guys and Dolls, Carousel, Annie, Get Your Gun.*" Her eyes flashed and she suddenly drew her chin down into the hollow of her throat, drew one hand across her breast, her palm outward, held the pose and looked up at us with her eyes flashing. Suddenly she emitted a yelp which rose upwards and increased in intensity until, at the top of her voice and with her arm held high over her upraised head, her fingers flung wide, she began a high-pitched snarl with a low-class, jazzy sneer, her teeth clenched and the sound forced out—"Yee-ee-ee-ii! You cain't git a man with a gun!"

She was great. We screamed in pleasure. She could still do it! She projected like a fine pro. We begged for more, but she shook her head, yet pleased as if she were a small girl being praised. She got up and began to collect the plates, shaking her head firmly. "No," she said without a trace of self-pity, "that's all over. I help Duncan now." And she was in the kitchen.

"Aye, that she does! She helps me now. She's in the shop more than I am, and it's she that keeps everything goin'. She's a great one, Sarah!" Duncan stated in his emphatic way, smiling now as she returned with coffee and petit fours.

The doorbell rang, but before anyone could answer it, the door opened and a uniformed policeman stuck his head inside. He had already started to speak as he came toward the dining room.

"Mind if I come in for a bit? I've about an hour before I go on duty—" But he broke off as he caught sight of us and started to back out, his cap in his hands. "Oh, I'm sorry, Duncan. Didn't know you were entertainin' company—" His blond complexion grew pinker.

Duncan had jumped up and went toward him. "That's all right! No, don't go! Come in—here, take this chair—" and he pushed aside some dishes and pulled out a chair. "Now, do sit, Timothy. I mean, *Captain* Ross. Excuse me, Timothy—I forgot about your promotion." He introduced us.

Timothy's blond pink deepened. He bowed, and after acknowledging the introduction, apologized. "I'm so sorry to intrude. Didn't know you were here. I didn't mean t' bother anybody." He sat gingerly on the edge of the chair and refused coffee. "Just finished eating, hope you don't mind," he explained.

He and Duncan began an analysis of the pipe contest. I had the same sensation of wonder to hear this fresh agony, as loud and vehement as what we had heard earlier, and again without reaching any conclusion. There was no doubt about it: they were just hurt by the decision.

Timothy turned politely to ask what brought us to Edinburgh. I had scarcely finished explaining my genealogical sleuthing for Americans when Duncan erupted.

"That is the silliest thing in the wor-rld! I've seen those foolish Americans running around, wavin' a piece o' paper, tellin' anybody who'll listen they're descended from some lord or other, and I tell you, gir-rl, they just look plain silly t' us! *Why* do they do it? Don't they realize we don't *care?*"

Duncan's words were always emphatic; one visualized everything he said in capital letters, followed by exclamation points rather than a simple period at the end of his sentences. But even though he spoke in capitals, his thoughts were far from foolish. He didn't give the impression of being opinionated, looking for someone to disagree with, but of feeling many things deeply. He made a good deal of sense even when he misunderstood, as now. He was really asking to learn, in that way he had.

Sarah glanced anxiously in my direction, then relaxed. I waited until Duncan had finished, smiling at his fury. Timothy nodded agreement, his pink flush rising and receding. He was a magnificently blond, good-looking man. His features were delicate and sensitive, though strongly masculine. His coloring was really elegant.

"What most Americans don't understand," Sarah put in, "is that we live with these things all the time: lords, dukes, people like that. It's not unusual to us. But nobody speaks about it, you know. We think it's impolite to keep telling people . . ."

I nodded. "Maybe I can explain—" I got only a few words out when Duncan rose.

"There's no need to sit here stiffly at the dining table. Come, let us sit more easily. Let's go t' the livin' room." He led the way and we trooped behind and arranged ourselves, disposed of small glasses of whiskey that Sarah passed around, all except Timothy, who begged off because of his job. When we were all quiet again they looked to me for my thoughts.

"I think that Americans are a bit like adopted children. All Americans, with the exception of the Indians, of course, came from other places. For years they deliberately turned their backs on what they'd left. I've often wondered why they forgot who they had been."

"Probably better that way," Duncan said, nodding vigorously. "Some of 'em were cutthroats and ruffians. Didn't want anybody t' know."

"Probably. But not all. Some left rather distinguished lineage. You can bet that they wanted to forget something . . . people just don't get up and leave where they're happy. I think when they got to America they were too busy to think about it."

They listened like children. Then Timothy shook his head slowly, and the light from the windows caught yellow highlights in his hair and sent a ripple along a closely clipped wave. "Why do they come back, and rush up, all excitement, and tell us what they've found? I've seen many of 'em, and I don't understand."

Again there was the childlike feeling among them. Gilbert tried to answer. "Perhaps it would help to tell you about a man I know who was adopted, told when he was twelve or so. He couldn't stop fretting over it; he'd talk about his 'real parents' to anyone who'd listen, wondering day and night who his father was, if he was an educated man, what kind of man, a good man—that kind of thing. If he was good, why hadn't he taken care of his son? And if his mother was a slut—all kinds of thoughts like that. He was so obsessed that when he grew up, he went a long distance to another city to try to find his father—he thought he'd look him up and talk to him on some pretext, find out what he was like. Very irrational."

"That's true," I said. "I've known several people who were adopted —the same thoughts seem to run through all their minds. I knew a wonderful woman, adopted into a family that gave her love, education, material comforts and cultural advantages; when her first baby was born, she said, 'You don't know how good it is to have someone who really belongs to me!' "

Suddenly, out of silence, Timothy said, "That's th' reason I can't adopt a boy—I know now, and I've thought of it for a long time. I never could! Ann and I have thr-ree girls, and ach-h! what a time she had with each of her pregnancies! She is so sick, so sick! But she'd have another baby because I wanted it, if we could be sure it'd be a boy!" His pink color grew deeper.

"That she does!" Sarah said. "Oh, how sick she gets, poor Ann! And d'ye know, Hortense, Timothy is so fond o' boys that he takes a whole lot of orphan boys out t' the field three evenings a week and teaches 'em to play cricket! He's a fine mon! He loves boys so much— he'd love a boy of his own!"

Suddenly Timothy jumped up. "Say, I've got t' be gettin' on duty— I'm going t' be late!" He put on his coat, and with his cap in his hands he bowed to us. "I'm so glad to 've had this opportunity to meet you." He disappeared quickly from the room.

What a breed of men these Scots were! Their tenderness, their strength, their realistic evaluations of their limitations. No one spoke for a few moments.

Then, sounding somehow belligerent, Duncan broke into the silence. "You Americans have the most beautiful country in this world, and what're you doin' with it, eh? Makin' a mess o' it—a mess! Ugly, polluted, full of riots and troubles! Now, what d' ye say to that?"

"I agree with you."

He looked surprised. Slightly modified in tone, he continued, "Those race problems—ach-h! what a mess! You're in real tr-rouble, my lass, and what're people doin' about it? Makin' things worse, not better!"

"I'm afraid so, Duncan, but America's the growing tip, the part of mankind that's working its way into the future. It's like an adolescent these days—all that pain and soul-searching, anger and anguish."

Looking less angry, he shook his head. "I mar-rvel at Americans! D' ye know, I marvel! Because, with all that race trouble," and he jabbed a finger at me and waggled it back and forth, "with all that tr-rouble, not once have they said t' us, *This is all your fault!* And it is, y' know. And I don't know why they don't. Because the slave ships were British, and the slave traders were British, and they started the whole bloody mess!"

"That's true," Gilbert said, "and I don't know why it never came to my mind before. But isn't it the nature of Americans to look ahead? If they don't remember what they left, they don't remember that. They live in the future, not in the past."

I thought about it. Did those people who first went across that wide sea have a dream—that because they had suffered, they would try to start a new way, where men could forget and grow into the future? The future, only. It takes a lot of time. They criticize themselves more than they're criticized when they don't meet the ideal, and what advantage comes from blame?

Duncan suddenly asked Gilbert our plans. When he understood the question, Gilbert explained that I had to go to Inverness for research.

"Ye leave t'morrow?" Duncan was aghast, and he got up suddenly. "Then, come! Let me get out the map! I c'n tell ye about places you must see. Come—look here, lad." He spread a map on a bookcase at the back of the room, and the two men bent over it, Duncan's voice coming dimly from across the room: there was a barman at an inn in Pitlochry named Harry; no, he didn't have a last name, it was just Harry. "No bartender in Great Britain has a last name," he said, affectionately clipping Gilbert on the shoulder.

Sarah got up to fill the glasses, and Philip said good night and went upstairs. When she sat down again, Sarah asked, "Do you know you're going up to that part of Scotland that's most nationalistic?" She was watching me closely, although her posture was easy, one arm resting across the back of the chair, her glass easy in her hand.

I shrugged. "Oh?"

She nodded. "There's a bunch of Scots up there who think we can break away from England and start our own government."

I may have looked astonished. "Can you?" I thought about it for a moment. "Come to think of it," I finally said, "perhaps it's not so surprising as it first seems: the British Empire hasn't exactly grown of late—India, Nigeria, trouble in Northern Ireland now. Do you think Scotland can do it, Sarah?"

She tossed her head. "No! It's a laughingstock. The ones who're the loudest are the worst—I hate to think of them trying to represent me in Parliament." She sipped her drink, her eyes dancing. Suddenly she burst into laughter. "They're so funny. They do us more harm than good. They don't know what they mean, when they get a chance to talk."

"Could Scotland be self-supporting, Sarah?"

Her gaze was instantly level and sober. "No." She tipped back her head, and the lamplight outlined her strong jaw line.

I looked at her and suddenly said, "Why don't you stand for Parliament, Sarah?"

"Me?" Her astonished laughter burst out like a cork from champagne, and the men turned around from their map to see the reason. "Hortense just asked why I don't stand for Parliament," she explained.

"Not so silly, Sarah," I said. "It's time for women to take a place."

Duncan bowed low. "Yes, indeed, Madam Sarah. Do stand, dar-rling!"

"You could do it, Sarah. You're smart, know how to get an idea across. You know how to do things, and what people need," I insisted.

"Oh no, you don't! I'm not standin' for Parliament!" Sarah grew sober and sat thinking about it, and the men lost interest and turned away, Duncan exclaiming occasionally over a good place to fish, or a friend to look up in some beautiful bypath on our way.

I called out to him, "Duncan, we're going on a working trip, not a fishing jaunt."

He turned around. "Yes, yes! So you say! But if you're goin' up there, you just as well might be dead if you don't take time t' see the greatest beauties the good Lord ever created on this earth. Where's your heart, woman? Are ye goin' t' leap into your car and gallop away wearin' blindfolds?"

When the laughter had stopped, Sarah was regarding me closely, and this time she seemed puzzled. "Up there in that nationalist country, there's a man—at least I think he's there. He's an American, too. I think he is. Maybe you know him—his name's Malcolm Cromarty."

"Hmpf. Doesn't sound like an American. Still, you can't tell. I don't know anyone by that name."

She waited for a moment and began again to speak. She seemed cautious. "I'm not sure which he is. He's spent a lot of time in America. I thought you, being an American, might know him."

I thought with a sudden astonishment of the provincialism of Europeans. What strange ideas some of them have of the size of America, translating it into their own size. Other Europeans had asked me, from time to time, if I knew so-and-so, thinking if they knew someone in California, I would also know him.

Suddenly Sarah jumped up and returned with the whiskey. "Oh, it's good for you—you'll sleep like a baby tonight, and no bad head in th' mornin', either." Then she settled down and sipped her drink. "He's wearing the Royal Stewart tartan in his kilt, you know. Nobody wears that tartan—nobody Scottish. Only Americans do. They don't know any better."

"Does he have a full beard? A bit white?"

"You *do* know him!"

I shook my head. "I've seen a man who looks like that portrait of James the Sixth in the gallery, but I don't know him. I saw him in the hotel last night; and before that, in England."

Duncan came toward me, folding the map. "Here you are, all planned out. Don't try to drive too fast up there. Just let the beauty sink into your soul."

It had been a rich evening. We had shared both laughter and deep emotions that had moved us all. We were moving through the hallway to the front door, where we paused to say our thanks. I hated to leave this great couple on such a serious note, and I grinned suddenly at Duncan. "D'you know, would you believe—the solution for all the problems we discussed tonight has just popped into my head! Pollution, riots, heartache, traffic, employment—everything!"

His eyebrows flew up. "Ye don't say? And what might it be, pray?"

I drew myself up in a dignified pose, and in a voice used by the chief of protocol at court, intoned, "The authorities of all great nations shall immediately issue proclamations: no cars are to be tolerated ever again! The horse shall become the only allowed means of travel!" They were beginning to laugh, and I went on, back into my own character, nodding and pulling the ideas from the top of my head as their eyes sent out sparks of amused delight. "Just think of it! Freeways torn up, gardens planted—fresh food on the table, which means improved health—" I stopped, interrupted by Duncan.

"And much natural fertilizer—" He bobbed his head, his eyes sparkling.

Sarah, her voice choked with laughter, yelled, "No smog! We'll get rid of all that black stuff!"

Gilbert caught on and yelled. "And the troublemakers will have to stay close to home—"

"—where everybody knows 'em, and they'll not get any attention," Sarah agreed, one fist punctuating her words.

"The end to riots!" Gilbert called, triumphantly.

Duncan's face went serious. "But what of employment, madam? What about wor-r-k?" He poked a thick finger at me.

"New industry! Saddlemakers, blacksmiths—that's no trouble!" Gilbert shouted as if he'd not get another chance, "And chestnut tree planters!"

"Yes! And gardeners, grooms, footmen, stablemen—" I stopped, out of breath.

"—and flies! Flyswatter-makers!" Sarah shouted, supplying another job and opening the door at the same moment. She was still laughing as we went down the steps. Before we closed the car door she called, "Hortense, dear, *you* stand for Parliament!"

When we got back to the hotel and Gilbert had disappeared into his room, I sat with brush in hand at my dressing table, the remembered image of the Scot unexpectedly coming between me and my reflection. Who *was* he? I came to, seeing again my own face in the mirror with a perplexed furrow on my forehead. Why did I see him, even where he was not? Strange, I mused into the glass, we'd encountered him twice on this trip. The country was swarming with people we'd never seen, yet this one—this rather unusual one—twice in as many days. And Sarah, now, wondered too.

I smoothed on face cream and watched my expression change to bland. I studied my face. Yes, my complexion had stayed rather good, I had to admit: the result of these nightly rituals. Discipline, I said to myself, screwing the top of the jar back on. The best place to employ it is on yourself, Hortense. Stop being puzzled; it only makes you wrinkled. I made a face, pulling hard to tighten the neck muscles.

I tossed the tissue away and stood, pushed up by my hand against the rigid tabletop. Oh, if I only didn't have this hip! I regarded my figure: I *must* extend my regimen to include exercise! Either that, or cut out the nightcaps which Gilbert and I both enjoyed. I stood very straight and held in my stomach, did three deep knee bends, and touched my toes twice. I could still do it!

It's really too much to expect to quit drinking! I didn't look so bad; I had fewer excess pounds than many women of my age. It was just that part of my territory had been ceded south of the border, not divided equally between North and South.

I saw myself grinning, and stood watching, like a teen-ager who has just discovered herself. Anyway, I conceded, I was still firm in bust and had a definable waistline. All to the good! I'd work on the hips and abdomen as soon as we quit riding about the countryside. And when the hip feels better. After all, one needs *room*, I nodded to the woman standing in her skivvies, who began to laugh.

You aren't so bad as you make out, you know, I said to her. You've been assuming a false identity. You really mustn't—just because you once got to feeling dizzy. You feel quite all right most of the time. Now, you do.

I laughed and something changed in my face; it lost twenty years. What a strange realignment of muscles brought about this near miracle! I remembered a critic who once wrote, "—a youthful quality that belies the many years we have watched this fine actress," and he had actually gone on to try to analyze the quality in print. Which, of course, was impossible and had come off very badly. I remembered that it had embarrassed me.

I leaned toward the mirror. I had seen this face for over fifty years, and I had never understood exactly what really took place when I laughed. The parted lips revealed teeth slightly askew; far from a perfect smile. But the smile put a glint into the eyes. And the face muscles on the up-pull did bring out some youthful look. How to describe it? But it was going frozen. I needed the association with people. I missed the stage, I admitted to myself, stopping my glass gazing and hearing my voice say, "Remember to smile oftener, Hortense!"

And then it happened; there was a twist of the neck, the chin thrown up, straightened spine, facial muscles up, and then I saw what the critic had tried to explain. It was gone in an instant.

The good mattress was pure comfort, but before drifting to sleep the face of the Scot floated into mind. Who was he? Malcolm Cromarty? An incredible name. Why did he keep coming to mind? But at least the images were not of red-carpeted hotel corridors.

I had made my goal and turned back. What Rose had said was true —I might walk until I dropped, and would come to no houses on the moor. It was a safe place to let me walk alone.

When I got back to the lodge I saw a car in the back at the service entrance. Nobody was about. The lodge might have been inhabited by a caretaker only, from its appearance; it looked deserted. I wanted to get the license in the hope of investigating later, after I got away. Cars had several times come, but never before had there been a good opportunity to identify them, glimpsed from my window, the view too foreshortened, or too far to see the number. I went back.

The car was a small sedan, and the tag had been concealed by a metal plate attached by wires, fastened too firmly to be pried loose without an implement.

I went to the main entrance, thinking how clever they were. They'd expected that I might try to learn something this way, and were taking no chances. I had learned only a few things; the puzzling facts still eluded. I missed Gilbert. He would have thought of something that I didn't.

When I came up to the front of the lodge, Frances stood at the corner peering toward the back. As I appeared, she retreated into the lodge. So I was watched even when it didn't seem so.

IV

As a way to improve appetite and muscle tone, moor hopping can't be surpassed. It was good that a few simple exercises had been a part of my regimen all along, even if I hadn't actually gone in for Air Force Isometrics, or I could not have managed as well as I did. Now I felt better than in years.

But rain was falling in heavy sheets, the sky shrouded with black and gray, some paler-colored whitish clouds nearer the horizon. They made a more interesting pattern than a rainy gray American sky, but I eyed my window and became terribly restless as it continued, the only change occurring when gusts blew the rain against the window glass. I needed a change, and went down to the lounge.

The kids were in class in the dining room, a gentle hum of voices coming through the door. Someone had forgotten to turn on the chandelier, which made the large room even more gloomy than my small one had been. Even the fire had died down.

This was less comforting than my own room. I was about ready to go back when one of the lads came up from the hallway to the rear, evidently on his way back to the class. I decided to risk the encounter I'd planned now. I had overheard this fellow several times; his voice was tremendously confident; this was no frightened fawn.

I had to call his name twice before he realized that I spoke to him. Then he turned abruptly, half facing me, withdrawn and refusing to move closer, away from the dining room door, which he had very nearly reached. His manner was curt.

"Yes?" He waited.

"Colin, could you tell me—do you have any idea why I'm being kept here?"

He eyed me speculatively without answering.

"Please, Colin," I began again, hoping to get a slight warmth in my tone, to ignore the chill he projected, "surely you must realize how it feels to be detained without knowing why, or not to know how long I must stay. It's really unnerving."

He continued to look at me. I could sense his mind dividing between the class on the other side of the door, where a sputter of quick words erupted and died down, and the necessity of making a reply. Finally he spoke.

"You're not one of us. I don't know why you're being kept, and how long. Why did you come here? I don't know—you came by mistake. You're an American; you think you own the world. You are very smart, and you are wily. You have learned about us—you know us. You cannot go, madam. It's as simple as that."

I tried to ignore his surly answer. "But Colin," I protested, a sudden move forward and my hand on his arm, "I'm not here because I wish to be! I'm held against my wishes! I don't know what you do, who you are—I've only scant knowledge—" But he shook off my hand with a quick, angry motion.

"You are a liar, madam. You must realize that some of us are on to you—that r-ridiculous pose of yours—your shambling gait—you put it on. What else would you suppose we think than that you're a charlatan?"

He opened the door and went inside abruptly, and my hand flew to my cheek as if he'd slapped it.

I stood alone in the dreary room, my eyes roaming across it for something, anything. If I had spared Frances's feelings, he had not spared mine. Perhaps I had asked for this, but not really. Not quite so rudely, so unfeeling. I gave a short laugh, as much for my mistaken plan as for my hurt feelings.

Someone had left a pad of legal paper lying on the low table in the bow window, and I picked it up and climbed the stairs listlessly. My mind felt disorganized, out of sorts, heaped all together like a badly pawed-through bureau drawer. I would try to organize some of my thoughts; perhaps Colin was right, and I did know something more than I realized.

I began to write rather aimlessly facts which I'd noticed: these kids were different from other hippies; they looked clean. They didn't smoke pot, or take the new drugs, so far as I could tell, but they did drug themselves on whiskey. I had seen some of them in the lounge at times, their expressions blank, their muscles gone lax. They were sticking to the tried-and-true drugs. As I was, too, I chuckled to myself. I'd forgotten how long since my last drink.

They were standoffish with me, constrained by what they knew that I wasn't supposed to learn. I suspected that their reserve was imposed by orders from Rose. Where had she gone? I hadn't seen her except at the beginning of my prison sentence.

Usually she was to be seen, sometimes as I went through the lounge. Or her voice would cut a thin slice through the rooms, that slender, high tone like a silver knife slicing through an overlay of hubbub while the kids milled around, perhaps waiting for dinner. She had either left, or she was sick.

I shook slightly at the thought of Rose, I noticed, and it was terribly disquieting. It was strange to be dependent on someone's good will, especially when it was as thin as hers, to be a captive. It made a stifled squeeze in some inner core, a hateful feeling, deeply frightening.

I turned my thoughts to the kids. I could think about them without that nerve-tremor reaction. If only they would allow friendship, I was sure that I would like them. They showed easy good humor with each other; sometimes they talked lightly and flippantly, but when I was near it was always in Gaelic.

Their moods didn't yet include the opposite traits: of sorrow, despair or gloom. Too young for that yet. If someone was unhappy, the antidote was to be sat beside for a time. Tenderness, passion and affection were evidenced often—the kids probably thought these feelings "real." They touched, embraced. Several times on going through the lounge I had rattled the cane to let them know someone was near.

Pity, compassion, sentiment—but I may not have seen enough; or they may have been too young for these deeper emotions to have developed. They were devoted. They had a Cause. I had listened often to the sounds coming from the classroom, but I hadn't learned what they discussed. They usually showed businesslike industry, their good-looking young faces serious. Later in their lives they might show the traditional dour look, but now they looked appealing, their brightly colored complexions and brilliant hair healthy and well cared for, their clothing clean and pressed, their work done quickly and competently.

I sighed. I felt no wiser, still full of question marks. Why I was here, what they did, how long I must stay were trembling, snaggling, fearsome questions. Colin had said that some of them were onto me; that implied that others may have defended me. Perhaps there were friends among them, and when I passed among them, there was no feeling of threat. Yet the doubts which Colin aroused pressed hard. I must be careful, must watch. It would be a mistake to feel too easy. Perhaps when Rose was around I managed my part with better technique. She was like a sharp critic, holding me firm to a good performance. I must not relax.

I looked up from the yellow pad. The sky was still dark, as heavy as it had been on the day when Gilbert and I had left Edinburgh for Inverness, and Duncan's plans for our sightseeing had been spoiled, the moors forbidding, beaten by heavy rain and pushed down upon by the dark sky.

I let my mind go back to that day in a respite from the unknown facts I had been seeking. The dark sky that morning had seemed to cave down on us, a heavy, ominous blue-black. I remembered that I had shivered when the little car climbed higher, seeming almost about to be flattened by it, and I had pulled the new head scarf I'd bought in Duncan's shop tighter. Gilbert had sighed, and turned on the heater, on his face that familiar look of resignation.

We passed through Pitlochry without stopping, forever the poorer for not meeting Harry, but arriving just at afternoon closing, a cup of tea no substitute.

"Some other time," Gilbert said. "British bartenders are professionals. Harry'll be there the next time."

In Inverness we found good rooms at a modest hotel, Mrs. MacIver pointing out that the tourists hadn't really started yet, and the sun coming out just as we entered.

It had been like a blessing, that sun, streaking yellow after the dark gloom of the entire trip. We had wobbled up the wide stairs to our rooms, cheered with the spacious look of the dining room and the delicious smells coming from it, something to be enjoyed in a little while, something to make up for the long, cold trip.

The rooms were airy, facing the river, the view in both directions fluid and open and romantic, spires and trees piercing the opposite skyline, and green, well-tended lawn to look out upon. There was a wonderfully warm connecting bath, and I decided to get into the tub, feeling creaky in the joints.

I lay back in the hot water, nearly floating free in the huge tub. The tub was regal, far different from the English bathtubs, which were shaped like antique grave covers, so elongated and narrow at the end. This one was extremely wide, made for people with huge bodies, wide and long enough for a giant. A child could swim in it. Thoughtful and sensitive of the Scots, to plan for all of the different sizes and shapes.

Even the water was different. It splashed down from a high faucet and made a chuckling sound. Of a light brown color, it was pigmented by the peat through which it had recently flowed. It smelled different: of earth, and it was pungent not of chloride but of open land and wide, changing sky. The bath water in England had spurted fitfully, with reluctant snarling sounds, and afterward had sucked down into the drain with ominous sounds.

We had taken a wrong turn on our way, and had to backtrack about five miles. The signs in a small village were badly placed and hard to see. We made the turn just as the sun broke momentarily through the clouds, and it illuminated the dark red, wet brick of an old building, on which was scrawled that strange sign in chalk. Like a child's drawing of a purse, its strings up in the air.

I had lain in the tub and thought of what the sign meant, had seen it again in the thatched hut. The pamphlet which I had kept had proved to be a disappointment. That good design was on the cover; inside was a short paragraph in a foreign language, Gaelic, I imagined. The sign had said KEEP GAELIC ALIVE. My goodness, these kids not only kept it alive, it was jumping!

The short paragraph was followed by a translation. It was in biblical language, purported to have been written by St. Brigit, enjoining the faithful to keep steady on the course, to seek the truth, and to be ready to battle in defense of freedom.

I snorted. Nothing new or different. There were too many educated snoops around these days, made compulsive by their Ph.D.'s to search for odd tidbits even when it produced only more of the same well-known thoughts. So a patron saint had written that message, and it had been buried for centuries: what difference did it make? It was signed in abbreviation, and the name of St. Brigit written in italics, parenthesized. I don't know what I had expected, but this was a disappointment.

I had found it the next day, when we visited the thatched hut, I remembered. The first evening in Inverness we had emerged after dinner for a stroll, and had been lured by the snarl of bagpipes. We had crossed the river, surging between cement-lined banks just across the street from the Glen Mhora, on a suspension footbridge, very long and wide enough for two, but most easily navigated singly, each hand slid along the heavy rope railing. It was after eight o'clock, and growing quite dark. The sky was thickly overcast by clouds of navy blue and purple, and the wind blew strongly. It was bracing. I called to Gilbert that the exercise would do us both good.

The sound of the pipes and insistent drum crackle almost took visual form: like a stiletto speckled with clinging particles of metal; it at once coaxed and repelled. It also recalled a smell of distant skunk floating on a current of warm evening air in the Midwest, at the same time good and repellent, overlaying the odor of fresh-cut clover hay. As a child I had shivered at the combination of smells, and I shivered now. The insolent, piercing whine and snap overlaid the water's surge and the rushing air.

We walked through a park of clipped grass and under some trees. We emerged into a clearing, suddenly filled with a silver wash of light. It grew brighter. At the apex of the sky the clouds had opened to reveal limitless, lustrous blue, a deep pool of space. I felt dizzy with a sudden expansion of vision, a reversed depth sensation. I staggered and leaned on the cane, pushed it hard into the gravel, unable to withdraw my eyes from the sky. Gilbert's warm hand was placed under my elbow, and I murmured thanks.

Something had changed. My mind staggered, pulled gasping out of my skull. It was like a revelation of pellucid truth, or breathing pure oxygen, a dive into sky depth, as shocking as a dive into ice water.

One hears of city dwellers in the mountains, gasping the fresh air and describing their feelings as exalted and joyous. Science might say that oxygen, passing through millions of tiny air sacs in the lungs, mixes with the blood and produces an elevation in its oxygen content, a side effect being a sharpening of the perceptions. Gilbert might agree, after clearing his throat, that sharpening of the senses is a spiritual effect. But that is too cautious. I know that my vision cleared. As surely as I see at all I felt as if thick scales dropped from my eyes, and I gasped.

The opening in the clouds grew; light pulsed down; it seemed to breathe; it was animate. Near the earth, dark clouds of purple and blue piled beneath that high opening, where at great distances fluffs of gold and peach reflected the already set sun; beneath were layers of gray, white and silver. They moved gently, like near somnolent beings. The sense of depth and distance gradually grew and pulled, feeling like an extraction of the sense of sight. I felt intoxicated.

Gilbert's face glowed pink in the reflected light. It seemed nearly surprising to be standing here, smiling at each other. We had been a long way away.

Drawn forward by the sound of the pipes, we followed the path to where several converged. Here, sheltered by trees, a bandstand was faced on three sides by bleachers which formed an enclosure where the pipers marched.

They were filing toward us as we entered and took seats. They wore black velvet jackets and caps; their kilts were white, with red and black crossbarring, the red picked up in the ribbons of their caps and the Royal Stewart tartan of the pipe bags. They turned expertly with military snap, passed through their ranks and reformed, keeping steady drumbeat and step. Their elbows flashed jauntily and the hems of their kilts swayed in time. They looked cocky, and they looked very small. The band was made up of women and children.

I must have gasped this realization to Gilbert, for a man sitting next to me explained. "The men have their own band. The women and children got tired o' sittin' at home while they went off and had their contests. So they formed their own."

They had evidently practiced much. They were assured and precise and smart, and they paraded back and forth as they played. The flouncing of their kilts emphasized the drum snap and the jounce of their elbows and beat of their feet. It was hypnotic.

They filed off, flourishing drumsticks. The audience broke apart into separate individuals. We joined the throng out of the gate and down the curving paths toward the footbridge, and emerging from under the trees were bathed in that astonishing flow of light. How strange to know that the hour was close to eleven at night, yet still that brilliant sky. Air, sky and water were gold-layered. The strong wind had changed to a gentle surge, and the water, dark blue and gold-speckled, flowed in a steady rippling sound.

We paused at the bridge for our turn to file across. Halfway across, a slender young woman stopped in front of us. Standing in one spot, she began to jump.

At a standstill on the bridge behind her, we saw her jump higher, hitting the footspan violently, her knees drawn up and legs thrust out again like a jackhammer. The long span caught the rhythm and began to swing. Its small undulations became wide arcs. It shook and moved violently from side to side. I grabbed the hand rope and yelled, thrown against Gilbert. Behind us many others were yelling.

The woman made a final jump and hit the bridge with her total strength, gave a yelp and pelted away. We could not walk, but clung to the ropes, terrified and thrown from side to side and against each other. And suddenly I was back in childhood, on a hot evening at the foundations of a new house, where a raw lumber plank made a footbridge, hearing children's screams in the dusk and feeling the earthquake vibrations of the plank, and I laughed aloud while we clung and waited for the shocks to stop.

With our feet finally on firm land, the hotel ahead, it seemed nearly ordinary; yet the episode at the bridge was quirky and odd, and that extraordinary light poured down from overhead.

"What a place, this Scotland!" Gilbert looked at me and grinned, his face bathed in the color from the sky, and the electric light in the hotel entrance making only a pinpoint of yellow, a drab color with all the color from the sky.

"Here's lunch," Frances said, setting down the tray and bobbing off. I sighed, again aware of today. The sky was as dark as it had been earlier, and the yellow pad held only scribbles about kids and pot, whiskey and some sentimental notes about emotions. Must have exercise; hardening of the arteries, first thing you know, rigor mortis. I wished the rain would stop. Dark skies, dark thoughts, idleness and isolation were no good. Memories were better.

I had not been able to sleep much that night in Inverness. Light came from the sky and bounced back from flooding lochs and firths. Had a strange perceptual alteration really occurred? Did I see everything more clearly? I could not say.

All that night the light had been lucid. I woke to wonder what was happening, who was in my room. I saw no one. I stood by the window and saw the water flowing and the light, and the air surged around my body. The surge of light and air pervaded, the mood unusual, quiet, mysterious, and yet lucid.

I stood a long time there, looking and waiting. Waiting for what? I listened and could almost hear; I looked and almost saw. Some transcendent thing will be revealed, I thought; it will happen quietly, between breaths. It pulses gently. It does not frighten.

But nothing happened and I went back to bed, only to raise up on one elbow and peer again into the semi-darkness. I had not seen or heard. But I felt as if all things were to be made clear, and the way made plain.

It had not happened that way. Instead, all things were clouded and the way made twisted. We had gone to the thatched hut, then to the battlefield. Nothing had been clear since then. What a place, this Scotland!

"Well, so much for rain," Gilbert had said as we left the battlefield and mushed our way back to the car. There had been no sign of the

Bruce link, except for the name cut into a fieldstone near one of those hummocks. The rain had flowed like sudden tears, a force that began about as soon as we'd gotten out of the car. It seemed symbolic. Battlefields and graves. That was all.

Our woolen coats had become soaked as we stood looking over a long slope of wide expanse that fell gradually to a ravine and rose again beyond in high mountain peaks. The grass looked manicured by sheep, but they weren't here now. I could see men marching over that long slope, see them form and run, and their ranks thinning as bodies fell. Fire cracked and smoke puffed from massed artillery. Men fell and rose, an arm was held up and someone ran on with a claymore in his hand.

Another crack and puff and he dropped. Shields flapped feebly and then more feebly. Spears and swords fell. Again the crack and puff. The ranks thinned.

"Even the weather's mixed up," I said later as we rode in the car. "Look at it! Just a minute ago, while we stood on the battlefield, it poured rain. Now the sun's out! Those poor men! All that space to maneuver, and not a chance. The English used massed artillery; the Scots had small arms, and very few field pieces. Swords against mortars. I could cry."

Gilbert rolled the window down. "You and your ghosts!" The air blew in quite warm. "Stop trying to swab off the windshield; it just bothers me."

"Gilbert, I do not see ghosts! I don't see any white things floating around in space, or stuff and nonsense like it. There is a sense of people and space, swinging into position here, drawing back there. That kind of thing."

"Well, if you say so. I guess you'd know."

"If we scratched away the grass and a little dirt, we'd find broken spears and pieces of steel. All mixed in together, that's how they were buried. In their clans, right where they fought and where they fell. It was a massacre."

"That's what I read."

"Even the cairn marker. It was sad, too."

He looked at me quickly and back at the narrow road. He didn't answer.

"Just ordinary fieldstones piled into a great round tower. It's awkward. Ugly. And that grass, just sticking up on top. It looked like it needed a haircut, waving in the wind like that."

We were passing the thatched hut again. "I didn't learn anything up here today." I pulled off the woolen head scarf and shook it out.

"Well, I guess it's the county records for you now?"

"Did you see anything strange in that thatched hut?"

He swabbed at the windshield with the back of his hand. "That little place? Some people there. Looking around, same as we were."

"Not that. And yet, yes. Remember the sign out front?"

"Yes. I read it."

"Was anyone there?"

"What do you mean—anyone there?"

"Were there two men talking, in front of it?"

"I don't know. I read it. It called attention to a stone marker down—" but I interrupted him.

"Oh, not that! There were two men talking, weren't there?"

"Were there?"

"Oh, Gilbert!" I thought about him. How had he gotten the way he was? Genes, or science? I took a deep breath and then sighed. "Inside; who was inside?"

"Some people like us." He sounded bored.

"That couple with the packs—they were too old to be hostelers."

"Hortense, you think of the strangest things!"

We had arrived back at the Glen Mhora. The dining room was good, and our capable waitress served a hearty lunch. I couldn't stop thinking about the hut. What was it that snagged my mind? I couldn't discover why I kept thinking about it.

I set down my coffee cup. "Well, I'm off to the records office. Are you going to nap, or do you want to come?"

"Do you need me?" He looked very sleepy.

"No, not really. It's just up at the end of the street; that old castle. They made it into the shire records office. It's a good cement walk. I'll be fine."

I poked along the sidewalk rather sleepily, myself. The wind and rain, then the hot sun and heavy lunch. I was sluggish. Maybe I should have napped, too. Puritan conscience. The walk would clear my head. It would be an afternoon of reading.

If those American Bruces were linked to the great chief of the old clan, it would mean a lot to them. A tie with aristocracy is valuable to certain types of Americans, worth nothing to others. In Charlotte, if they'd done what I suspected, struck it rich, this would put a nice finger on everything they did.

They were paying me well; I shouldn't judge. They were paying me handsomely; my private bathroom proved it. If they wanted to swagger a bit more broadly than they had been doing, perhaps they needed a little bolstering among wider swaggerers.

I don't suppose they'd do anything very much different from what they had already done, really. It would give them a feeling which they'd value; a coat of arms would appear in their home, hung discreetly so that visitors could see it fairly well, without craning their necks too hard. Hung among family portraits of smooth women, their hands folded neatly, and strong-looking gentlemen; a tacit statement to anyone who entered their house.

There might be some small allusions: nothing blatant, of course. They'd probably had money enough for some time, and had gotten to know how to get their point across. Yes, I agreed with myself, to those to whom such things are important, this added authentication would prove a telling point.

I wondered, as I pushed open the door, if maybe a son or a daughter was getting married. Maybe into some snob line. Yes, that might be the reason they felt the need to swagger a bit wider. Or some of the ladies at the symphony ball might have dropped a few choice remarks about a forebear, and a noble curiosity had been started. I chuckled.

The clerk brought out the volume of records that I requested, and retired to his desk behind a counter. I carted the book off to a long table and opened it up. Now and then the clerk glanced in my direction to satisfy himself that I wasn't making off with the unwieldy thing.

Here were the lists of names by clans, long lines of names written in spidery handwriting in fading brown ink. The lists were long, the writing badly faded. The light from overhead was so poor that I felt my eyes cross in the effort to read.

I sternly told myself to stay awake, and felt my eyes gradually slipping down in my face. Twice I pulled my head upright, vexed at my feeling of indolence. I commanded myself to work. Get to business; this was no holiday. Yet my curious languor persisted.

When my mind and body conspire to work against me, I should by now have learned to give in, but I am an old fool. But two against one is no even match. One *what?* I asked myself. Hortense, you are in a bad state!

Mind and body. That's it. Mind and body. What else is there?

A snickering, like small children peering into a room where hushed adults sit solemnly . . . a scurrying, outside drawn curtains, heavy draperies . . . many small feet scampering and the sound of giggling, and little hands poked around heavy red portieres, and small eyes peeking out from around the edges.

What else is there? What else is there?

It had taken on a lovely, musical singsong. What . . . else . . . is . . . there . . . what . . . else . . . is . . . there?

The singsong became higher and the giggling grew and faded. Little feet scampered up some stairs, down long corridors where dust curled, and doors lined long walls, and a window gleamed dully at one end. Doors opened, and the high squeals came faintly.

What . . . else . . . is . . . there?

Children tiptoed down the hallway now, white starched hems flashed from around corners, long-stockinged white legs, feet in polished patent leather Mary Janes, dresses with sashes and ribbons. The giggles. Fair hair brushed up to tops of heads and caught in stiff, giant bows. Long petticoats, two of them. Starched stiffly. Stiff, harsh to soft skin, rubbing under armpits.

And crying; childish petulant crying, and a slap. Arms forced into openings. Faces severely scrubbed; the smell of the musty washcloth; the eyes burn, the face rubbed hard, the dress patted down.

There! Now go on down! Go on, you're ready, now. Go!

The hushed room; the solemn adults. The feet pushed; a stern hand on a shoulder and the feet sliding, sliding. The feet resisting. Little feet sliding down a polished hallway, stumbling down the stairs. A gasp, a deep sob. Smarting eyes. The stern hand. You're all right! Stop that!

The heavy red portieres; the room; stiffly sitting adults; black suits; stiff white collars. Those solemn faces, many faces. Leaning forward. Lean back. The hand, again. Faces alike. Dead. Solemn, important faces. Dead smells. Ladies in high collars, their hair brushed up into pompadours. Bowing forward, rows of bowing ladies with high collars. Smells of powder. Smiling stiffly; smiles alike. Bowing.

Curtsy! Bob down; one foot behind; starch scratches. Bob back up. Smile. Smile. Come now, smile! That's better. Nice. Good. Smiles.

Now go! Go. Be quiet, but go. Get out. Back to the hallway. Out where the others are. Out of the room.

Here they giggle. Here they grab, push, make faces, laugh. Alive. They scream and push. Funny. Funny faces.

Hush. Heavy adult steps. Draperies open. Firm hand on the dark red portieres. Eyes round.

The hallway exposed. Nothing. The little faces have gone. The hallway is clear. It gleams, polished and shining. Empty.

"Time to close," the clerk said, his hand on my shoulder.

Startled, I shook myself and looked up. His face was tired and drawn, and above, over his shoulder, I saw the dim yellow globes in the ceiling, now looking brighter in a darkening room. On the table my notebooks glowed white.

I gathered my papers up stupidly and crammed them into the brief case, on the floor at my side. I had found what I'd come for, anyway. The record showed that Stewart Bruce had fallen on the battlefield in 1746.

There had been two brothers, apparently. Alan, the younger, must have seen his older brother fall, for his fading initials were there beside the name of Stewart Bruce.

I picked up the book and carried it back to the counter. My face must have turned to mush, I thought, trying to rearrange it into a waking expression. I smiled as I handed him the book. He nodded, a bit tired. He was through with his day and in a hurry to leave; one couldn't fault him.

I stood for a moment and noticed the long lines of his face, how deeply etched they were from the edges of his nostrils down to his lips. He regarded me quietly, and seemed to be patiently waiting for me to leave.

I don't know why I didn't just say a quiet thanks and go.

"The Stewart Bruce branch of the family died out, didn't it? I mean, he had no children, did he? I think the record shows that he fell at Culloden."

"I believe he did not marry, madam. These were our young men, you know." He held the volume patiently. A small sagging muscle at the corner of one eye twitched.

"Is there any other record? A later one?" I was feeling ashamed of my nap, and was trying to make sure that I had done my job. Guiltily.

"This is the record of those who formed the clan regiments, madam. I trust that it was helpful."

"But can one be sure of the death, when the initials are signed after the name?"

"I believe so, madam. That is the way records were made in those days." He shrugged and turned away. When he faced me again, he said, "Of course, you must realize that it's a long time ago."

"I just wanted to make sure. To know for sure. The American Stewart Bruce line is going to be in for a nasty jolt." I nodded my thanks and went out.

I stumped back to the hotel in harsh wind. For some reason the wind whipping against my body seemed fitting. Perhaps it was a kind of chiding, a rebuke for being so careless. I was vexed with myself and the afternoon. I was supposed to be working, was accepting pay for it, and I had napped over valuable old records.

The brief case and my handbag were more than I wanted to carry; they hit against my legs on one side, while with the other hand I held the cane and tried to hold my long coat together. What a waste of time! I'd have done better to stay at the hotel and nap. Why hadn't I? My Puritanism sticking out again! I had needed a nap, and had gotten a poor one in the records office. When are you going to get some sense, Hortense?

My coat was flapping; it blew wide. The brief case picked up the wind and twisted me to one side. I grabbed for my coat again, the cane flipping out. I felt like a full sail as I pushed my heavy bulk against the gale.

What had I really learned? That a man named Stewart Bruce had died. Yet he hadn't. The American family had Stewart Bruce as its forebear.

But the record clearly showed it, and the man said it was right. He had fallen in the battle, and his death was verified by his brother, Alan, whose dim initials lay on the page beside the name.

Surely, somebody had lived, to begin again in North Carolina.

The brief case banged my leg. It was good that the hotel was just a short distance ahead, I thought, pushing on. A few more staggers, and I'd make it.

But what about that man in America? Who was he? People don't just materialize like ghosts, Hortense!

Oh, everybody knows there are names taken. Not everybody who claims a name really inherited it. Everybody—talkin'—'bout—Heav'n —ain't—a'goin'—there—Heav'n!—Heav'n—Goin'—t'shout—all—over —God's—Heav'n.

"Oh, stop it!" I said it aloud, angrily. Isn't it enough that you goofed off when I was trying to work? Now you've gone daffy on me, singing that old song! Of course I know everybody talkin' 'bout Heaven ain't a'goin'—going! there. Stop! What *about* that man? Shall I just write and say they're a bunch of bastards?

You can't do that!

That's not quite the way I'd put it. "I'm very sorry, but the record shows that the man whom you suspected to have survived, died on the battlefield in 1746. Ergo, and thusly, you must find some other man. Families come from men, and so I am sure there is one, some-where, who begat your rather distinguished line, the scions of the cotton trade in the worthy city of Charlotte." How's that?

You're feeling tired, and you're being nasty. Can't you just tell them in a nice way?

Maybe I can tomorrow. I can't right now! I'm clutching my coat, and the wind is trying to pull it off my poor old frame, and my eyes have turned to jelly in a face made of soft putty, where even my nose has slid down someplace so that my glasses are falling off!

I stopped and pushed my spectacles up. I had passed the hotel. I turned around, exasperated by myself beyond comprehension. How could I have gotten so wound up in thoughts that I'd stagger past, against that terrible force? When it blew from my back, I nearly flew into the hotel entrance.

"Hallo! Find what you were looking for?"

"Hmph. Maybe."

"What d'you mean, maybe? What's wrong? You look a bit undone." Gilbert was freshly shaven and his trousers were neat. He had dropped the paper when he glimpsed me in the doorway, and he glanced up over it. It lay flat and elegantly untouched-looking on his knees.

"Well, if you knew how exasperated I feel!" I snapped. "That wind—!" I tossed my head over my shoulder. "I nearly got blown off the face of the earth. I think it had it in for me."

"Here." He rose quickly. "Let me have that," taking my brief case and purse while I yanked off my scarf. His eyes, which had been smiling, dimmed into a look of concern. "I say, Auntie! You need a good stiff one right about now." He gestured over his shoulder at the bar. "Come on in. They just opened a minute ago."

"It's about time they did!" I snapped. "That silly law! Closing all bars all over the country just because some foolish workers drank too much on their way home from work. Close at two-thirty and open at six, indeed!" I had started to follow, but then drew back, my hand to my hair, which surely must be disarranged. "Great heavens, Gilbert, I can't go in there looking like this! What'll they think of me?"

He laughed and took my arm. "Not much more than they did when you came, you old fraud!"

He had me inside and sitting on a barstool before I realized it.

We ordered our whiskeys and I sipped gratefully. After a time warmth signaled up from my stomach and I felt better.

"Gilbert, I don't think we can go just yet. I'm not satisfied. There's more to this than I've found out today."

His mouth pulled down at the corners. "Time's a'runnin' out, Auntie. My classes—" he waved a hand in the air.

"We'll make it. Just one more day. It was hard to find out much today."

"It's your trip, but I've got to be in Washington pretty soon; there's gobs to do before I can fly off to the wild, wild West."

"I know. One more day."

In the morning Gilbert was going to have the car greased and checked before we left for London, and he drove me to the records office. Sunshine lay on the rooftops, and the women were finishing with their scrubbing of their doorsteps. Everything looked very much like an innocent American summer day, except for the coolness, and I enjoyed the short ride to the records room. I had really become discombobulated yesterday. This time I would work.

The round light globes were lit again, but this time morning sunlight poured into the big room and it looked quite different. I hung my coat on the rack inside the door, cheered by its brightness, and went over to the counter.

"Hello!" I said in surprise.

Two young bearded men stood behind the counter instead of the man who had been there yesterday. One wore glasses and was dark; the other, a little younger, was blond. Both wore their hair cut just above their ears, and their beards were trimmed. They stood quietly watching my approach, and at my surprised greeting the dark-haired fellow moved to the rack and pulled down the big volume I had read the day before. He handed it to me and bowed.

It is pleasant to be recognized in your hotel, to have the porters smile as you pass, to greet someone with whom you've made acquaintance, perhaps in the lounge or at the bar. It is nice to be recognized by a reception committee where you've flown to make a speech, coming down the airplane ramp. It is not quite the same to be recognized for no apparent reason by a person totally unfamiliar to you.

Feeling my smile change to a perplexed expression, I carried the book to the table, sat down and opened my brief case. I spread out the notebooks, bent again and brought up my purse and fished out my pen. As I did I could see the young men talking quietly with each other. I felt distinctly self-conscious.

My hands hovering over the materials, I tried to place the chaps. Surely they were strangers! Had I seen them in the hotel, in the park? I shook my head and began to work.

The room was quiet. Occasionally someone came in, spoke in undertones with one of the young chaps, and left. I wasn't disturbed by them, only aware that I wasn't alone. I reread the same columns which I'd pored over before. There were the names in faded ink, the initials of Alan showing his verification. I riffled through the pages, hoping that there would be more about the Clan Bruce, but the volume was arranged alphabetically and there was no more. I gave up on it.

But perhaps there was something else, another record. I picked up the book and took it back. Now only the dark-haired fellow with the glasses stood at the counter.

He listened as I inquired, accepted the book I held out, and replaced it. Then he disappeared behind a row of stacks, and I heard a low discussion. Somewhat later he reappeared, carrying a smaller volume.

"This may be better for your needs," he said.

I took the book and went back to my table. This was an old history, published in 1795, recounting the many battles between the Scots and the English. It proved to be enormously interesting, and I read of the Treaty of Arbroath, signed in 1320 by Robert de Brus— the French spelling of Bruce, no doubt of that—and the moving words: "We desire no more than is our own, and have no dwelling place beyond our borders, and we, on our part, for the sake of peace, are willing to do all within our power."

There were records of battles that began before men had learned to write, when they became legendary, told by parents to children in front of fires in the crofts. There were battles swirling between the two countries as far back as the knowledge of men existed.

Certain kings had emerged, who, like Malcolm III, led their people to greatness, and who were loved and followed. Others were not so smart. Malcolm's great-grandson, William the Lion, had gotten caught in a ruse by the English when he had forayed far south of Scotland and had let his men run off to pillage.

The Scots were really a different race from the English, it was quite clear. I turned the pages and read on, fascinated to see, spread out under my hands, this long record of struggle between two peoples who were so unlike one another, and yet so much the same. Different, and living in the small confines of an island. Under one monarch now. This present system seemed to have held ever since the battle of Culloden.

There were names I recognized, and names new to me. The Scots were from a different breed, their land separated from the southern half of the island by a thick, high wall, built far back in ancient times by a Roman emperor. I had seen parts of that wall; it was an immense work, built to keep out a barbaric people, to keep them from plundering.

My mind snapped back to the present: the Scots were *not* barbaric! Not any longer. I smiled, recalling how very warm, how civilized they are. And they had not lost that marvelous capacity to have fun. Like children.

A nudge came from a dim recess; my dream of the day before crowded into my consciousness. A child had been forced, a compliance imposed. There had been fun in the hallway; the children had made faces and laughed. Inside the dim room, those older ones conformed stiffly.

Oh, come on! Don't fall asleep again!

I looked up from the book. I am not falling asleep! But I should go to the rest room. And I'd better stop reading this fascinating story. It's a waste of precious time; I can read it elsewhere.

When I returned it I obtained another from the youths, and settled back to further study. This book was more specific; it was a local history, and suddenly I grabbed my pen and started making furious notes.

"Not all of those believed to have fallen at Culloden were actually killed. Some, wounded, feigned death rather than to run the risk of certain death at the hands of the English. Some of these warriors, bearing the notable names of great Scottish clans, crept away under cover of darkness and were aided in their escape by sympathetic crofters. So great was the wrath of the English at the uprising that survivors were pursued into their private domains and into the far corners of Scotland, where they were mercilessly put to the sword. Even children and women were killed, and their houses set afire, their livestock killed or driven away.

"There followed a period of such savagery as to be scarcely believed. Whole families were murdered as they fled into the glens. The survivors, wounded, were hidden in barns, which were set afire.

"One duke, hoping to gain favor at the English court, pursued as far south as Linlithgow Castle, where he and his men pillaged the most beautiful castle of the Scottish nobility, and set afire what remained. It stands today a hulk, with few reminders of its former beauty."

I shuddered. I had stood within that castle's walls, that blackened and shattered ruins, wondering at a difference about it, some atmosphere not shared by other ruins. Always I had shuddered, and had wondered why.

I read on. "Some of the clansmen were able to make their way through the Outer Hebrides and across the Irish sea to Ireland in small fishing boats. Others fled to the mainland of Europe, where some changed their names and tried to forget their nationality. Some went to Normandy, and their names were kept. Many were able to get to the New World. Some of the greatest clan names were thus transported to other soil where they were able to begin new lives. Among the names thus transplanted are Cameron, MacDonald, MacAlpin, Bruce . . ."

My hands shaking, I scratched the words onto my papers. Here was my verification, perhaps my missing link.

But which Bruce had gone to America? If it really was Stewart, my Charlotte employers had it made. Yet he had fallen. Still, this book cast some doubt. Maybe he hadn't.

I went back to the counter. "Isn't there some other list of the men who died, another regimental listing? I'm not completely satisfied

with my research. These books are very good, but there's some confusion. Perhaps I should explain." I began the involved explanation,
seeing their bland faces, the eyes that didn't change expression as I
spoke.

Again I felt that unaccustomed self-consciousness. I felt like a daft
old woman pottering among things I didn't understand for the sake
of my own eccentricities. I chided myself for my feelings as I
struggled along with my explanation. Surely, Hortense, you will not
let these young men force you into being something you're not!
They're intimidating you. Come, you've lived long enough to know
what you know. You're not daft, and you're not eccentric. Slightly,
perhaps. But not crazy.

"You have the records, madam. Remember, it happened nearly
three hundred years ago—quite a bit of time. Our people were de-
moralized, surely you understand? Records were made in haste; there
was a certain amount of concealment. The aftermath of a bloody
holocaust—"

The dark one, an arm waving and his eyes blinking behind his
glasses, regarded me with a faint smile. There was a trace of con-
descension.

"Of course. I realize what it must have been. I do, really. Persons
disappeared, families were mixed up. It was horrible." I had one hand
up on my cheek.

Hortense, put your hand down. Stand up straight on two feet and
stop looking like you're not very smart. You're sure. Act sure. Something's still missing. It's your job to find out.

I dropped my hand and placed both of them firmly on the counter.
"What you say is true. Yes, I read the records, and I thank you. But
they indicate doubt about all the deaths listed. That's why I question: I must verify with certainty the death or life of Stewart Bruce."
There, I had said it, straight!

"My dear lady—" the blond youth began. I turned and started
back. There is such a thing as a generation gap. I did wish that the
younger ones would try a little harder to overcome it. I had done
my best.

"It's all right; never mind. I read that some survivors went across the Channel. I'll just have to check in Normandy."

The two looked at each other. Then one of them turned and went to the stacks. The other glanced down at the counter and rubbed it with one palm. Hesitating, undecided if they meant to do more, I watched him for a moment. He continued to polish the wood, and when it seemed clear that he had no intention of pursuing the matter, I went to my table. I had notes, and unfortunately for me, there seemed more work yet to do.

I put my papers together slowly, trying to think what was best to do. It came into mind that my old friend Gretchen Meeks would be in Normandy just about now. I would write to her and ask her to search out the records there. It was a long shot, but it might prove to carry pay dirt.

For another moment I watched my fingers picking up my materials, and then I made a quick decision. My hotel room had no desk; I'd sit here and use this table for that letter to Gretchen.

I tore out a sheet of lined notebook paper and began the letter, explaining my problem and the dilemma over Stewart Bruce—the whole puzzling affair of survival. I asked for her assistance, flattering her a bit and pointing out how well she had worked out the tangled De Montagne lineage, promising to help her if she ever needed me. I asked if she'd calculate her time and bill me for it and her work, whatever she considered fair.

I concluded by saying that we were in a hurry to get Gilbert down to London, and I'd have crossed the Channel myself for the work except for the shortness of time. I didn't want to indicate in the slightest manner that I was already feeling Gilbert's leaving, feared the crossing alone and my difficulties with the French language. No sense setting myself in her thoughts as growing old and incompetent, no matter how these young chaps here thought.

I gave her a London address where her reply would reach me later, signed the letter and folded it. I found an envelope in the brief case and wrote only her name, suddenly realizing I'd have to find her Saint-Malo address in my address book, which was with my things at the hotel.

I hesitated then. I could carry the letter back in my purse, or I might slip it inside the brief case. In this moment of indecision I became aware of the eyes of the two young men, a distinctly eerie feeling. Still holding the letter, I turned to see them better. They moved a little, fading backwards into the stacks.

Again I wished there were some way to bridge the visual impressions made by the old on the young. I could have related to those two, if only they would let me. They looked clean-cut, intelligent, purposeful. If they'd smile, if they would let me talk with them. If they didn't relegate me to a category.

If! Still holding the letter, I thought how many times we older ones had judged by a haircut, or the lack of one. Or some who were put off by beards, having grown accustomed to smooth-shaven cheeks. If only all of us made more effort to communicate.

I smiled at how I'd taken up that new cliché.

I made my decision, which would return eventually to bring me grief, dropped the letter into the brief case among the notebooks and papers. I decided I'd make another effort to meet these young men on better terms. They were partly visible, there in the stacks.

I picked up my purse and moved to the counter. "You were good to help me," I began, my voice raised a bit because they had moved back into the stacks. "I thought I'd like to come up and say I'm grateful for your help."

They looked at me without comprehending my motives, their faces as impassive as before. The blond one started to come forward, and then he hesitated and stopped halfway down the tall stacks. He smiled a little uncertainly and nodded. Then, seeming restrained by the immobility of his companion, he stopped. Both regarded me quietly.

I struggled to find something else to say. But a conversation made by one person alone becomes a monologue. I had said thanks. I was being put off again. They were a certain kind of snob, what kind I didn't know. I've learned to use the snobbery of snobs against them with telling effect, but these young fellows were not the usual kind. They didn't try to impress by outward symbols, either hinted at or alluded to; they weren't trying to make me feel insignificant, not really. There was something else.

I turned and made my way to the rest room once again, pondering their strange behavior. It was as if they guarded something they didn't wish me to know. I thought about it as I washed my hands. The symbols weren't right for snobs of either money or age. Those illnesses had other symptoms.

I couldn't quite figure them out. Young, but not too young; mid-twenties, I'd judge. Could their status symbol be their lack of age? Had they pinned on me the complications of dotage, an eccentric potterer, or of dilettantism?

I dropped the towel into the laundry bin and shook my head. Hortense, some things are not determinable, even by you. You're a snob, too. You think that you understand people; you think you're infallible. Forget it. It doesn't matter.

But something nagged. All right, I conceded as my hand reached out for the doorknob: I'm a snob about getting close to people. I use symbols, too: smiles, attempts at graciousness. Was I appearing ingratiating? Did I look foolish and silly? For some reason I could not fathom, I felt that way.

I went to the table, got the brief case and then my coat, turned to say good-by. The two chaps had disappeared.

The outside air was sharp; purple clouds were piled on the horizon. On the walk to the hotel, I consoled myself that I had done my best. Gretchen would search on the Continent in my stead, and it would work out.

Gilbert was all packed and ready to leave; he insisted that I give him my bags so that he could pack the car. I flew around putting everything in in a rush. During lunch he spoke of flying back to the United States as soon as we reached London, and from the eagerness of his voice it was easy to see that he looked forward to returning to his own life. I couldn't blame him. He had been a great help, but he must have often felt that this compulsive search of the past was less interesting than what he saw in the future.

For me, I felt a bit at loose ends, unraveled. Until I heard from Gretchen, there was no more work to do. It would only be a short time until I heard from another client and got started on a new commission, but I wished that there were a more definite errand now.

As soon as we finished eating Gilbert settled the bill and ushered me to the car. I suddenly thought of the letter in the brief case. It was too late. Gilbert was a perfect beast about unpacking, once he'd stashed things in. I said nothing about it. I would mail that letter as soon as we were in London. To stave off the Charlotte Bruces' anxiety, I would write them and explain the delay.

V

I sat beside Gilbert in the tiny car and thought. I thought about those men who had gotten away to unknown land, and after it had become familiar, had called it "home." Many of those forgotten warriors had escaped after the last battle at Culloden, floating away in small vessels under cover of darkness, and later concealed by fictitious names, some of them not daring to admit to a stranger who they were or where they had come from; even where they went.

The women and children had fled into the valleys through which we now drove. They had put the wounded into barns. When the barns were set afire, had the wounded cried out in the flames and falling timbers? Or did they make no sound?

I shuddered. I was getting morbid, too long reading of the battle, too long poking about in graveyards in search of family skeletons. I would rest in London; see ballet, theater and hear the symphony. Then, if nothing new developed, I would go to Chipping Cranford and the Queen's Arms, stay until the bobby got to know me properly. With good luck I'd make the acquaintance of the people who lived in the newer house behind the wall. If not, I'd get books and study architecture, learn when the old ruin was built. It would be comfortable and I would be busy. Later there would surely be another commission from an American who had begun to wonder where he came from, and I would start out again.

Those questing Americans, once they had grown up enough to stop finding out who they are, and turned their thoughts to wondering who they had been, seemed a little wistful and sad. They were all Displaced Persons.

True, they had not been put into concentration camps, and few had faced hostile mobs whose own small spot on a piece of dry soil gave only a scratched-out existence—the way it went today. The soil in America had been soft and yielding, for the most part. Even if savages remained, they had fought only briefly and had moved away or subsided; the other white men might not have been greatly welcoming, but the new ones were able to make places for themselves. They had done this at great sacrifice of energy and toil; the tears they had shed must have often fallen from nostalgia for those left behind, and the dear places they remembered which they had fought for.

Nostalgia faded when they realized that life, itself, was the most precious possession. When would men learn not to fear each other? What horrors this had given as a legacy to future children, now developed into a mushroom cloud! The differences of some men might complement the needs of other men.

I shook my head. I must have been struck by that light! I had experienced an opening out, not only a visual impression. We were descending from high moors, rolled across by dark purple clouds, into low places which held water. Sun streaked over the landscape and brought out shades of the palest green, tinted the water silver-blue. Mists in the air faded into mist in the sky; the view held all the colors of the cool side of the spectrum. Ahead we saw mountains, their tops concealed by dark clouds.

I began to sing and my voice quavered. "The hills . . . of home; the hills . . . of home—" and Gilbert took over and sang in his strong baritone, "My prairie home is beautiful, but oh . . . I long to see the mountains that I know . . . Their lofty summits veiled in misty rain . . . The hills . . . of home . . ."

Listening to him, I wiped my eyes and hoped that he didn't notice. What a beautiful country this was, and what a terrible sadness it had known. Would people ever learn to work together? To use the yearnings of their souls, to honor the artist as well as the automobile maker? All of us had emerged from the ooze like this we saw around us now. Were we in a spring thaw, thrusting up in countless ways, learning where we had come from?

Science classified the things learned, became categories which some men now worshiped. Science probed and catalogued. Thrust upward in spring thaw. Cathedral spires against gravity, the mind against the unknown.

Could we hold steady a bit longer? Wait and try to understand? The ground beneath our feet seemed to tremble in the spring thaw and thrust. Were there glimmerings of summer ahead? From worm-eaten effigies to spires and the sky. Today, the newspaper had said, a man floated out into the space, his arms and legs wide open and encased in white, his head in a glass bubble.

From where he floated we were invisible. He saw only a round ball of blue softly wrapped in white. We crawled in darkness. We had come from chopping blocks and armor, spires pointing up to space. Man: body, mind, soul.

The road had dropped low near a loch and bright diffused light flowed from overhead. All around us the land was dark, but on the water sunshine speckled the ripples gold. A bend in the road, and ahead we saw a castle of dark stone set close to the water. In the foreground bright buttercups splashed yellow mass against emerald grass. The black walls of the castle were heavy and dark against purple clouds. Then suddenly a mist dropped between us and the scene.

I blinked and wondered if I had really seen the castle, the yellow buttercups against the green, the black walls and purple sky.

"You're awfully quiet," Gilbert said.

"I do wish I hadn't put on so much of that eye cream last night. It slid into my eyes; I can't see clearly." I blinked again. "Do you know, if I lived here, I think I'd begin to believe in the Little People. Gilbert, wasn't that a castle?" I felt terribly moved; only commonplaces might be said.

"It sure was! What a sight! What's the matter? Think you're having visions?"

"Yes. I had a vision."

He turned slightly to look at me questioningly, then pulled his eyes to the road, puzzled when I said no more.

I sat wondering if the hippies, the kids who freaked out, the men with beards and the girls with long hair and outlandish clothes sensed something like my vision. Had they discovered something, or lost everything? When they blew their minds, did they discover this sense of soul?

We had to start speaking of this third part of us again, without apology or smirks. The new trinity: body, mind, soul. Every crop of kids has to learn for itself, and did it only seem that the new crop were expressing negatives?

Suddenly I said, "Gilbert, there were several young men in the thatched hut, there in Culloden . . . weren't there? You saw them, too . . . didn't you?"

He glanced up at me and quickly back at the road. "Oh. So you're back there, still." He was having trouble with the car.

I glanced from the window at the sky, still blowing rain and heavily laden with clouds. It had been awfully long since I had gone outside. These bearded lads and long-haired lasses seemed to know why I was here, but they kept the secret. I had no friends, but there were no enemies, either. I occupied part of their space, but I was not a part of their Cause, whatever it might be.

It was peaceful and orderly and quiet. Many people would have felt glad for a life such as this; to me it was a terrible vacuum. I felt like an old relative. Yet old people who live with their children get a chance now and then to be with the family, even if they don't participate. I needed a good laugh now. And hearty conversation. There was no threat, no fear of being carted away into the night, but it was a frightful bore.

I put down the yellow pad, hearing someone fumbling at the door. The sounds were different from the businesslike ones Frances made, and in a second I saw why: this was a girl they called Dorcas, with straight, Dutch-cut yellow hair, stolid, matter-of-fact in a primitive way. She set down the tray with a resounding clatter.

"Is Mrs. MacPherson gone, Dorcas? I haven't seen her for a long time."

She walked deliberately toward the door before she answered, then stood with her hands on her hips, to eye me speculatively. She seemed unwilling to answer.

"Well, it's just that it seems strange . . . she told me she was in

charge . . . and I haven't seen her for so long . . ." I wondered what
was passing through her head, and hesitated to arouse her suspicion.

"It's not really any of your business, is it, ma'am? I mean—you're
not supposed to know . . . are you?"

"Of course not. But I did wonder if she was ill." I felt humiliated
by her manner, ashamed of my curiosity. Yet why did I have to
apologize? I held her with my eyes, and for a moment she stared
back. I thought of suggesting the loneliness of my room, and decided
that it would make no difference with this angry young woman, who
watched me defiantly.

She started out of the door, but just as she was about to disappear, she stuck her head inside. "She comes and goes, you know. It
happens quite a bit. We manage quite well, actually, without her."

She shut the door.

So Rose had gone, and this young woman already was infected
with something akin to the defensiveness of Americans who jump
the moment an occasion comes up in which they are seemingly
called to account. I stared at the yellow pad for a long time, feeling
like a pillow that has been pummeled to put it in good order: perhaps better for the fluffing, yet with all my feathers disorganized.

The room had grown awfully dark, and finally I got up and turned
on the light. Then I sat for a long time thinking before touching the
food. When I had finished the supper I got my coat and boots. The
rain had ended.

In the lounge only a couple of the kids were wandering, aimless
after their dinner. The outside air was washed clean, the night sky
translucent, glorious. Pale pink clouds floated near the horizon, and
overhead the blue opened for a million miles, space that pulled you
up out of yourself. It was evening of the first day after Creation.

My head reeled with the look of it and the freshness. Wet oozed up
from under the tip of the cane and the boots. A curlew called, and
its sound melted upward. The faraway bens were outlined in strong
dark lines against the low backlight. I walked toward the high line
of dark that surrounded this low land, my thoughts busy with the
sudden change inside my head, which Dorcas had seemed to set in

motion. With a sense of wonder I saw that there was anger here; if it sometimes was directed against me, only the kids could say why.

But the anger which I felt seemed to move me off dead center, and propel my vacuous thinking into a sort of organization. For the first time all the impressions formed, organized themselves like ectoplasm, becoming a being—an entity. I was frightened by the lines and shapes that formed, and yet, like a curious séance-goer, compelled to await whatever fateful outcome might emerge.

I remembered that they had spoken of Malcolm Cromarty. I had no idea who he was, but if that was the same man who had told the unforgettable story in the Queen's Arms, he had directed me to Duncan's shop. I had liked him tremendously: if he wore the taboo Royal Tartan, that was all right.

If the kids knew him, or had just spoken of him from hearsay, I couldn't tell. I wished that I had learned Gaelic—it had seemed a dead, archaic language; who needed it? Now I needed it.

But that didn't cut any ice, as mother used to say. I must go on intuition and a few facts: Malcolm Cromarty was in some way connected with these kids; he had been in Chipping Cranford with Rose; I had seen them.

I knew that I made an assumption that Malcolm Cromarty was the same man I had talked with, the man Sarah had meant, the man the kids spoke of. Yet it seemed to hold some awesome logic which I could not logically explain. In retrospect, as I thought of the long hallway and the opened doors, his being there with Rose seemed to be some sort of business arrangement. I was certain of it. It had nothing to do with the sly-eyed suspected-closed-door-rendezvous type of meeting, and the slight fact of that overheard conversation, the glimpsed upraised hand was corroborating. And the Queen's Arms was too homey for a clandestine interlude.

As to what this might mean, I could only surmise. I stumbled through the sullen streams and climbed awkwardly over the rough hillocks, and I began to put many small pieces together.

These kids and the ones at the thatched hut in Culloden and at Inverness had many things in common besides beards and long hair. I had nudges, and not much else, coming off word-poor. I decided that it was a kind of fanaticism, a devotion beyond ordinary living, like a distraught mother with a sick child. A Cause.

What was the Cause? I had no idea. I reverted to instinct; sophisticated instinct, to be sure, but not factual knowledge. Sarah had said that we went into the part of the country that was most nationalistic. I could still hear her voice. The Cause might be political.

There are many kinds of politics, and as with economics, medicine, jurisprudence and mathematics, this area falls into a category of human endeavor where my knowledge comes up lacking. I am such a natural-born idiot that I don't know the difference between Whig and Tory, when they existed or if they still exist, and if either bore a resemblance to modern-day Leftists and Rightists.

I nearly fell into the ooze, got up and brushed off my wet leg, where the brown wet peat still clung, angry with myself for not watching my footing, and angry also with the dead-sounding, undescriptive labels of modern political thought. Why weren't these groups given identifying names that would help one to understand them—like WE LOVE YOU, NO MATTER WHO YOU ARE, and THE EVERY MAN FOR HIMSELFERS?

That would have helped. My consolation, in the company of serious politicos, was to dwell quietly in the beautiful world of metaphor —the stage, books, painting. Illusion left them all in left field, stranded. The bores. They took themselves terribly seriously, made a business of everybody else's business with a dilettante's knowledge, lived in a world of their own making not so real as mine.

The kids had that kind of feeling about them, the fanatic's eye-stare. It was either politics, or the world of selling. Perhaps they were attending a sales conference.

I had learned of these selling classes years ago when I'd stumbled into a New England inn in early spring, and had found myself in the company of star supersalesmen of a large insurance company. With some consternation, finding myself surrounded by men, I had noticed that they disappeared from the dining room promptly at nine in the morning, to reappear at lunchtime with their faces shining a peculiarly zealous brand of holiness known as New Ideas. There was this look on the kids.

Even church retreats were different, the communicants emerging from their meetings starry-eyed but haggard, humble, apologizing. There was no sentimentality here.

The difference was hopefulness, awareness, a self-value judgment akin to that of the insurance salesmen. The kids emerged from their meetings with a fierce, tooth-baring purposefulness. Insurance could be their Cause, yet I knew it wasn't so.

The blackboard in the dining room was always wiped clean. But on that day when I had talked with Colin, there were scrawled lines and smudged abbreviations. If this was insurance, I would have gotten a glimmering, recognized something. Equations I could have understood. Court lineups, juries, the legal system would have given some small clue. I understood nothing of what I had seen.

It was politics, I was certain.

Then why had they captured me? A mistake—a case of mistaken identity?

But I was the apogee of the unpolitical—an Innocent, so completely unpolitical that I had once voted for a new courthouse and a new fireproof addition to the old one!

What could they want with me? My world had to do with illusion —with hopes and fears, angers and tragedies. I thought of the funny, the queer, the odd—the way ordinary people lived, the dreams they lived for. I had often wished that the writers and artists could take over governments. Perhaps the world would be better.

But Scottish nationalists? It was to laugh, as the French say. Culloden had finished that idea for good, done in everyone who thought there should be a Scottish throne. The two countries were welded together geographically, economically and parliamentarily for longer than America had lived.

Even in America the blood had melded; people said they were Scotch-Irish, or Scotch-English, not realizing that scotch meant whiskey, the people being Scottish.

It was political; who was behind it? Perhaps Malcolm Cromarty. That brought up Rose again.

Who was Rose?

I said, "Rose is really Anabel MacPherson. She told me that much. She was in Chipping Cranford. So was Malcolm Cromarty."

So you're talking to yourself. Daft. Time you left this place. Get small. You can.

I looked up from the dark earth. The lodge was a mere speck; I had walked a good distance, and darkness spread upward from the land. The hummocks were almost indistinguishable. If I meant to go back, it was best to go while the brilliant sky still showed the way.

I mumbled aloud and hopped quickly. The light was soon to go; I had stayed out longer than I should have. Surely Gilbert had sent the policemen. I gave up on linking him with the crowd here; it was too much out of character for him. There was no reason why he would be a part of a Scottish nationalist movement, and he had been my friend in many ways, had proven himself so over the years.

Leave. Leave tonight. Don't wait any longer.

But how? I'm nothing without a car. This hip—would it take me across the endless miles? Where to?

Try. Rely on yourself. You can. Look—the lodge is a mere speck; you're a speck, too. No one can see you, it will soon be dark. Walk away. Try.

The inner voice had stopped, and I trudged toward the lodge, feeling totally deserted. If I left on foot, I must lay plans. Through the darkness light shone from the windows of the lodge, and the kids milled around, looking much like they had when I had first entered the place.

When I came inside they didn't seem to notice. They called to each other in a happy mood, and were bringing in trays of glasses and bottles of whiskey, giggling and full of high spirits.

The upper hallway was empty, and the sounds from below were gay, enticing. They were going to have a party; maybe the class was graduating. From their relaxed manner, it seemed to be something like that. I had longed for a hearty laugh this afternoon; why couldn't I sit on the balcony and listen? Nobody would know I was there; it would do me good. Yes, that was it—I'd go to their party.

I went quickly down the hall and dropped the coat and cane and boots, then crept back to sit on a large antique wooden chest, intricately carved with roses and thistles and entwined branches. I could see almost everything from here.

They had already begun to drink, and the whiskey was going down rapidly in the bottles. Small groups sat closely and chatted together, then laughter erupted from a cluster of kids and brought a call from across the room. For quite a while there was nothing special that could be made out, from the general hum and buzz in the lounge below.

Then the voices got louder and laughter rose more frequently. They had stopped talking Gaelic, and occasionally I could catch a remark over the layer of sounds. From a small group sitting directly below, the laughter erupted with an explosion. The others stopped talking, enticed with its sound, and a lad called out, "Ar-r-rgh! Alex, here!" He swatted the arm of the chap who sat beside him.

"Hear! Hear!" the crowd screamed, begging Alex to share his joke.

Finally he stood, waving his glass high. His face was flushed red, but he shook off the girl's hand on his sleeve, intent on making himself heard. Before he could begin, one of the chaps sitting near doubled up in a fit of mirth, recalling what he'd just heard, the effect intensifying the others' curiosity. The crowd now shouted, urging him on.

Finally he succeeded in obtaining quiet, and he stood, glass in hand and weaving slightly. He said, "And now—if you're r-ready t' hear—" And paused just long enough for the cries to break out a bit, then went into his joke.

> "There was a young widow in Crewe
> Who said, as the Vicar withdrew,

'The Curate's more tender, and taller and slender,
And more of a spender than you.' "

Screams and laughter flew up like bubbles in champagne, drowning out for a short while anyone's remarks in the swarm of sound. The limerick had the effect of pulling the kids together, and after their laughter died away, many of them shouted lines, remembering verses they had once heard, or trying to create new ones.

Finally another chap stood and waited for quiet. It was Robert, the chap from the records room.

"There was a young lady from Perth
Who kept a red hen in her berth.
When asked for the reason, she said that the bees in
Her belfry were bad for her mirth."

He dodged a barrage of small cushions sent flying, caught some and pelted them back, and the room below was for a time a confusion of swirling, brightly colored pillows. But the trend had started. Soon another chap jumped up and bowed in the grand manner.

"R-robert, that unfor-rgettable poetry was not so offensive t' our tender, slender ears as Alex's br-reach o' pr-ropriety, an' for that we say thanks—" But he had to dodge pillows. When the catcalls stopped, he went on with his limerick.

"There was a young lady from Perth
Who kept the Black Knight in her berth.
This reason espousing—his season of jousting
Had made him a man of great worth."

It called forth shrill screams, and I chuckled, hardly able to restrain a hearty guffaw. But it wouldn't have been heard. The kids were roaring, and now the limericks became a contest. They stood and shouted across each other, waving their glasses like rapiers, verbally fencing. It was worth a price of admission.

And then one was heard above the others:

"There was a young man from Dundee
Who followed a bird up a tree;

And from that lofty perch, with a grunt and a lurch,
He kicked a bad egg on the head of the church,
And they made him an English Grandee!"

They pounded each other and screamed in high excitement. Evidently this touched a spot, meant more than the others they had heard. The noise had barely subsided, when someone began another.

"Cromarty walked up to MacMarty
And said, 'D' ye know you're a smarty?'
And from that day and then
From the glens to the bens,
MacMarty's kin's skin has been arty!"

Now one of the girls stood, her glass high.

"There was a young lady in Scone
Who was left to herself, all alone.
Until she went crazy, ran off, joined the Navy,
Washed up in brine-bath as a crone."

Their clever replies zinged swiftly, one after the other. It was hard to hear some of the ensuing limericks, and sometimes I caught only a portion of what was called across the crowd below. They demonstrated lively wit, and it was impossible not to admire these kids. I giggled to myself in my lofty perch. They were smart, and they were quick. What was it they were up to?

They were passing around the bottles down below, and there came a short period of general talk and laughter, until someone again stood and commanded silence with another limerick.

"How remarkable is the small weevil
Who nibbles along with his sneezel.
He can gobble his way through a ben and a bay
And a mouthful of prickly pine needle."

The shouts that followed were quickly followed by this—

"A certain young countess from Perth
Had a waist of unusual girth.

It defied a hand-span, and cried out for the man
Who enlarged it, to fill out her purse!"

There were cries of, "Oh, Alex!" and a man's voice shouting, "Kill the bastard, and give no mer-rcy, I say!" and then a general fluff of noise, of lines being tested, begun and left hanging, and someone taking one up and trying for words, rhymes begun. Suddenly a loud voice took over.

"What a good filling food is plain haggis!
Th' mashed turnips and whiskey supplied us!
These good Scottish foods have sustained all our broods
And made us a nation of giants!"

There were loud shouts of, "Hear! Hear!" and tables were pounded, and the fury below was greater than it had been. In a moment someone else rose and shouted down the noise. When everyone was perfectly quiet, he began:

"And there was this Malcolm Cromarty
Who stood for the good of the party.
A'wearin' a skin and a grin, served the gin
In a tin painted bucket so arty."

The laughter below was punctuated by screams of delight, and the lines flew back and forth so fast that I couldn't make one out from another. Then the sounds ebbed, and another voice, a man's, began.

"From these great Scottish bens, lochs and traces
We emerge at long last in th' races.
A'swarmin', our beards growin' up t' our ears,
And a shot o' straight whiskey t' brace us!"

There were cheers, screams and huzzahs. Someone stood and shouted, "That one can be better! I say, Douglas, that can be impr-roved! Listen t' this!

"From these gr-reat Scottish bens, lochs an' river-rs
We swarm out at long last without shivers!

A gr-reat band! Our beards growin' up t' our ears!
No Duke this time splinters our timber-rs!"

Their shouts grew until the room bulged with sound. When things had quieted down again, another sturdy male voice began:

"Oh, come t' the sound o' the piper-rs
A'skirlin' the damn British Isler-rs!
We'll send 'em a'flyin' all over the island,
From Or-rkney to Dr-rumore, the vycktors!"

His distortion of the last word brought down the wrath of the room on the head of the poet. I peered over the balustrade and saw some of them pounding at him, and he raised his arms to fend them off. Their laughter was still hearty. They hit at him and berated his mispronunciation, and I heard his voice raised, claiming the right to poetic license.

Then I sat back, and for a long time their talk swirled, breaking away now and then into that Gaelic language. Another glance confirmed that they were finishing up down below. I rose, prepared to scoot the moment one of them moved away. I had heard a lot. Suddenly the whole thing made sense.

But someone, in a last-minute flare of wit, had risen to toast. I leaned back as faces turned in my direction. But they were looking at the speaker, almost directly below, his glass in his raised hand. A couple of the girls, collecting the bottles, waited while he shouted.

"Th' curious sign o' the thistle
An' th' clear sound o' curlew's low whistle—
They tell us t' grow, over Highland and Low,
T' be wor-rthy o' wearin' the thistle!"

The kids jumped up and shouted. In the wild chorus of "Aye's" and "That's right, Jock!" I went quietly down the hall to my room. I had heard enough now. Many pieces of the puzzle were coming together: what they did and why, what they belonged to, my perplexity in the records room at Inverness, those vacant-eyed young lads at the thatched hut, the strange mark on the pamphlets. I had seen them.

Then I had not seen them. The pamphlets had been taken away, probably by the vacant-eyed young men, who had seen more than they seemed to.

And I knew exactly what I must do next.

VI

I poured out my large handbag upon the bed and sorted through its contents. It had everything in it for comfort: two miniature bottles of whiskey which had not been consumed on the plane flight, several packets of crackers not eaten with soup in restaurants, a couple of packets of Handy-Dandies, as they call cleansing tissues in Great Britain, my comb, hairbrush, pens and pads of notebooks, a folding toothbrush, the antique keys, my Swiss knife, my nail file. I planned to become a mere speck, to follow that inner voice tonight. I would get smaller and smaller, like Alice, until I had gotten far away. It didn't matter how long I must walk, but I would walk. The hip had managed all right so far, and if I took it slowly enough, I might make it.

I had food and sustenance of a limited kind. I hoped for help before my strength ran out, but if I were picked up at dawn on the road, I would be free, alive, and only in need of rest and nourishment.

The lodge was absolutely still. I had heard the kids straggling up, laughing and calling to each other. Now they were sleeping off the booze. The key had been left in the entrance door after my return. I had only to turn it and go out.

But before I left, I must learn what was in that pine closet in the basement. It contained a secret that I could not leave without learning, the key to the mystery that was becoming clear.

The lobby was as quiet as death, and the WAY OUT sign glowed its dull red at the end of the hallway. I moved smartly toward the basement door. It was unlocked.

There was no sound as I went down the stairs, my breath held, listening. When I was safely at the bottom I resisted an impulse to hurry and waited, listening again, until I was sure that I had not been followed. Not a sound came. While I waited I began to wonder if the closet was stocked with jellies and jams. I saw that someone had been at work down here. The boxes which I had seen earlier were flattened and stacked beside the wall.

For some reason I was sure that something more important than pamphlets was inside the closet. It scarcely seemed necessary to lock them up. I pried at the padlock with my Swiss knife, and it was fairly easy to open. The door swung wide soundlessly, and I pawed on the walls for a light switch, touching shelves of the slick papers in neat piles. I finally found a light bulb dangling from the center of the ceiling. It was as I had expected: shelves on each side were stacked with the pamphlets.

I studied a sampling from various places, but it did not hold me for long. I could not read the Gaelic, and any with translations were like the one I had filched—innocuous, inspiring and allegorical. Every one was printed with the simplistic drawing, which I now realized represented the Scottish thistle.

The sight that drew me to the end of the closet was an antique black metal trunk. It sat importantly on the floor at the end of the aisle between the shelves, seeming to be ensconced there. Four locks were spaced into its heavy lid, and its body, tarnished brass straps and chunky legs were corroded heavily, but the curving, interlocking overlay of Scottish work could still be seen.

Nicks had been made around the locks, and the front edge of the cover was more polished than the body, where hands had lifted it. It was a treasure of a cask.

This was more like it! Blood surged through my ears in a steady, pulsing roar. I knelt beside the chest and dumped out my handbag, scrambling the antique keys together at one side, so eager to try to get it open that my hand shook when I tried the first key and scratched deeply into the scale. The cut removed a bit of the encrustation and revealed a small medallion. I held off my curiosity about the contents, even more curious about the decoration, for it could show to whom the trunk had belonged. I scrubbed at it furiously. Enough of it emerged to make it out—the lion rampant. I chuckled with happiness. This could only mean the property of the Bruces. I had hit pay dirt.

The first key I had used did not fit anywhere, and I threw it aside and tried others. Some were obviously too large or small, but there was still a goodly number of possibilities which I tried with undaunted zeal. I found one which entered the third lock, finally, but in spite of my strongest efforts, it would not turn. I had felt enormously cheered that it seemed to fit, and the resistance of the lock dampened my enthusiasm momentarily. My method had been so random and exuberant that I was not sure which of the keys I had tried.

I began to sort them out, lining them up on the floor according to size, and began again with systematic trial and rejection. As the possibilities dwindled, dismay set in. Then hope supplanted it as a key penetrated the first lock. But the result was as before: this one also held; no lock opened.

I tried it in the two vacant locks. It took the fourth, where it refused to turn. I put it back into the first and studied the trunk, exasperation growing. The two keys stuck up from the lid, a snaggle-toothed, mismatched pair. I now began to doubt if my scheme was feasible. My life had left me badly prepared for this kind of work. I bared my teeth at the miserable success so far achieved, the prize seeming as remote as before I had started. I had used all of the keys which had seemed possible, and stared at it with hostility.

Then a memory slowly oozed up from many years past: I was a child in a museum, watching a guide pointing to a similar antique chest; his voice droned about a sequence. I was back in action.

I twisted the keys alternately, seeking patterns, successions. Suddenly the first lock snapped open. What had I done? I closed and opened it, then the third. Nothing changed; nor would the fourth open. I could not find the right combination.

Agonized by this small triumph, I went through the reject pile, again without results. There remained only the keys I had first put aside, obviously too large or too small. On the chance that a trick had been devised by the locksmith to fool the eye, I began with the discards.

One, about the size of a modern door key, took the second lock.

But, though I twisted all three, trying to remember the sequences as accurately as I could, the result was unchanged. I leaned back in complete frustration. I hated to admit it, but I was baffled.

Slowly. Keep on. You should be aware by now that your purchases were guided. It's a clear case of precognition. No need for you to rationalize about wall decorations. Remember. Think back again.

I snorted and began to repack my handbag with the welter of things on the floor. Clairvoyance is an idiot's explanation for coincidence! I bought the keys because I liked them, most of all the miniature key with finely made, polished tiny teeth, on a long and elegantly shaped gold stem, a minute lion on its tip. It was in my coin purse; when I got out of here, I would have it made into a lapel pin. Gilbert teased me about it, saying that it needed a magnifying glass to be seen. There was no place on this trunk for a tiny key like that. What if each of them bore the lion rampant? A Scottish decoration, seen everywhere. What was I supposed to remember? The floor was cold, my knees stiffening, the hip starting a dull throb. What had I forgotten? I couldn't open the trunk; I'd better admit it. What more was there to remember?

As always, to think of the little key had a soothing effect. I sat on. Had I missed something? I studied the thing again, trying to find anything I might have overlooked. I don't know what kept me at it, except that sometimes I had done what I thought I could not do. I tried to move the trunk to see all around it, so that the light might shine differently on it.

It was of heavy steel plate, and clumsy to move. A lengthy examination of the four sides proved nothing new was to be found there. And then I thought of the bottom.

It was more difficult to topple it over on its back. The bottom, also, was heavily strapped, of the same thick plate. There seemed to be nothing different. Then I stiffened and brought my face close. In one corner, nearly concealed by the triangular leg understructure, there were faint marks. Closer inspection showed that a small plate, hung on an inner pivot, had worn those tiny marks at one side.

The plate moved upward to reveal an inch-square enclosure, a small lock hole in its bottom. The gold key was right. It wobbled for a moment, penetrated, took a firm hold, and clicked the lock open.

I grappled the chest upright and began to turn the keys. The second lock opened. The third had to be shut to open the first. I had found the sequence. The lid came up with a protesting squeal.

Layers of documents were inside, some old and frail and yellow, in Latin, the ink faded. Others were newer, and I lifted them out and put them to one side to study later.

I had long known that quantities of Scotland's official records were confiscated by King Edward in 1296, when the English lugged off the Stone of Scone. Scots used the verb "stolen," and have since then resented its loss, their ancient coronation stone. Perhaps the English believed that to take it might unite the two countries; the thought is probably charitable. It had the opposite effect.

The theft of the records was as hateful. Anger was kindled that is alive today. It had always seemed strange that such strong emotions could persist for centuries, to become the cause of bloodbaths between the two countries, which supposedly was settled by the thrashing the Scots had taken at Culloden in 1746.

I was seeing some of these old records. The first glance proved their value, papers with the red wax seal of the Bruces. My eyes raced over lists of famous names dating back to 1066. There was no doubt but that they were authentic.

I read "new" and startling facts: in the eighth generation following the Conquest a marriage had taken place in secret. From this had come Stewart Bruce's line. Following his name was a record of many births, the final one dated 1915. No death was recorded for this male descendant—evidence that the man I had been researching in Inverness had survived the battle, and evidence, too, that his line still existed. Alan's name was followed by the words "Removed to America." There was no notation following, and it seemed a little sad, as if they had written him out of their thinking. This was the line of my American clients.

But in spite of the pathos of that, I felt cheered. I now had information which had eluded me, could make my report. I felt as if I should give quiet thanks to some unseen guide that had kept me at my quest in such an unlikely place.

I started to repack the chest, when a symbol caught my eye—an escutcheon with emblazoned crosses on the shield, its crossbarring, wreath and supporting crest with helmet and the scroll and its motto familiar since childhood. That same escutcheon had hung over my mother's bureau, seen so often that it had been taken for granted, like so many of the lovely things she had.

My hands shook so badly that it was necessary to put the papers into the trunk lid to be able to read the fine, spidery writing. I recognized some of the names of Mother's ancestral line, and suddenly my eyes seemed to have grown far out, ahead of my face, extended on antennae, and I heard myself panting. I could not read fast enough, or believe what the papers told. This was the line of the ancient kings of Scotland, the line which had, seemingly, come to an end with the Baliol turmoil. But it really had not. It went on: Mother had been a descendant, and I suddenly knew that if there were a throne, I could be considered a serious contender.

It was as if I had drunk too much wine. The small enclosure rocked and swirled; I panted as if struck by a tidal wave. I felt awash in a sea of intrigue, instantly aware of the way history obliterates and distorts facts not wished known.

I tried to focus on the lists, names of people I had read about and loved since childhood without really understanding why. I was exhilarated, like a girl who, in an unsuspecting instant, sees the man she has dreamed about. I wanted to shout, to run upstairs and wake the kids, throw my arms around them and proclaim blood brotherhood.

So Duncan had said, "We think you Americans are silly when you wave your papers and shout." Well, I wanted to shout, and be damned to what Duncan thought!

I remembered Linlithgow Castle, that empty hulk seven or eight stories high. Its stones—were they red? gray? yellow? They were of no color, of all three; they changed color with the light. The looming walls were streaked with black. Was it weathering, or had there been fire? Or was it changing skies that changed the color of the stones? They looked fired, flamed. Old, dead fires, long cold.

The entrance gateway: an elliptical arch between twin round towers, four battlements above it, in the spaces beneath them were medallions of wreaths, capped by crowns. In one the Baliol triple hearts, crowned, the rampant lion in another, and what in the others? Something indecipherable, queer—were there triple tiers of sheep? Hard to see, hard to remember. Forgotten, now.

The light changes as I watch, the colors fade from red to gray, and I walk into the courtyard centered with the fountain, its shape an ornate crown, set in a circle of yellow chippings in emerald-green grass. Windows loom from three sides, five stories of blanks like empty sockets in a skull—so many, so many on every side, staring down. I turn and see the carving over the Norman entrance arch; in the center is a grinning face in high relief; it looks like a pig, but it wears a Viking helmet; it has a snout. On either side are strange birds, but they are not birds; something droops below them; it makes me think of water, that drooping thing. A fish? But it has wings. An elf face at the top, above the helmeted face. Is it an imp? It is in low relief; the light changes and it is indistinguishable, gray against streaked gray stones, its details gone. It is cold here. The wind has come up; it is strong, cold, blowing.

I go quickly inside the great hall, open above to the sky. There is sky outlined by blackened stones; above my head thick clouds, framed by arches of walls three stories high. Fireplace hood arches hugely at one end; windows arch jagged stones against layered clouds; wind funnels through here. I walk on with a feeling of dread, no reason I can put a finger on, just a crawling under my coat collar. I try to catch up with Gilbert, who has gone ahead, not so interested in the elf face and Viking snout. I go far down the roofless great hall. In a deep window recess I pass a satyr sitting on the sloping sill, behind him the jagged arch, concealed by the stones of the heavy wall until I am abreast of him. He stares straight ahead, a young man with a beard. He does not see me; but he does see me. A satyr? But he wears shoes; he is a young man with a beard, sitting on his haunches, staring straight ahead at the opposite wall. He does not move; he is watching.

I move forward, in a hurry, too fast to notice the low step into the next room-without-a-roof and rambunctiously bang my feet on the stones, nearly falling and off balance, almost running into it. It is not a room, there is no roof. I try to walk slower, yet move hastily through to the circular staircase and climb up in its narrow darkness, around and around, to emerge five levels above the crown fountain set in emerald grass and yellow chippings. I waver there, holding hard to the slender iron railing and seeing down the vertical red-gray wall, past where floors used to be, all the fireplace openings along the inner wall, the entrance doorways gaping the long length of it, open space to the dungeon depth below, green with moss where the sun never shines; all silence; the wind surging. The walls are only gray, black streaked. The fountain is carved elaborately down beyond; the carvings are unrecognizable shapes. What are they?—different from any I have ever seen.

We walk skeleton hallways between gaping holes of rooms, glimpsing the fountain through empty holes of windows on the courtyard side, on our way to the tower at the far end of the high walk, the ruin around and beneath and above us. Here is the turret tower; a plaque in old, weathered letters is set: ". . . Queen Margaret's tower . . . in Linlithgow's bower . . . sat . . . and wept the weary hour . . ." And Gilbert has gone up there, and I cling to the sentry wall, the wind tugging at my coat, the great bulk of the handbag, and Gilbert calls, "Come up, Aunt; you must see this!" but I cannot move.

The wind . . . I shall blow down into the courtyard; it is eight stories down; the wind wants me to fall down there; I cannot go up the narrow staircase into the sky, the slender stair with a straw for a handrail, another story higher, higher than where I cling to the wall, alone. I am too high, I call, my words blown away by the wind; I cannot come up, Gilbert; I cannot climb up there! I am afraid! Gilbert, come down! Come back and help me go down! Help me from these walls, I cling to these streaked walls, I push myself against them; I am dizzy!

But I say nothing, and he is coming back, running down the

slender stairs. "Why don't you come up here, Aunt? No? Too bad; it was good; you can see for miles around."

The Queen sat there while her lord was away at the wars, and watched for his pennants to show flying out against the sky. How did she come down, too small a stair for anyone to go with her? Her maids waited where I stand.

Someone is watching, Gilbert. Something sees us. No one is here, but eyes watch. I feel them. Something knows that we are here. Let us leave! Oh, let us go quickly! "I am tired," I say.

Now I knew: the walls of Linlithgow were streaked black from the fires made by the Duke of Cumberland's troops on their way back to England. After Culloden they had slept at Linlithgow, foraged for food, plundered and rested their horses, and in the morning as they turned away, had put fire to the straw inside the courtyard.

They must have seen the black smoke rolling against the sky as they went triumphantly to report their victory. The smoke must have risen for days. The most beautiful castle in the land, Mary of Guise had said, mother of the Queen of Scots. The Queen was born there.

I held my breath. Aye! Reasons existed for my feelings at Linlithgow. Gilbert said that I saw ghosts. I didn't see, I felt. They had been all around us there at Linlithgow, nudging silently, trying to tell a story: "You are one of us! You belong to us!"

I shivered as I knelt, but it was good finally to know the reasons for the strange feelings I had had. I held in my hand lists of kings long gone, names belonging to my lineage, now not only names, but people. They were no longer here, but the places they built were, and their traditions, loves and hates, ways of thinking, even of speaking. I knew suddenly why as a child I had loved Scottish songs, why now my hair raised up when the bagpipes whined and the drums snapped, why I wanted to run and scream, why I gulped and tried not to show it. Now I knew the strength of racial feelings. They are too deep to explain.

The thought brought to mind other people—the blacks who banded together in America, the Jews who struggled to make Israel, the countless people for whom no papers, no records could ever be

found now, their clinging together for identity so fierce that sometimes others felt a threat in it.

But Scots had kept identity, kept their own land. It was under
alien rule, and they sought their own rule for their own country.
Here in the Highlands had been preserved their crafts and skills and
dances, songs and loves they had developed over centuries, and their
forthright ways. The kids were doing it. I wanted them to make it!

I picked up more records to study, wishing for a machine to copy
them all. If they could only be published, so that everyone might
know what had been obliterated! An insight emerged: the English
needed the qualities of the Scots—their warmth, honesty, humor and
kindness, their simplicity, their way of seeing into the heart of a situation, and into people. I recalled Timothy and his love for boys and
for his wife. And hadn't Duncan seen into me, when he had told me
in the truck of his love for Sarah? I had been given a look into his
heart then.

The English loved pomp and polish, grooming and fine manners, cultivated voices high-placed in the mouth. They overdecorated,
overrefined, both themselves and surfaces. They spoke from behind
the teeth; the Scots spoke from their guts.

Scots were no longer the brutes who had long ago ravaged the
borders; they had spent centuries working within limits, searching
for possibilities, and had become courageous and proud and warm.
They had correctly learned to fear the English, whose violence was
carefully concealed, but used with utmost brutality against their
northern neighbors. Many of them had fled—many to my own country; those who remained had to live with their anger. It fanned their
need to develop their own ways, and it had not died. These kids were
the proof of that.

The Scottish blood that had gone to America had built the sub-
stance of America, had cried hot for revolution when many of the
colonists were only lukewarm. Their loved names had been given to
places and people to be preserved and recalled, but a strong new al-
legiance was formed.

I smiled as I thought of our young, who called old-world history
"irrelevant," and asked why new and creative ways couldn't be found

to end disputes "over there." Twice we had tried to end those wars, and were vilified later, thought of as mongrels because of our mixture of bloodlines. It made me shudder to think of such a thing, the idea of racial purity as developed by the Nazis under Hitler grown into full-blown paranoia.

I felt exhausted, worn out from the emotions I had just experienced. It was similar to the feeling when the final curtain had dropped; it was time to become myself again, everyday and commonplace. I studied as I had learned my lines and made a few notes in the small notebook. There was too much to copy all of the facts; my clients would have to take my word.

The quiet study brought on quieter feelings, and I was grateful. It was good finally to have answers for so much that had puzzled me for so long.

I realized sometime later that much time had passed. How long had I sat here in the pine closet? I began to gather up the papers and put them into the trunk.

With the last sheaf ready to put in, one hand already on the trunk lid, the Sutherland name jumped out. I opened the papers in haste, anxious to leave, yet more anxious to read what it said that I had not known. Near the end of the last page I found my husband's name, his birth date, the record of our marriage and the date of his death. Someone had written a lightly penciled note after my name: "Suspicious. Keep under surveillance."

Far from being among kindly kids, I knew that I was in danger, and had been all along. I was among a crowd of young political fanatics. They knew why I was wanted, that I had been forced to stop here. There was a contest for the government of Scotland; perhaps they intended to set up a throne. Someone knew that if I chose, I could lay a legitimate claim to it. My presence must be a threat to their plans. While I had been going about my business, happily American and unaware of skulduggery and fear, someone had removed me from the world of the living, probably thinking that I knew more than I did, intending to prevent interference with their plans.

I threw the sheaf of paper into the chest and pushed down the lid with no effort to cover my traces, swallowing at the bitter taste in my mouth, and suddenly weak. I had a terrible feeling, as if a silver cone in the middle of my body had instantaneously become white-hot; it shot gray ganglia behind my eyes. For a second I could see only swift iridescent flashes and haze, blinded by sparks flying out in every direction, a rain of swift hammer blows inside my skull.

I tried to stand and tottered. A nightmare became real: I was in an elevator going up at high speed; the sides dropped away, and I was suspended in space, swaying crazily like an out-of-phase pendulum. My breath rattled a husky, two-octave whistle. I held tight to the trunk lid, quivering as if electric current passed through my body.

The cone gradually cooled, and I could see again. I reached for the light. I had to get out! I turned toward the door, and stared into the face of Rose Glasses.

She grabbed my wrist and pulled down sharply. I screamed.

"None of that! You've played the dotty dowager long enough!" Her grip was tight, shutting off the circulation.

I tried to get past, out of the closet, but was turned sideways and bent down by her increased pressure. I looked up, from my knees. She smiled, her lips pulled tight against her teeth. She held the pressure, then twisted and pressed down harder. I felt the tears start into my eyes.

"Get up! Now! March!" Her tone was cold.

I tried to stand, but she held me down. I struggled for some minutes while she continued to command me to get up, yet held her firm grip. When she finally let go, I got to my feet.

But she blocked the doorway, her arms folded across her chest, the strange smile looking frozen on her face. "Spying! I always knew you were a spy, Hortense! You had some of them fooled, but not me!" She hissed my name, and little drops of spittle flew into my face.

I tried to force my way out, but in the narrow doorway she leaned against me, pushing my body against the shelves, twisting with such mad strength that pain spurted across my chest and slithered downward. I didn't want to get sick, but it felt about to happen.

I swallowed convulsively and tried to say that I needed the cane. With a dry mouth, no words came out. I blinked as she twisted again.

She may have grown tired. Whatever the reason, she let up the pressure enough for me to bend. I brought the stick up and over my head. Instantly her hand shot out and caught me across the breast in a karate chop, and the cane flew up and ricocheted from the beams. I reeled back.

She kept her grip and reached for the light, turned it off and propelled me out of the closet. Free of the narrow room, I tried to move away from her. She tensed and pulled me up short, kicked the door shut behind us, and gave my wrist a sharp twist as she ordered, "Move!"

I went slowly, my handbag slapping against my ribs. I do not cry at pain, but I sagged downward and panted. Rose brought her toe sharply into my side. "Get up those stairs," she commanded.

Pushed by her in this manner, we reached the stairs. I tried to go up, but some things can be said and not done. The hand was sending gangrene signals, and as I quivered at the foot of the steps, I heard her cursing and commanding me to stop faking, her face muscles taut, her teeth bared and her eyes protruding. A death's head in pink glasses.

I wobbled up one step and she pushed from behind, one hand pulling up in a half nelson, her knee applied low. I had to stop. I knew I would never make it; not now, drained of strength by the pain and too deeply frightened even to try to climb higher under such conditions. I paused, hearing her curses and commands, and then suddenly I whirled out of her wrestling grip and caught her with the back of my free arm across the cheekbones. She staggered back, and then quickly flew forward and hit me amidships.

Pain erupted like Fourth of July fireworks, the grand finale ending. The sound as I crashed against the stair treads came dimly. I sprawled there at the side of the stairs for a long time. I could hear heavy breathing; whose, I don't know. It sounded like a death rattle.

Then came a quiet time. I put my hand to my face. My glasses were, miraculously, still on. Rose seemed to be searching for hers in the dim reaches of the basement. I must have hit hard, for she had a long search. I spent the time feeling my ribs through more than fifty years' accumulation of flesh: I was in some sort of order. My hands and fingers worked. I could move both feet from side to side. My head, responding to a command over the strong complaint of neck muscles, turned from side to side.

She had found her glasses and was coming back. She kicked my feet. "Get up!"

Though willing, I couldn't heft my weight. I grabbed at the stair tread and pulled up to a kneeling posture, and then, hands on the rail, tried to pull upright.

"No more playacting! Get up!" She brought a knee up into my back.

It had the opposite effect of her intentions. Completely off balance, I clawed frantically at the handrail. She was close against me, and I sagged backwards, unable to control any large muscles. I literally spilled backward onto Rose. The air rushed out of her as we hit cement. The sound made up for the pain in the old hip when I crashed. I wished that I could spread out and just blot her up. We sat still, neither of us able to move.

Finally she got up and stood over me, hands on hips. I felt like a beetle on its back, waving its feelers. Deeply afraid of her, I tried to get up again. She watched and kicked at me a couple of times. Then she suddenly shrugged, turned and went up the stairs.

In the respite I tried to direct my body from a mind cluttered with shreds of fear and pain. Where was the tiny voice that could assemble the various parts into a unified whole? Several times the legs seemed ready to hold my weight, but the arms became a problem. I realized that my handbag still dangled from the left elbow. At the casual thought, my arm moved upward, the fingers dropped, and the handbag slipped to the floor. I stared at it, fascinated. My feet, out front, moved gently as the weight fell off. I might have been watching a Pinter comedy of the absurd.

Don't try so hard. Rest.

I listened and watched my hand drop to one knee.

You can stand. Just stand.

I reached forward, elevating my rib cage, arms out as if to dive, and rolled, tipping gently to the left. I came to rest on one forearm and remained there, bemused by this new position.

Bend your knees. Yes, you can.

One foot was slowly coming back home. I tried the other.

Rose found me on all fours. I stared back at her like some old dog. She had my coat in one hand. She threw it. It hit me in the middle and I rolled over like a toy, gently onto shoulders and ample hips. I could see my feet moving back again in slow motion, still trying to carry out that command.

Rose grabbed the coat and pulled me up to a sitting position, her hands clamped into my sides. She finally succeeded in getting my hands into the sleeves, working them on like a mother dressing a child. When she had it on, she stamped off into the semi-darkness. I heard a door open, then the sliding of garage doors and the sound of an engine spluttered and pulsed. She came back, her feet pounding echoes which reverberated through the garage and again in the basement.

A few minutes later Malcolm clumped down the stairs. He wore a sweater half pulled down over his trousers in the back, and his hair was tousled, his eyes fogged with sleep. He took my shoulders and I smelled the odor of stale whiskey. Rose took my feet. I was in no shape to battle Rose alone; I could not fight the two of them.

They carried me between them into the garage and pushed me inside the car. The door slammed, and Rose drove out with a jet spurt, shifted gears and tore toward the highway, careening around the corner onto it like a race driver.

The headlights illumined the narrow roadway bending ahead, the boulders flying by and disappearing into the darkness. She took the turns with high speed. If she planned to dump me, she had plenty of opportunity and small chance of discovery in this land of ditches, gullies, endless bogs and deep lochs. If she stopped, I would fight with the strength I had, but she drove too fast to open a door and tumble out. Concussion was one accident I could avoid.

I must wait for a situation which would be more to my advantage. I didn't expect to see the lodge again, or Gilbert. If he succeeded in getting help, anyone who came there would have a fruitless search, more so than the first. The remaining hope was that they might find the chest and the Sutherland sheaf. I hoped they could deduce something from that, but the hope seemed vain.

I wondered if Gilbert were still working to help me. It seemed that he had given up, for there had been no other sign. I had only myself to protect me.

We were deep in the bens, and my teeth chattered without stopping. I shivered uncontrollably.

VII

Rose spat cherry seeds toward the sloping drain hole and eyed me warily. She looked like some queer monkey. Perhaps she thought me asleep. Holding the small basket in one hand, she filled the other full and tossed cherries one at a time into her mouth, cleaned the seed and ejected it with her lips pursed. She made pfts of sound with her mouth and the seeds dropped onto the stone with sharp taps and rolled gently through the hole. There was not another sound.

She finished the cherries and threw the basket behind her. If this had been a normal kitchen, it would have landed in a corner; since it wasn't, but the kitchen of a medieval castle, the basket simply disappeared into the gloom. Rose didn't come too near at first, perhaps afraid that I might spring at her, perhaps wondering if I was alive. Finally, as I remained unmoving, my eyes nearly closed, she satisfied herself that I was in no shape for more jousting, and she bent and scrutinized me, her eyebrows drawn together.

I had lain on this stone floor for what seemed many hours. After the drive of last night and the fight at the lodge I couldn't do much more than to clutch my greatcoat around my body, too exhausted to move except to shove my big handbag under my head. Someone had come out when we drove through the portcullis gate, a young man, I judged from his feel as he pulled me from the car and propelled from behind while Rose pulled from in front. They had said a few words to each other. He had not been surprised to see her. I surmised that they knew each other well.

We had grunted up a narrow flight of stone steps to this room. They dumped me, and their torches had bobbed away into vast blackness. I heard their steps fade in the distance, and then the clang of heavy iron; perhaps some gate. Then everything was still. I lay trembling, hoping to get quiet and gain enough strength to get away, once daylight came. I had no idea how, and feared the blackness to every side. There might be holes, there might be drop-offs. I stayed against the wall, its firmness a source of comfort in the impenetrable dark, where a lighted match only illuminated more dark beyond. I seemed to be in a cave.

In the car Rose gave a verbal barrage of abuse, then changed to questions that I had not answered. What had I learned in the closet? Had I behaved as a guest should? Had I obeyed her instructions to stay in my room, or walk on the moors, when I had broken into the closet? When I seemed taken by the grand mal complete with clacking teeth, she had turned on the heater with a snort of disgust, and the chattering of my teeth had finally stopped. But my leg muscles had quivered into a life of their own, the spasms persisting throughout the night. I hadn't known there were so many different muscles. The cold of the stones intensified their spasmodic contractions, and yet I had a feeling of triumph. I had learned much, and Rose didn't know. And I must get away.

The day finally came after much time passed. I suppose that only hours actually passed, since the discovery in the pine closet had been after midnight, and much time had gone into picking the locks and study. The drive in the dark had been long, though I was in no shape by then to judge time. Dawn had come slowly, whether from heavy clouds or from some unusual aspect of the place, I could not tell until light penetrated. Then I realized that I was in a huge medieval kitchen of triangular shape, set at an angle to a vast great hall, which I could just see into from where I sat. The kitchen occupied a space between the castle proper and another building, whose blank wall of heavy stones rose up opposite and made the third angle.

The fireplace was large enough to hold four Volkswagens; its hood, of the same stones as the walls, projected and sloped upward at second-floor level. There was an unfamiliar escutcheon centered in its keystone. With no trouble the fireplace could have cooked a full ox, several roasting fowl and many kettles, all steaming at once. I wished that it cooked something now, but it was cold and clean. There was no warmth anywhere.

The triangular kitchen rose upward for over four stories to the top of the buildings, its sides of enormous chiseled stones overgrown with moss. On the castle side windows opened into it, black apertures at all the levels, from which the lady of the castle might have watched her scullery maids at work here below, where I lay in one corner hugging myself in my coat.

It was dim and dark, the only light coming from one side very high, through narrow pointed slits in the solid masonry. Light came, too, from the swill hole, an opening large enough for a small boy to crawl through, looking somehow menacing, the sloping drain stones set into the floor across a wide arc, so that anywhere in that direction the slop would have been gathered together, to spume in a gush through the hole in the wall. The slope pulled the eye forward. A tilt could almost be felt from the appearance, and I visualized a char boy avoiding it, moving among scullery help when the castle was alive. A scullery boy could fall through.

On hands and knees I had crept there in first light, to halt suddenly and grunt, my fingers gripped around the stones of its aperture until they blanched. I looked down a sheer wall for two hundred feet to water below. When the sickening vertigo left, I crawled back, knowing that I was unable to explore the castle. I could not get out alone.

I watched Rose, keeping my eyes nearly closed. She came nearer, her eyebrows drawn together, and I pulled up my knees. She jumped back and kicked out.

"Ha! So you're alive!"

I remained silent, and maybe it was wise. She watched me for a few moments, then commanded, "Come on! Get up!"

When I continued to watch, my knees drawn up, she got uneasy. She moved a bit, then came closer and bent down slightly. "Come along. You'll have to get up, you know. You can't stay here."

It was a comfort to hear it, for this was not my splendid idea of a glorious holiday in a romantic castle. But it might get worse, if the alternative to a miserable existence is a miserable death. However, she was alone. If they had been intending to speed me on my way into the next life, she didn't look like it right at the moment. When she had come she carried only that cherry basket. She might look like a monkey and she might know karate, but I'd survived her attack before, and just might do it again.

And so, shaking again, I got up to a sitting posture. I realized that I should have spent the past twenty years playing handball instead of eating Swiss cheese sandwiches at lunch hour over a book of medieval history. I was doing so badly at getting to my feet that she finally made an exasperated noise and came to help. She was rough, but she got me up. I swayed more than usual, dizzier than usual. The cane had been left behind in our rush from the lodge.

Half pushing me, half supporting, we moved into the large adjoining hall, a room which towered in height, and of several hundred feet in length. A wooden balcony banded the two long sides very high up, and under it at irregular intervals, soiled banners slowly moved. They did not look jaunty or celebrant; rather, they seemed left behind when the castle's inhabitants deserted. Pale light came into the hall from narrow slots under the roof, and as we went down the long distance I saw that tall windows of grayish-green glass were deeply recessed in the thick walls at one side, and through them came distorted views of a courtyard outside and a high bailey wall beyond. The other wall was solid, except for the slots at the top.

We did a slow two-step diagonally across the room, stopping often, the effort to advance great. We came to the end of the hall, where a dais held two ornately carved chairs, placed side by side. In the corner behind the dais Rose opened a door into a round turret, and pushed me in. I looked upward through murky shadows at a spiral staircase, its treads worn into shallow basins, and stood still, appalled at what she clearly expected me to do. The stairs wound abruptly upward into the gloom, and were widely spaced. I was sure that I could not climb them.

That was what Rose clearly had in mind, and she hissed through clenched teeth and applied her shoulder. We climbed. I must give the devil his due—she was brave. I could not have gone up without her, was not sure that I wanted to go where she intended me to go, but at least it was up, not down into a dungeon, and almost anything seemed better than the stones in the drafty medieval kitchen.

We passed the first level and kept on. She stopped at the second and opened a heavy oak door. We faced a smaller hall, seeming to be on the opposite side of the castle from the great hall, though after the spiral climb, I wasn't sure. We went through it toward two doors at the end; she opened one and we faced a large room with a single narrow window placed high in the wall. Sunlight poured in.

There was one item of furniture—a very old, high, intricately carved poster bed, its hangings and spread dusty. I sank onto it with relief, and the dust rose up in a cloud. Rose watched with her hands on her hips, then turned and went out. I heard the heavy sound of a beam dropping across the door. It was completely quiet after that. In my mind a dimly remembered poem formed; I was asleep before I remembered it.

It was dark again when I awoke. Something had awakened me. I was afraid, with a lurching fear, and for a few moments I remembered nothing, but sat up, trembling at something strange in the room—a restless, noiseless squirming. The air puffed about in little gusts, and there were scraping sounds. In a few moments I heard heavy thuds which seemed to come from the floor beneath the room.

There are ghosts in the old castles, ask any Scotsman. Some are fierce spirits, evil and malevolent; others are quiet and timid, and come seeking. To know which kind of ghost you've encountered is reassuring, like the discovery that the stranger poking in your room is really an old friend in search of a cigarette; it puts you more at ease. Which ghost was here, trying to manifest himself? Evil or companionable? Threatening or friendly?

Air buffeted my face, and my hair prickled up. I put out a hand and brushed against something quickly moving and gone. I screamed and the motion stopped suddenly. The sounds, after a short interruption, resumed.

I sat up and listened, feeling my skin prick into gooseflesh, and the air currents began again. It seemed as if the ghost was high overhead. I ducked as a thing brushed across my forehead gently.

I struggled onto my feet, holding the side of the bed, my plan to deal reasonably with the spirit world forgotten, and wobbled toward the window, where the sky showed a faint light. As I moved, the air swirls stopped.

The window recess was about six feet deep, I judged from its feel, one hand sliding along it for support. I held tightly to the wide stone sill and panted, for the eddies began again. In a moment a thing passed rapidly up, over my shoulder, moving to the left.

I told myself firmly not to panic, but in spite of it, I frantically felt for a way to get the window open. It was built solidly into the masonry.

The clouds shifted, and I could see into the courtyard. Something was directly below, a dark object of considerable size, revealed for only a second before the clouds fanned together. But the brief light had also revealed fluttering wings silhouetted. Bats!

I took a deep breath, relieved that the room held only natural creatures. One world at a time. I stood by the window and hoped for another glimpse of what was outside. The bats continued to fly toward me, and just as they seemed about to hit, swerved to the left.

The sounds continued with intervals between them. As much as I disliked standing where bats fanned near, I wanted even more to know about that dark thing below the window. I felt sure that the sounds would make sense when I learned what it was.

My stomach rumbled. It had been a day since I'd eaten. I was dismayed to have fallen prey to unreasoned fear. Hunger had dulled my wits, and even my muscles trembled. I would get my handbag and eat crackers. Whiskey would help, too. They were better than nothing.

I turned from the window to feel my way to the bed, where the handbag had been left, but just then the clouds were parted by a high wind. Weak light came from the opening. I pressed close to the window and stretched up as far as I could, trying to see close to the side of the building outside. It was a canvas-covered truck backed against the wall below. The scraping sounds were louder here, and in a few moments were followed by thuds directly under the room. No one could be seen, the truck too close for the restricted view. A high wall jutted out to the left and cut off sight in that direction. Then the clouds closed and I could see nothing.

I groped back to the bed for my handbag, and at the crinkly sounds of the paper, the bats stopped. The thuds and scrapes had stopped, too. I got back to the window just in time to see a flash of headlights turned on and immediately off. The motor started gently, and in the semi-darkness the truck rolled forward and made a turn about toward the building, to disappear directly beneath. It snarled in low gear up a grade on the other side of the building, and whined higher, to fade away in the distance.

So the portcullis gate was close. My impression, when Rose had propelled me across the great hall, had been correct, and I had gotten the layout of the castle pretty well in mind then. It was reassuring to know that my brain had been working even though my body had not.

The bats began to fly toward the window, veering off suddenly to the left. I held my hand to the glass and moved it, trying to find an opening somewhere, but there was no tiny flow of air. Rain pelted the glass suddenly, like pebbles tossed.

But the bats had found a way to get out. If I might trace their flight, perhaps I could find an exit for myself. I now knew what lay on the right side of the window recess; now I had to learn what was on the left side. I could see nothing in the thick darkness of the room, and wished that I had been smart enough to have brought along a torch. There was much in the handbag, but only matches for light.

The little flame was only a pinprick which emphasized the dark, but I held it out at arm's reach. I could see only its brilliance. It burned my fingers. I dropped it and placed my burned fingers in my mouth, and in the quick reflex motion dropped the handbag, spilling it out across the floor. I let it stay and moved slowly forward, hoping that my eyes would grow better accustomed to the dark, and feeling with both hands the wall on the left side of the window.

Suddenly I gasped. The wall had ended, my hands feeling only open space. In sudden panic I drew back, then forced my hands to move cautiously forward, where the wall came to an end.

I realized slowly that there was a turn. My fingers explored it, my body following them slowly forward. Suddenly my ankle struck a sharp corner. I was bent double by the pain, and crouched, rubbing the ankle. When the pain was less, I felt forward on the floor, touched a sharp corner above floor level, then another. There were steps going up.

I sat on the first and moved upward like a child who has not yet learned to climb. After three, the steps came to an end, and I sat on the top and patted to each side. It was frightening, and I sat very still. Should I go on?

But the floor was solid, and as my hands moved upward on each side, I felt walls. It seemed to be a narrow enclosure. My pulse quickened. Where did it lead?

A dread of closed, restrictive places descended like the darkness. I could not go into that narrow place without seeing; neither could I endure the hours until daylight came. Hands flat on the floor at each side, I crouched and felt the sweat break out and become cold.

When the emotion passed, I began to feel ahead carefully, letting my body follow the seeing fingers. The floor was coated with dirt and the bat droppings, but it seemed solid and firm. No holes, at least not yet. The walls were as cold and firm as the walls of a prison. The narrow place seemed endless.

I crawled on and on. It seemed a long time later that I glanced back toward the room. No glimmer of light showed from there, not even the faint outlines of the window. Fear flooded, like a dike bursting. I held myself as if I cradled a child and sobbed in low grunts and groans, rocking back and forth. I had crawled into my grave, into a narrow place I would never get out of! I was alone, deserted; nobody in nothing. The terror gripped for a long time.

Then I wiped off my face and went on, both hands exploring first the floor, then the walls. It seemed terribly important to know where this passage led! Suddenly bats brushed against my head, and I recoiled, struck out in reflex action, hit something, pulled my hand up in a jerk, and struck the ceiling. This hole closed up on itself!

I screamed, and the sound died instantly, as if it had not been made.

I could skitter back to the room. But I would not. What was it that I had touched when I had struck at the bats? It had been up from the floor level slightly. I felt for it again, cautiously in the dark, forcing my fingers not to recoil as they encountered the hard, cold object, but to become my eyes, to sense the shape of the thing. I patted it, then gently rubbed. It was curved, low, hollow.

As it gradually took on a visual aspect, a familiar shape, I began to rock with hysterical laughter. I had crawled into this narrow enclosure, absurdly afraid, and now I was gingerly and carefully smoothing a chamber pot! Of course! This passageway was a "necessary"!

I had read of these places, also called "garde-robes," where in medieval times extra garments were also stored, for the benefit of the aromatic fumes which were then thought to prevent moths. I laughed until tears flowed.

Somewhat restored by laughter, I could now notice a flow of air, laden with moisture. It must come from outside. I slid my fingers along the slope of wall where the ceiling came low, and felt a narrow niche, just wide enough for two fingers. This must be where the bats flew out. The stones were much rougher here than those nearer to the room.

I felt my way back a good bit relieved. I had not fallen into a hole, and with daylight I would learn more. I went to the door and tested it. Just as I had known, there was a beam on the outside, which I sensed from the resistance of the wood. In addition the door was locked. I could not possibly get out through the door, even if I picked the lock.

At the foot of the steps into the garde-robe my handbag spilled its contents across the floor. I took the last swig of whiskey from the small bottle and crawled onto the bed, my feet tucked under. Sleep was out of the question, so I began to sort out all of the impressions that still puzzled.

That dream in the records room; what had it meant? I could only conclude that I had remembered an instance of coercion from childhood, but none of the faces was revealed as familiar. The curtsy and kissing had been compliance, in spite of slaps unobserved by those who waited in the parlor.

There seemed to be some connection with the English. I saw again the mother in the Queen's Arms, smoothing that child down into a chair, and then the bobby and the dream of corridors in so many colors, really daydreams those had been, while Gilbert and I were on our way to Edinburgh. Yes, there was a quiet certainty that they were related; now that I had learned of English control, these quiet nudges of the subconscious made sense.

The English controlled quietly. They had erased the Scottish line; their bright colors obscured the twists and steps of corridors, just as the bobby had drawn attention from the ruined manor to the roses. Now it no longer seemed odd that signs in the English cities called attention to public toilets and crematoria: they were greatly concerned with disposal. Even bathtubs shaped like coffins. Subtle ways reveal thought, the lofty spires pointing to the sky, while inside effigies of the dead line the walls. Intense love of the past preserved in stone. The macabre effigies, their shrouds drawn back to reveal grinning skulls and empty eye sockets, bare pelvic and leg bones—and overhead a mighty thrust of arches.

The clammy air and my dark thoughts were making me shiver, but I couldn't take my mind from the cathedrals. Surely they were England's greatest art; there could be no doubt of it. I remembered lying flat on my back in Ely's beautiful Lady Chapel to study the bosses of the ceiling from the horizontal of a pew, no one there except Gilbert, who had laughed because of such unconventional behavior.

Was it coincidence that the master artist had carved not angels up there, but villains? That the greatest counterthrusts were borne by rough men? I saw again a face of a pirate, red hair blown to one side, his eyes straining and his brilliant red tongue stuck out from the corner of his mouth in a perpetual leer. This gleeful menace had triumphed over the heads of worshipers for generations.

The cathedrals induced a compulsion to dwell on the Black Death, plagues, superstitions and witches, murky things of gloom not understood. They underlined fear. Hidden thoughts crawled out along the gargoyles' snouts and scales etched against the sky. Even the banners whiffed gently, hung from crossbeams and moved by air warmed from passing bodies below, admonishing with cobwebs.

The Scots said it quite differently. St. Giles in Edinburgh had no effigies, and the banners there were four-square and sturdy. They emphasized clan support, were less flamboyant and hung between arches and columns starkly bare. Unrelieved. Even the statue of the founder of Presbyterianism was hidden behind the High Kirk.

Did they speak more of soul? Less of carrying the eye to ceremony and pomp, to the obscure? Surely their banners took less time to see, and were less of a pain in the neck.

I wished that I had brought more whiskey; I was morbid, cold and thinking of all the wrong things. Rose had outsmarted me. Why had I been so sure that she had left the lodge, that I would not be observed down there in the pine closet? I burned with frustration and anger. My body ached with its exertions. I rubbed the back of my neck and longed for daylight and a change of thought.

The Scots were certainly open about things, even if they had used underhanded methods to kidnap me! If daylight ever came again, if I could find my way from this terrible room where bats flew; if my wits worked better than they had yet—maybe then my way to escape would somehow be found. I tried to sleep, but the bed linens were musty and old; they smelled of decay. The somber thoughts of grotesqueries had not been comforting, and I sat with my coat pulled tightly around my legs and watched for the first signs of daylight.

My face felt like jelly and my hair like a pack rat's nest when the first light penetrated the dim window. But I had been right about the layout of the castle: the room did face east. And now the unremembered poem came to mind.

"Hortense the fair, Hortense the lovable, Hortense the fine old dame of Astolat, High in her chamber up a tower to the east, Guarded the—" And my voice trailed off. What did I guard? The knowledge that I could be the Queen of Scotland? What an absurd thought!

I got off the bed and found the small items that had fallen from the handbag spread over the floor near the steps to the garde-robe. I combed my hair and ran a tissue over my face, hearing my stomach rumble as loud as the timpani in a symphony orchestra. I was so hungry that I shook.

By noon I had decided that Rose planned to starve me to death, and it was a slight relief to have her come with a bowl of bread and milk, which she set down on the floor and left, slamming the door behind her and bolting it with a heavy thud. She had not looked at me.

I waited through the long day standing at the window, then curled up on the bed. Nothing happened. The bailey wall jutted out about seven feet above my window and a bit to the left, a walkway on its top, a sentry-way in feudal times. It enclosed a huge courtyard of about four acres. I could see where it turned back toward the castle, to about where it joined that part where I must have spent the first night. There was a stone dovecote far toward that side, in green grass. Near my window were cobblestones, which edged off into gravel.

I made several pilgrimages into the garde-robe. Even though the light here was quite dim, the small opening in the stones where the bats escaped was to be seen. Their droppings speckled the floor. I needed badly to wash, and longed for soap and water. But Rose was apparently determined to keep me on a subsistence amount of food and care. I was angry, frightened, aching in muscles and joints, but I was determined to get out if I could only find a way.

The bowl of bread and milk had steadied me slightly. I stood by the window and peered into the empty courtyard and considered the thoughts I had mulled over in the dark of the night. Perhaps I was muddled; if I was less than clear in my thinking, it would not have been strange. I longed to see someone outside the window; I would have broken the panes and screamed for help, would have stuck a tissue in the opening to be fluttered by the wind. But no one appeared out there.

I had been thinking of England's cathedrals as her finest art form, yet concerned with death and decay and pulling the attention from it to the sky. What was America's art form? Did we have any?

We were the amalgam of many people. We hadn't aged enough to return to the past. We borrowed from Greece and Rome; now we borrowed most heavily from Africa. Was the man in space America's art form? If so, America looked to the future. Rather, wasn't it perhaps the future of humanity, itself—all the fears, the aspirations, all of the increment of so many people? It was still in the making.

Humanity, itself—America's art form? God help her, then!

I went from the window back into the garde-robe. There was something about this narrow enclosure that aroused curiosity. I knelt near the end where the ceiling lowered and inspected the stones, chiseled roughly and placed with less care than those at the opening. A few seemed worn. On others the marks of the chisel were as clear as if they had been cut only a few years ago; this was especially true at the back of the passage. I wondered if it had been hard to set them, and decided that it had. My neck was aching from the inspection; surely the mason's would have ached worse.

I crept low, nevertheless, and studied the stones carefully. One seemed much smoother and slightly darker than the rest. It was fairly large, almost two feet across, and it was low in the wall. Too low, certainly, to have been worn by passing hands feeling their way here over the years. I couldn't decide what to make of it, of its patina and dark luster.

I stood again at the window wondering how in the world to get away, if I ever would get away. I needed to sleep; even though the bed was musty, I ought to try. But after a short time I got up and went back to the narrow passageway, and bent to study the stones at the end.

The sun had moved across the courtyard and the light in the garde-robe was becoming dim, yet even in the dimness, that one large stone seemed to have a polish and a glow. Surely it had been rubbed over a long period of time. It looked much like sculptures that are passed and touched, where a toe or a finger or a nose takes on a luster not shared by the rest of the stone. I felt of it, of its smooth surface, wondering again why it was so polished, so that even in the fading light it had a deeper glow than the others. It was almost square in shape, about a foot up from the floor, a most unlikely place to develop a patina.

I finally got tired and got up and went back to the window. There was no one to be seen. The place seemed deserted. And something about that privy passage kept pulling me back there.

Puzzled, I felt again of the polished stone, then pushed it. It was very snug, heavy and secure. I tapped it. No sound but a brief, heavy reverberation. I pushed it. It stayed firm. I knelt and put my shoulder against it and held all the pressure I could bring to bear on it. It didn't budge. Yet for some reason I kept at it, again and again. It had meaning of a special kind. It was firmly a part of the wall, too low to have been rubbed by passing hands. And why was this one so polished? Why not others on either side, or all around? That stone didn't make sense. That was what bothered me.

I placed my fingers along its lower edge. The stone slowly swung into the wall and out of sight. Startled, I moved back and peered through the hole it left into a mass of cobwebs and dark obscurity.

My answer had come so unexpectedly that for a few moments I doubted my senses. Perhaps I had gone daft; perhaps hunger was too much for me. The stone had slipped back into the wall at a touch, disappeared without a sound. I bent and peered again into the hole. The stone was balanced far back there in space, and it seemed to be waiting now for me to do something. Only I did not understand my part.

I could see very little because of the thick tangle of spider webs. Did the space just drop away? If I stepped inside, would there be something firm? What if the stone moved back into place, for some reason? Would I get out? If I did, get out into what? And if I did not, I was a prisoner, anyway.

I studied the hole and the stone seemed to be studying me, waiting for me. I reached out gingerly and swept aside the nearest webs. In the dim light I could see a blank wall straight ahead. I looked upward and saw more tangled spider webs and a chink of high light.

I slid my hands into the opening. They encountered horizontal stone thickly encrusted with dirt, or perhaps it was lichen. Whatever it was, it was rough. I put my head and shoulders into the aperture and peered up, and drew back as dizzying vertigo attacked. I had looked up tremendous height, emphasized by the stark parallels of the walls. There were steps up, at right angles to the opening. Narrow and steep. In the other direction the stone blocked off the view. It would have to be swung back into place in order to go down. I sat back in the narrow privy on my haunches and tried to make up my mind.

I felt terribly afraid of the steps. If they fell apart under my weight, if they teetered, if they were unevenly covered by lichen so that I lost balance, or mossy so that I slipped! I imagined myself tumbling all the way to the bottom. Dear God, let me be killed! To be injured, to lie between those heavy walls for a long time! I am a coward, not half so sure of myself as I try to seem. How long would I last? I would have gotten myself neatly out of their way. Who were "they"? Could they even find me?

And what was the bottom? It was darker. How would they find me? Could I be gotten out? I wished that I'd never left America. Involved antiquity my foot! Dungeons were exciting seen from the outside, when you could shake your head and make little disturbed noises and leave. Stories of prisoners were interesting in the third person, not the first!

And if I stayed where I was? I could manage a long time on one meal a day of bread and milk. It might do me good. I hated being shut away, not being where I wanted to be, not seeing friends, wondering about Gilbert, wondering why I was a prisoner, wondering how long. I hated it, but it hadn't killed me. Rose could have done it if she'd wanted to. There was poison, which would have been simple. She could draw and quarter me if she wanted to, and I had no doubt but that she knew how. This ancient way of killing was to hang the prisoner, cut him down just before he lost consciousness, disembowel him before his own eyes and cut off his arms and legs. If he was lucky enough to lose consciousness, he never knew that his body was then pierced on a sharp pole, to be carted through the streets for all to see, and then placed atop the city wall for the crows to eat. Dear God, people had done this to people!

I was angry at my morbid thoughts. Rose could have done me in a long time ago! She was sadistic, but she waited for orders from someone. What had I done—what reason was there for keeping me a prisoner? If I knew, I'd be a step ahead. If I were set free, whoever gave the orders surely would expect me to head for the police and the embassy, surely would expect to be searched for, would know the law's clout sooner or later.

What should I do? I had lost track of time. My watch had stopped. From the way my stomach was feeling I judged the time to be around five o'clock. If I had found an escape—if it *was* one—I'd better get to it while there was the help of daylight. I set my teeth and entered the hole head first.

With hands on the rough stone, keeping my weight well back on my legs, still in the privy, I tested the strength of the step on the other side. The first one seemed solid enough. It was not slippery with moss, and the lichened surface was something of a help, not uneven, but rough over the entire step. I would have good traction. I got both legs over the ledge and sat there, breathing hard. The steps made a steady pattern up the wall. A dim light came from that narrow chink in the top of the castle wall.

I determined to try to go up. I could not go down without getting the stone out of the way, and that meant shutting off my escape to the privy. That would have to come later, after I got up my courage. I would take my time and go by easy steps. No plunging about.

I stood and looked up. I didn't dare to glance down between the steps; I might see too far. I found that I could keep my hands on each wall, and I carefully placed my feet on each step until I learned if it was firm. After I had taken only a few I realized that this castle was as solid as Edinburgh. Behind me I saw the entrance stone sitting there patiently, almost as if it had personality. I began to like it very much. It seemed to wait for me.

The steps climbed abruptly and were rather widely spaced. I went up a good distance and stopped for breath, not daring to look back now because of dizziness. Several feet higher, the steps leveled out. To one side was a heavy wooden door with rusted straps and a large square lock with a circular handle. I twisted it and pushed the door. It grunted open onto the sentry walk along the top of the bailey wall. I went out and looked down, held onto the sides of the parapet, sick with vertigo. The vertical wall under my hands sliced down the side of the bailey to a black moat.

I forced my eyes toward the distance. The castle was set low on the side of a long slope which rose up behind it. The area was uninhabited. I could see not even a road. In the other direction the bens rose in magnificent jagged lines of purple and blue, and nearer were the dark waters of a huge loch. The sentry walk had disintegrated at some distance further on, the bailey wall crumbling from weather and lack of upkeep; at one time it had continued on around the wall which encircled the castle.

I peered cautiously down into the courtyard. A car was drawn up near the portcullis gate, a small English make. There was nobody to be seen. I could see my window. Under it and far below, was a wide door, and I guessed that it was here where the truck had unloaded.

The sky was heavy with dark clouds, the air cold and wet against my face. I stood, holding to the parapet, and wondered what kind of escape this had proved to be. I could not get down from the sentry walk without diving into the loch or the moat. If I had been only a tourist, it would have been thrilling to stand and admire the huge castle. Its defenses had protected it for hundreds of years, but it was not to be gotten out of any more easily than it could have been taken. Even across the top of the keep were the slotted apertures through which arrows could be shot. I didn't expect arrows, but the defense was excellent.

Then the main entrance door opened. A slender middle-aged man emerged and walked toward the car. Rose Glasses stood on the top step. I dropped to a crouching position. Rose had faced directly toward me. I hoped that she had not seen me, or my quick motion. I heard the car door slam. They were not far from where I crouched, but far below, and I realized that if I had been in my room, I would not have seen either of them, or the car.

The man called, "Just keep her here, and look in once a day. I'll be in touch. If she makes any trouble, you might throw her out of the window." He gave a short laugh and started the engine.

That voice, cultivated, placed high in the masque of his face—something of what he said—my memory stirred. Suddenly I heard that voice coming from the grandfather in the Queen's Arms, his humorously modulated tones, and a querulous little boy, the man saying, "Look, old chap, if you don't stop that grumbling, I'll have to throw you out of the window." He was English. There was no doubt in my mind.

But Rose worked for the Scots! This was strange—the man was without any question an Englishman. What were the English doing, mixed in with this? What was that grandfather doing here? Was Rose working both ends against the middle? Suddenly I grabbed hold of the centuries-old dirt on the sentry walk and retched.

The car snarled and skittered on the gravel, then went through the gate. I peeked over the side of the wall. Rose was turning and starting back inside. She looked determined. She might be coming to my room! I had left that stone ajar!

I bent down and ran toward the sentry gate, hoping that she wouldn't notice me if she looked up, swung the sentry door back in place and scrabbled down the stairs in haste, not half so afraid of falling into the depth as of Rose coming and finding me gone and my escape hatch open. In the garde-robe I tried to pull in the stone. I didn't know how; it wouldn't budge. I could already hear the beam lifting at the heavy door to my room.

I exited the privy, brushing back my hair to take off the waves of cobwebs. I fell onto the bed, my chest heaving, remembering that the stone had been left slid back into the opening, that a hole gaped down in that narrow hallway, just as Rose opened the door.

She came toward the bed, her face set, the muscles firm, and she studied me for a long minute. I was trying vainly not to breathe so hard, and feeling terribly vulnerable, as if she might divine where I had been, and about the stone. I didn't dare glance toward the garde-robe, but kept my eyes fixed intently on her.

For a few moments she regarded me, seeming puzzled. Then, all at once, she seemed to make up her mind, and with an exasperated short motion of her hands and shoulders, she exclaimed, "Oh, why don't you stop *acting*? There's nothing wrong with you, and you know it better than I do! You can't fool me again! Sit up!"

I got up on one elbow. I hoped she'd leave, and not go exploring my privy. It was a relief to know that she thought I was trying to act.

Finally she said, obviously irritated, "You're an idiot! If you were smart, you'd have known a long time ago to leave well enough alone. There's an old saying: 'Let sleeping dogs lie!' If you had, you'd still be at the lodge; eating fairly well, actually. Make up your mind—you'll have nothing but bread and milk here, once a day."

I blinked and nodded. "All right, but please, may I have some water?"

She placed a fist on one hip and made an exasperated sound. "You're a prisoner. You'd better find that out. You had to go snooping around; well, here, you can't. Prisoners are locked into their rooms. You can have washing water once a week. If you don't behave yourself, you won't get it."

I nodded again. I wished that she'd go. She took pleasure in turning the screws, in knowing that I was uncomfortable. And I knew that no matter how difficult it might prove to be, I'd have to get out of here.

She seemed to think that I was repentant. "You'll find out precious little here! You can't go snooping anywhere, and from now on, you'll do just as I say." She looked down on me, and as I nodded again, she moved as if to go to the window. She stopped just short of the garde-robe door, while I held my breath, and turned, one arm held out in the grand manner, swinging it to indicate the bare room. "And how do you like your guest chamber?"

Then she walked quickly to the door, opened it and lifted her eyebrows in a supercilious manner. She inclined her head in a sarcastic bow, gave a high laugh and left. I heard the heavy beam slide back into place.

I sank back and took deep, relieved breaths. I was determined that when she returned, I wouldn't be here.

VIII

Should I wait for a new day? Could I negotiate the steep stairs after dark? I had no idea what they were like: where the steps ended, how far they went, what kind of terrain lay at the bottom, if a sally port existed. Supposing I crept through a door and walked right into Rose? I could imagine myself bowing and backing out, "So sorry to intrude," on my lips. I could laugh at the picture.

I thought about it while I worked at the stone. If I meant to use any of today's light, there was very little time to waste. Inside the hole, the stairs were in dimmer light than when I had come down them only moments ago, and I suspected that even with brilliant sunlight outside, those steps would be dim. No, I didn't dare chance it. I would sleep with the bats another night, wrap my head in my coat. In the morning I would probably feel more rested, anyway, for my grand exit. In truth, I still ached from that boxing match with Rose; or had it been a wrestling bout? I longed for a bath and a comfortable bed for the night, a quiet room, a rubdown, a stiff, long drink and a hearty dinner. I still had one small bottle of whiskey, but it must be saved for an emergency. If I had allowed it, I could have felt very sorry for myself; instead, I made my attention focus on the stone.

It almost seemed to glow, back there in its hole. I leaned way out and pressed all around it, to no effect. I didn't like to let it stay open all night. I was pretty sure that no one else knew about it; if this exit were known, I wouldn't have been locked into this room. I didn't want to take chances, either. That gaping hole in my privy, the dark night coming—the opening in the wall, if I could not close it, seemed to open some floodgate of fear deep inside of me. If it was to be my secret exit, it could also be some stranger's secret entrance.

It had to be closed! There must be some way! I must get the wall together.

I leaned far out and pulled at it many times. I pulled and pushed at the top, an effort to touch it at all without falling face down on the other side, my fingers just short, unless I stretched for as much as I was worth. I tried gentle pulls: top, sides, underneath. No results. I wondered if any of the other stones, the smoother ones which I had noticed before, could be the touchstone. It was getting very dim in the privy, and I moved around pushing and touching any of the more polished-looking stones. Again no luck.

I was dismayed. And I was extremely tired. I wanted to quit, and I dared not. I had to find the way to close up the wall. I sat down on the floor and leaned back for a moment to rest. Then a new thought came: surely there must be a touchstone on the other side. If a lover departed, the lady slipped out, if a warrior fled—surely some arrangement had been provided to close the wall behind them.

I stuck my head into the opening, most of myself in the garderobe, and cautiously felt around the hole. I jumped back inside as the big stone made its dignified and soundless slide into the wall. Just in time, too! It had very nearly caught me.

I regarded the wall, my heart pounding. What had I done to operate the mechanism? I might have been flattened, like a fly squeezed in a doorjamb. Could I find the touchstone again, when I needed to? Well, I had done my job. I was too tired to fuss around with the thing any longer. There would be time for that tomorrow, and I would *have* to find the mechanism. How lucky I had been to have seen the stone coming forward!

I pulled my coat high over my head and lay down on the bed. I must have fallen into a light sleep, although I remember trying to put aside all thoughts of the harrowing experiences of the past days, even to put Gilbert out of mind, as precipitous vistas opened in my mind's eye, where Rose seemed to twine in a serpent shape and squirm around with the circling bats overhead.

It was very dark when I was aroused by the scraping and thudding noises. A glance from the window showed the dark shape of the truck. What did they unload? I might be able to see more from the sentry walk, but I didn't dare to go up there in pitch darkness; besides, I *knew* what was being taken from the truck: it was ammunition. I knew, without knowing how. Any attempt to learn for sure would be foolhardy. Perhaps I had already done enough of that kind of thing. Hearing told almost as much as sight might have revealed, and logic confirmed. Such heavy thuds weren't made by crates of eggs; nor of furniture—surely not by night, and the castle was not being refurbished. Even coffins could not have made such deep, heavy thumps.

You are brainy and logical, fair Hortense. Hortense, the brainy dame of Astolat.

So you're back! Where were you when I needed you? Last night, and the night before? All day today? You deserted me. I've been in a state. I don't need any more going over, but go ahead—have a try.

I've been here. You were too upset.

Oh? I only wept myself into a pool, there in the garde-robe. I needed companionship then, more than most times you come. I've always been afraid of closed places. You ought to know.

You made out all right. What's wrong with a few tears? You felt better afterward, didn't you? You even laughed, later.

Who needs to cry if there's a good chat?

You resent something? Come on out with it.

You might be understanding, at least. A little warmth—

Wait a minute; I'll play Hearts and Flowers. Are you trying to make yourself feel bad again? Provide warmth and understanding, eh? It's you, you know.

Me? Do go on.

You must be quiet. Pause. Listen, and think. Light comes from within, you know. You must admit that you went off at a gallop with drawn sword when you went down to that pine closet. You were determined to find out what you wanted to find out. You did, and you were caught. What did you expect? Logic, Hortense, logic!

I thought about it; it was so, I had been proud, full of my own knowledge, full of my need for more.

Well, I learned something! I have a commission, remember that. Should I have been a coward quivering in my room like a dotty old dame? Hortense the dotty dame of Astolat? Rose has been trying to arrange my affairs. I'm not used to that kind of interference.

No, you were right. There might have been a different way to do it, but you're not dead yet. Keep on. You're on the right track. You expect to finish your task; Rose tries to prevent you.

Aha! That's it! But why?

Down below, the truck had unloaded, I guessed. The sounds had stopped. Its headlights blinked on, and would in a moment go off. I was ready to leave the window, anyway. The pattern had emerged; there would be nothing to see.

Suddenly four young men bounded from the castle directly beneath, silhouetted for that brief instant before the headlights disappeared, their arms and legs flaying out wildly. Shots erupted in a volley, six or seven in rapid succession. The engine roared and the truck shot forward with a splatter of gravel, screamed on a turn and disappeared under the building.

I could see nothing, although I peered for a long time. If anyone lay bleeding below, he could have bled to death. If help came, I couldn't see it. The courtyard was as quiet as if it hadn't happened.

The morning dawned with brilliant sun, a light, gay yellow spread over the brilliant green grass. Below my window were marks on the gravel, deeply dug into it where the wheels had grabbed. There was nothing else to see.

I gave up trying and got myself ready for the day, chuckling as I did so. There was no water; I made my "ablutions" by rubbing face and hands with one of the tissues, combed my hair and polished my glasses. I felt better afterward, and I smiled at the forces which habit exerts.

I waddled into the garde-robe at once and began pushing at my stone. I would have plenty of time and a wonderful light to scout the lay of the stairs and plan my escape. If all went as I hoped, I'd have my bread and milk, then leave. Once outside, I'd play it by ear. This evening I'd be hiking in the hills.

> Oh fare-thee-weel, my only luve!
> And fare-thee-weel, a while!
> An' I will come again, my luve,
> Tho' 'twere ten thousand mile!

I sang softly to myself. I wondered what actually had happened down there last night. If I hadn't known it happened, heard those shots and seen the men, I would not have believed it. There had been absolute silence after the truck pulled off.

The stone slid back and waited, glistening in a ray of sun emitted by that high chink. Good old stone. He sparkled like a polished granite Buddha, blinking stolidly in that bright light. He looked wise and smiling. Perhaps he had seen many men slip through the wall. Many a lover, too, I bet. Oh ho! a lovely thought. I entered the hole jauntily.

It was chilly in the dusky stairwell, and I was glad for my coat. I suddenly remembered the handbag, on the bed, the small bottle of whiskey and the crackers. I hoped that I wouldn't shut the wall and not be able to get it open again. I must wait for Rose and her bowl of bread and milk. The hours until noon stretched ahead into eternity.

I raised up on tiptoe and tried to peer over the stone, but it was impossible to see anything at all. Even the bright sunlight pouring down through that high chink revealed nothing of what lay below, or of the stairs going down. What if I couldn't navigate them? What if space opened up, a gaping hole? I trembled at the thought, and forced myself back into the garde-robe and shut the stone as I had done.

I sat on the bed and refused to admit that I could not manage, now that a way had been shown to me. I quivered with impatience;

I could leave now just as well. Yet if I did, Rose would be there with that meager dinner, and if she found me gone, my chances to escape unobserved would pass into limbo. I must wait.

I stood in the window recess, trying to divert my mind, to watch. But there was nothing to see, and the sense of impatience and lack of action was harrowing. I paced the room and timed my steps. I was ready to go. It was hateful to wait.

When the sound came of the heavy beam lifting on the other side of the door, I was standing in the window. I hoped that I seemed to be whiling away the time in idle observance of the sky, but my heart was beating so fast that I felt my body quiver.

Probably Rose intended just to set the bowl on the floor inside the door, but as she did, she glanced at me. Perhaps something about my appearance changed her mind. Instead of leaving, she advanced, a look of watchful curiosity on her face. Her glasses caught the highlights from the window, giving her an ominous, flittering appearance. If this did not go well for me now!

I moved quickly toward the bed and perched there, inwardly defensive, hoping that she wouldn't go into the window recess. It was too close to the privy exit. The wall was closed and I knew it, but the way I felt about that place may have been plain on my face.

She regarded me steadily, without speaking.

It is awfully hard to be looked at steadily. When there are guilt feelings, it is terribly difficult. What did Rose notice? Had my color deepened? Did I palpitate? Was I in some way giving away my secret?

The thoughts sluiced through my mind, and I knew that I must do something soon, quickly, something which would throw her off balance. With a sudden motion, I started toward her, rising from the bed and moving forward.

She jumped for the door, misinterpreting, her eyes fixed on me. Before I could move more than a foot, she slammed the heavy door and dropped the beam into place.

I felt a smile coming. That she was afraid came as a little, happy shock. I was twice her age and could not have managed much of an assault if I had tried, but her frightened reflex was reassuring.

It took only minutes to eat the meal. Then I got my paraphernalia and went quickly into the garde-robe.

You're ready. It's a great day for an escape.
The best. But last night . . . I think that I heard shots.
You know that you did. And now you're smiling.
Aye! It's good to know she was afraid.
I pushed the edge of the stone. Oh, God, let there be safe steps down.
Now think.
I just prayed. You might not have realized, but it was prayer.
I did. Take time; think carefully.
I am. But I need particular attention right now.
You already have it, you know.

I reached for the place where I had pushed last night, and pushed. Light shone in tiny sparkles from the stone as it glided back into the wall.

I stood at immense height, looking down steps, slabs that projected jaggedly out from the wall like the uneven teeth in a six-year-old child's grin. Their abrupt descent was spaced wider than those going up to the ramparts. They were so deep that the bottom was lost in darkness.

Oh my great aunt! This is a fix! Cherries and monkeys, karate and shots in the night! Lovers, indeed! It looks as if there've been battles on these steps! Someone's been rampaging down there with a claymore! They're half torn up! Slabs of stone knocked clean off the castle! I can't get out this way.
Try.
I clung to the wall of the castle, my mouth filled with salt water. I could see down to blackness, see far enough to get that dizzy feel-

ing again. I was desperately hungry and terribly aware of it, shaking like a nervous spaniel. I couldn't go down!

You're afraid. You can go back and tell Rose you're snooping again. Tell her you're sorry you're naughty.

I can't do that!

I started down. Rose be damned! She could eat her bread and milk.

The steps were even at first, and heavily covered with lichen. I clung with one hand to the rough wall, but there were places ahead that sent up my blood pressure. I'd do what I could do, take it one step at a time. I didn't dare to think of the great drop beneath. It was black, but maybe something would show up in the distance. I shuddered and placed my feet carefully, sliding my hand over the sharp chiselings in the stones.

Here was a place where a step had dropped out. I gritted my teeth together and forced myself not to look down, keeping my eyes on the next step so far forward. If only Gilbert were here, standing below with a hand stretched up, his young face smiling expectantly!

I did then what I often used to do in childhood. I sat down on the step and slid to the edge, pretending the ground was close, swung my feet forward and far out, pushed and jumped.

I made it.

The sun had moved and no longer shone through the chink. The air was clammier and there was a strange odor of closed places and decay. I went on, determined not to think. I could not go back now in any case, could not get up over the wide spaces which I had hopped across. Forward with persistence—upward and onward—though in this case, it was downward and onward. My hand on the wall was the only firm perception that I had.

I jumped from a triangular chunk, one side mortared into the wall, and landed on a wide step. From under my left hand, pressed tightly against the wall, there came a slight movement, and a stone edged out across my way. I looked through the space it left into a big room on the other side, full of long wooden boxes and rows of guns and grenades in neat stacks. Beyond the ammunition, five or six young bearded chaps gaped. In the split second that I peered through the hole, their expressions changed from astonishment to consternation. They were far to the opposite side of the room, but they had seen me, and instantly they moved forward.

I pawed frantically for the spot on the wall. The stone began a slow, steady move into the hole.

I went down the gaping steps as if the devil pursued, slid from broken slabs as if I did it regularly, had practised for this, hopping from piece to piece and keeping on like a rabbit that has seen his pursuers. I was an expert rabbit, hopping and landing, bounding forward from one slab to the next across the wide empty spaces. I could hear nothing except my own panting breath. The castle might have been deserted, its walls so heavy that a bomb would have to burst for the sound to penetrate to this side.

There were many chaps in the castle. I had seen several through the hole, and those last night. How many others? I didn't know, didn't take a count of them, but the thought of infantry pursuing whizzed across my mind, while my feet automatically moved. I sat, stuck out my legs, scooted off a step and jumped on.

The lads must be batting at the armory wall, perhaps were prodding it with crowbars. I hoped that they had to search for crowbars; I was sure, as I jumped and panted ahead, that they already had them. They were likely trying to tear down the walls.

But it would take them some time. They hadn't spent hours studying the walls, as I had—it had taken them by surprise. The stone had slid back like magic in front of their astonished eyes, while beyond, I looked into their munitions cache. It must have brought on near panic; perhaps they prodded wildly and wasted time, I hoped so. But they would come after me; I had seen how the castle was used, and knew that Rose knew, and I had seen many of their faces. The place was an ammunition dump.

The thought pumped up blood from my heart and made me race faster.

Ahead, two steps were out. It was quite dark here, and it was necessary to stoop and peer far down. There was a sound, a gurgle of moving water. I finally saw that I had gotten close to rushes and reeds, and some kind of ferny growth that reached up in long tendrils around the bottom of the steps. There seemed to be a thin slice of wet earth near the steps.

I jumped with both feet and landed on slippery muck; hit it hard and slid in oily mud. I splashed frantically and grabbed at the rushes. They slid out of my hands. The water was deeper than it had seemed; I was in it up to my eyes. My glasses slipped; I pushed them back on with one hand, and with the other lashed around for a firm hold.

My fingers grasped something hard and firm, and I pulled. Suddenly it came loose. I fell back, gasping, still holding to the long, narrow thing. I pushed it down into the soft mud and used it to pull myself up. I climbed out and panted, soaked through, and let my body lie there.

Now I saw what I had held. It was a sword, and it swayed back and forth, its point stuck into the bank, its hilt basket-shaped, made of interwoven narrow metal strips in an ancient design. I stared at it. It must be very old, yet it had not rusted and disintegrated, and suddenly I remembered a Virginia friend who told of finding Civil War swords pushed up from the ground by spring thaws each year, in the land of his estate near Front Royal. He had had a theory that the earth had protected the metal, and I had listened and shook my head in disbelief. Now I believed.

I had lost a shoe in the mud, and I stood, my coat dripping black streaks and my dress clinging, to feel around in the mud again. I found it finally, firmly wedged down, and turned it over and dumped out the water, then took it back to the steps, where I racked it against the stones until it had a form again. It went on with a squishing sound.

The sword caught a gleam of light which came from one side. I must hurry, the chaps might descend at any moment. I had to look for escape from the undercroft of the castle. Yet I could not leave the sword. It had saved my life. It was beautiful.

I pulled it up from the mud. If the chaps found me, I would use it to defend myself.

Where I had plunged into the water, the reeds had been flattened.

A glint showed beneath them, and I bent and pushed them aside. The glint came from a large piece of metal. I pulled at it and brought up a round shield covered with runic engravings and centered with a large stone, all under an overlay of green encrustation. It was heavy and cumbersome. It came up to reveal part of a skeleton.

I made a soggy retreat, the shield in my right hand and the sword in my left. I am not afraid of skeletons. I had looked into the stream long enough. There were living skeletons over my head, clothed in flesh, who were seeking me. The Scots have strong loyalties, but these had not had time yet to form any with me.

I tried to follow the stream. It must pass under the castle and out again, and its exit might also be mine. I heard no sound of the men or of Rose, but the thick walls possibly shut it off. The main body of the building came down below here; no doubt stairs wound below into dungeons, but wherever I looked, the walls were solid. The stairway which I had found might be the only one into this part of the undercroft.

I crept under some large dark bushes which had grown rank at the low opening in the wall, going a good way beneath. Enough light came in to encourage the tall growth of these bushes. I went to the wall, where from the stream's edge I could not be seen, and took off the wet coat and wrung it out, then settled down beside the wall.

If I ran outside, I might be seen. If I waited until dark, the wait would be long, but that seemed the safest course. The stairway had not yet been found, and I was hidden from view. I needed time to plan.

From the mouth of the stream the land dropped swiftly. The water fell in a little rushing sound among heavy, thick undergrowth. I could peer out from this protective greenery up at the side of the castle. High above was the lip of the slop hole where Rose had spat the cherry seeds, not another opening on this side. I had a good hiding place. My biggest problem was damp and chill.

I remembered seeing the moat around the castle when I had been on the sentry walk, and a crenellated turret at the far end, overlooking this side of the bailey wall. The bushes on the outside of the stream's opening grew down the slope in rank profusion, and would make good cover. This area had been ignored, possibly had not even figured in their plans. With this for concealment, and in darkness, I might make my way up the bank to the road unobserved. Luck seemed to be with me this time.

No one came bellowing down the stairs. I was getting very hungry. The crackers were soaked, but the whiskey was fine. Its warmth rushed through my blood so that the tips of my fingers tingled. I put the shield over myself and waited, feeling safer than I had in days.

I wondered if they would ask the local police for help, and decided that they wouldn't. They would hunt alone. I had weapons now. If they found me, they couldn't do much more than they already had, unless roused to fury. It was good that the chaps were searching, and not Rose, alone.

The sun moved high and its rays struck close to the opening near where I sat. After some time a car roared out from the castle onto the highway, and the sound faded in distance. There was a long period of silence, and then there came shouts which eventually stopped. I dozed, awakened by rustling sounds in the bushes outside my hiding place. A chap roamed in the bushes below, on the slope near the moat. Apparently he was satisfied that nobody had come through the rank undergrowth, for he left after searching. Had I tried to go through that tangle, a path would surely have been left in the matted vines and grasses. I was glad that I had stayed.

The afternoon was long and quiet. Sleep came in fits and starts; the damp prevented it from being restful. Nothing seemed to be happening, but just at dusk there was a loud hallooing. Perhaps they had found the sentry door, and if that was so, it would be only a short time until they discovered how to come down. The day was at its gloaming, and dark would come soon. Time for me to go.

I stood and flexed my knees, then did fists-to-shoulders. I would have liked to take along the shield, but its weight was too great, and I picked up the sword, which might be used as a weapon if I needed it. I crawled out of the opening in the wall.

I looked up from under the tall bushes toward the castle wall, and saw why I had remained undiscovered by the fellow who had roamed below: the hole through which the stream flowed was completely covered by the tangle, and even the stream could not be seen. No one could have seen me where I stood, even peering directly from the slop hole.

I moved down a little distance, following the stream and keeping under the cover of the thicket. There would be a climb soon, when I would have cover, and then at the top a wide expanse of berm which was clipped, where I would be in view. The road was beyond.

After about fifty feet I looked back. It seemed that someone stood on the turret top toward the loch, but in the dusk I couldn't be sure. I grasped the sturdy trunks of the shrubs and pulled myself up. This must be the slope which I heard the truck climb.

It was rough going and it winded me many times. Twigs cut across my face and grabbed at the damp clothing. I stopped to rest, then climbed again, going slowly. There was still a little daylight. I heard no sound, and reasoned that I remained undiscovered.

The sky was streaked with that rare afterglow from billows of high clouds. Near to the ground, dark clouds moved upward. I got to the top of the copse and here I rested, waiting for the dark. I would be completely in the open on my next move. The berm lay ahead.

The clouds moved steadily and gently, and brilliant light poured down. It gave a feeling of repose. I would soon run across the open space, and the feeling of serenity was comforting, reassuring. I needed the comfort, and was grateful.

I could look down on the castle from here, its battlements below me and about two hundred yards distant, the foundation of the walls far down, and the realization came quietly at how little I now feared vertigo. It had something to do with being close to the earth.

Then the clouds drew together and it was dark. I bent and ran up the slope. Just over the rise was the macadam road, a turn and a dip into a swale. I got over the rise, felt the hard pavement under my feet, and jogtrotted down the curve into the shallow valley. I could no longer see the castle. I was free.

The mist began gently, and if I had dried out slightly, I was wet in a short while. I felt light-headed, needing food and sleep, yet relieved of the tensions I had so recently felt. I reminded myself to stay watchful, for someone would surely pursue. I did not want to be dragged back to the castle, and had no idea where I walked to, but the sense of freedom seemed enough.

The road ascended slowly, and I doggedly kept on, and when rain began to fall the path ahead obscured badly. I saw objects in the blackness ahead, and then realized that there were boulders beside the road. I must not let myself be frightened. There were miles of road without habitation; it might take a long time before I found help.

I had come to the top of a slope and a small light came from overhead. I saw miles in all directions, miles of desolate land pocked with small pools of water. Not a croft in sight. Peat had apparently been dug, for the ground had a torn appearance. If I had been born here to live out my days, I would have piled stones atop each other just to make a record of once being alive, as the ancient Picts had done. How could the human soul endure such isolation?

It looked like the day after Creation, and God had not yet thought of man. I, alone, was filled with the knowledge of evil.

A hundred years before, this land which I walked was dotted by small, thatched huts, and little pockets of gardens with vegetables, and sheep belonging to the crofters. The government had moved out all the people in the Clearances, and they had gone to the cities and lived in tenements, their children cramped into tiny rooms high in buildings, without any sanitary facilities and among many other people. The cow was tethered in the courtyard on cobblestones, her refuse piled with theirs in a heap at the doorway.

The people needed the land. They had been better off here, even with the scant living it afforded. Here they had the wide sky and changing clouds, their gardens. I wished that some of them had stayed: I would not need to fear them, could have knocked at the low door of the croft, and it would have been opened; I would be greeted by a burry voice: "Aye, lass, what a nicht t' be oot! Come inside!" There would have been simple hospitality and quiet comfort.

I moved along through the dark. I needed a lift to my spirit. The sword was heavy, the handbag a dead weight on my arm. I understood now why medieval armor had died away. There came a fantasy of a fully armored knight rattling down the jagged staircase, and I heard his mail bump, his heavy feet clang on the steps. Had any of them knocked a head against the lintel of the doorway? How could he have endured the ring inside that metal helmet? What a feat it must have been to climb defended walls. Hollywood must have used paper-mache for its extravaganzas.

No wonder that the knight crept lightly clad to his lady's bower. But, of course, they did not wear armor inside the castles, even if movies showed it that way; it was field dress, the soldier's uniform.

I was so weary that I knew I staggered, yet my feet continued to move ahead. I let my mind explore the fantasies of medieval life. I must not think of my fatigue, of the distance I might have to go, of my weakness.

The mind can amuse even when the body is worn. I knew that my fantasies were absurd, and yet I must be indulgent toward my body; if this helped, let it go on.

Little knights on horses we had seen in the shops, some made of metal and others of plastic, on sale for children's toys. Some of them had been quite beautiful, the metal ones more expensive, but even the plastic ones attractive. I wondered why the toy makers didn't make small turrets with spiral staircases inside, and a knight who could be placed at the top step, to rattle down and emerge at the bottom. It would make a clever toy.

I remembered the privies high on the sentry walls, some of them even higher than where I had stood—square, boxlike stone enclosures made onto the walls, their lower reaches open, the seat only four parallel iron bars. Had ever a knight vertigo such as mine? I had looked down through space along the sheer bailey wall for hundreds of feet to water below, and I had grown dizzy.

I was getting wetter and colder. The road widened into a lay-by, and the boulders at the side were so high that a car might pull into them and never be seen again. It could become rust; nobody could have discovered it. I remembered the boulders Malcolm had driven into. I had had a reprieve; here I might stay until I became a skeleton.

But I sat on a rock and leaned back against one of the boulders. My heart chuffed like the W.C. tank high on the wall, trying to fill up. I shivered and tried to rest. I must not fall asleep, but find shelter and dry clothing.

Was Gilbert in distress? I suddenly wanted to weep. He was young, in full flower of manhood. I was old, and until now my life had been full and rich; no great loss if it came to an end.

Suddenly I realized how morbid my thoughts had become. I stood and went through a small series of exercises. I must keep going. Would my mind have strength enough to keep my body moving? I must think of something, force my mind to think, try to remember something, even the lines of a poem.

"So live, that when thy summons comes—" I had thought of a bad poem. "Elaine, the fair, Elaine, the lovable, Elaine, the lily maid of Astolat—" This was better. I moved ahead. Lancelot had a lovely name, the best part about him; he was a cad. Leaving a young girl with his shield and making love to the king's wife. Up a tower to the east the lily maid waited for him to return.

I had not been pursued. Or they went the wrong way, were lost. Or they walked in the rain as I did. They couldn't find me. No knights on black horses came charging across the rain-swept moor, riding on the highway . . . riding . . . riding . . . up to the old inn door.

I seemed to be scarcely moving, and I knew suddenly that my mind had sagged as badly as my knees. I must remember some funny thing, something that would lift my spirit. The night was pitch-black, I was shivering, teeth chattering. What could I remember? Warm rooms, and laughter, many people—surely I could remember something amusing. When had I laughed? There was a time . . .

Yes! A crowd . . . a party at the close of a long run, and a huge mansion belonging to rich people . . . a wide staircase of marble, and marble steps going up from a great entry hall, and people milling about there . . . waiting . . . waiting for Gregory Dixon, that famous English actor, to come down . . . he'd gone up to change . . . so famous that a room had been set aside to let him use . . . he always came off soaked wet with sweat, and yet from the audience he always looked virile, elegant. The crowd milled about in the entrance hall, and I stood among them, the steps gleaming in the light from the high French chandeliers, at their turn at the bottom a beautiful Ming vase, a treasure . . . Gregory comes to the head of the stairs, his magnificent head thrown back, the cords in his neck showing strongly . . . he has changed to a wine-red brocade jacket, his collar open, and the people look up and worship, and he knows, he savors it. He moves toward the wide steps that gleam as if they were carved of ice, and begins his elegant descent. How I dislike that man, so egotistical, so knowing, so sure of his beauty . . . and he comes down, a glass already in his hand, smiling at his public who wait here below for him. He steps gently. And then his foot skids. He topples, and the crowd draws in its breath. Gregory tumbles down the full length of the curved staircase, and falls onto the Ming vase. It shatters into pieces, and suddenly the rich woman rushes toward the vase, and all eyes follow her in consternation, for she is picking up the pieces and screaming, tears in her eyes, crying for the vase.

Somebody dusts off Greg, and he looks foolish and says that no, he isn't hurt. I go with the others into the dining room for food, smiling silently because of the spectacle and the way it has turned out. Sir Gregory, fallen from his pedestal, and answering solicitous questions, embarrassed now for his lordly entrance, his plan of a grand entrance collapsed about him.

I was grateful for my life on the stage, for the experiences I had had. I had treasured many things, planning someday to take them out again and examine them, when the days were finished. This remembrance had been enough to move me ahead a few more feet. I had been privileged to have had interesting things to do, a life to live after my husband's had ended. For many other women it had been different.

The road wound endlessly. How far had I come? Surely someone was seeking me, someone must have started out. I could not move fast, but I was lost. Where did I walk to? How far must I go?

I thought that I heard a car in the distance, but no light showed and nothing came near. I knew that I was having delusions, but the sound kept on and grew louder.

I must make my mind think, make my legs move forward. What could I remember now that would keep me moving?

I remembered my husband. He had been a noble person, but he lived simply and quietly, identifying with working people while not becoming just like them. He had taught and planted crops, making

his life education and farming, and he had chosen a way of hard work.
I recalled the simple tablet we had seen in Westminster Abbey—it
might have been set for him; it said: "Thank God for John
Frederick Leigh!" That was all, and yet it sang. I wondered who he
had been; was he like my husband? He had kept on until he dropped
of a heart attack, and he had never been too busy to help one of us.
I hoped that he heard trumpets sound a paean to his life in a mighty
welcome.

I could hear a car! I stopped moving, listening. I was in boulders
again, a place to strike fear into the heart. Headlights made a patch
of brightness in the distance. I crept among the boulders and back,
suddenly afraid to be seen. I waited until the car passed.

It was harder to go on. If I walked toward Ballachulish, there was
a hotel. But I was going up, into bens. Had I been brought west of
Loch Linnhe, or was I east? It must be east, for there were the bens.
It was folly to have hidden.

I could think of nothing now except death and misery. I dragged
the sword, and sparks flew up from its tip, and I carried it again.

My ears buzzed noises. None of them were real, just the spatter of
rain on the macadam and the sound of my feet slushing ahead. The
land had opened, and lay wide on each side of the road here. The
noises grew louder, a humming sound.

A car came toward me. There was no place to hide. I went from
side to side, trying to find any place, even a ditch, where I could not
be seen. But even the grass was short; I would not be hidden even
by grass on the flat berm.

The headlights became two, coming from the direction the earlier
car had gone. The car was near. I grasped the sword and met the
car head on.

It came to a stop a few feet before me, and the door opened.

A man emerged. Duncan! He was shouting, "Hor-rtense! My dear
woman, put down that damn swor-rd! Are ye just about t' attack me?"

I went toward him, sobbing.

IX

I watched the light move on the ceiling. Everything was very still. Young girls had been in many times to feed and bathe me; they had pulled off my soiled clothes and brought a little whiskey at first, and then porridge, and put me to bed with hot water bottles. I had been only half aware, and had slept deeply, such as I could not remember since childhood, and I had known that mother was downstairs.

Duncan had carried me up, assuring that Sarah was here, and would stay. Now I was fully awake, refreshed and well. I had not realized how desperately exhausted I had been.

Across the room the sword rested in a corner. The door opened, and Robert put his head in, the flesh between his eyebrows creased. He saw that I was awake, and came a little way inside, his hand still on the door, and hesitantly asked, "D'ye feel well enough to come down for dinner? I can bring a tray, if you'd rather. They sent me t' ask."

"I'll come down; no tray, thanks." I had gotten up on an elbow, and my voice cracked; it seemed to frighten him, and he started to back out. "I'd enjoy coming down, Robert, but please don't leave just yet."

He waited as if he'd bolt. "I just wanted to tell you that your limerick made me laugh. I liked it."

He let go and came forward a step. "Did ye, now? We dinna know you could hear us. We thought you asleep, that night."

"No. I don't need much sleep; I need people more. I sat on the balcony and listened."

"Well, there're people aplenty downstairs now. I'll tell them."

After he left, the girls came with my clothes. They had gotten my bags, and the change from the old things I had worn was nice. I hurried with the bath and dressing. When ready, I ignored the cane, and got downstairs without much of a limp.

There were Duncan and Sarah, Gilbert and a young woman "of surpassing beauty," as poets used to say, and the kids and the Scot. It was a surprise to see him. As I came down, they stood, and it felt like opening night of a smash hit. I didn't want to smile too much, but I began to feel like the Cheshire cat.

Gilbert, after a hug, pulled the young woman forward. He looked healthy and tanned, and extremely happy. "This is my fiancée, Elizabeth Forbes."

I backed away in surprise. "Engaged? Well, why not? And what good taste you showed!" It was true, for her eyes were clear and level, her mouth sweet. And now Duncan took one of my hands and said, "Come and sit, woman—we're goin' t' have a wee drop of spirits and a gr-reat deal of talk, a celebration t' be followed immediately by dinner, which is a roast joint of beef with Yor-rkshire pudding. I hope this meets with your approval?"

We sat by the fire in the lounge, the kids on the floor or draped on the chairs and arms of chairs. The Scot went to the window seat, where the sky behind him showed signs of blue. We raised our glasses in the traditional Scottish toast: "*Slainte Mháth!* To the glory of Scotland!"

I savored the fine Scottish skill with brown peat water again, the sip warming all the way down, and begged immediately for Gilbert to tell me what had happened to him.

Elizabeth looked up with laughter. "He said you'd be like that—I see what he meant," and she listened while Gilbert talked, her eyes shining.

"I've been traveling between Inverness and here, and Edinburgh and London. Got to know the people in the police stations and the embassy, and the air lines. I finally got the police to come, and then I found a Scottish rose in the Highlands."

The kids clapped, and Gilbert made a bow. "She actually found me in the Inverness police station, where I was yelling at a stupid sergeant who didn't speak English, and I couldn't speak his Gaelic, and was yelling in French!"

Elizabeth moved closer. "I'd been keeping an eye on him before you left, Mrs. Sutherland, but neither of you knew it. You didn't see me, but I had drinks at your hotel pub, and I worked at the garage when Gilbert brought in the car before you drove south. I knew when you left. When the police called that Gilbert had come back, I went over. He needed a lot of help; he was talking to one of the best men in the Movement, Sergeant Craig, who knew how to act stupid until I came. I was supposed to divert him, and I did my job, that's all."

"Aye! She diverted me." Gilbert chuckled. "She went with me up into the Highlands and down into the Lowlands; London, Stirling, everywhere. We even came here—you'd disappeared."

"That's when I leveled with him about you. And then we stayed and helped with the search."

I looked at Duncan and then at Sarah, who smiled across the rim of her glass.

"Do you mean, you worked with the police to keep them from coming?" I was astonished, and the two dropped their heads, and then shook them violently. "Oh, no! We *sent* the police!"

"I didn't need to go through all that? You knew where I was, Elizabeth? All the time?"

But Duncan shouted, "Silence, woman! Three questions at once are two too many! Stop beatin' your young nephew about! And that sweet lass, too! I will answer your questions, Hor-rtense, if you'll forbear with us; in good time you'll have your answers, and I hope that you'll find it in your heart t' forgive us much, when you've learned everything."

Why didn't he get on with it? But Duncan loved drama, knew how to achieve it, and savored his way of speaking. He sat down, and held all eyes. He was really miscast as a merchant. When he had cleared his throat ceremoniously, he began again.

"Now, the joy and beauty o' life is purpose, as you know, madam, bein' one who's found both in life. But before one finds pur-r-pose he must first know who he is—as you so ably pointed out just a few

weeks ago, a guest in my own home. And before you get to thinkin'
I'm merely philosophizing, let me assure you that a bit o' background's got t' come first, before I explain why you were so uncere-
moniously kept apart from the rest of mankind, to languish amidst
the young folk here, for 'tis important t' the whole affair."

"Aye! Right on!" The kids certainly related to this, if I did not.
They moved their feet on the floor until the stamping shook the
building.

"Well, I like having work to do, if that's what you mean. That's
purpose. Tell me why you rigged it against me."

" 'Twas not, madam! Nothing was r-rigged against you, even if it
seemed so! Unfortunately, you got in the way of our plans and it
became necessary to remove you from the scene temporarily, takin'
great pains t' see that you weren't unduly distressed, o' course."

I sniffed. "You're the one behind this! I think that I'm the one to
judge stress to myself. Duncan, I trusted you!"

He shook his head vigorously. "I assure you, madam, we are sorry
for the distress, but yes, I am behind it."

"If I was to be 'removed,' why didn't you keep me there in Edinburgh? Why was Gilbert separated from me? Why the high tower at
the castle? And for what reason?"

He lowered his voice. "About your nephew, madam: he was supposed to be with you; it was unfortunate that he eluded us, and we
had to improvise."

"So?" It was Gilbert who spoke. "Then you should have sent someone else to help fix the car—that chap didn't know a bloody thing! As
soon as I saw what he was doing, I knew. Got him when he
straightened up, and I trussed him with his own belt and tie. I went
the other way from yours, Aunt! Whoever you'd found were damned
inhospitable. I realized that I needed help."

He got a disparaging look from Duncan. "Spare us libel, sir! Let us
continue, without interruptions! Now, as to why you weren't detained in Edinburgh—we didn't know your errand, and when we
learned, you were in Inverness. You recall that you made some remarks about a certain famous man." He leaned forward.

"Well, y' see, girl, some people work against us. We thought for a time that you might be one of 'em."

"Me?" I was astonished. "Why, I didn't even know about you!"

He spoke in a conciliatory tone. "Don't act so aggrieved, Hor-rtense. There were actually two points: someone's been lettin' the bloody English know each move we make. Now, stop shakin' your head—we know it wasn't you! Now we know, but at the time we didn't."

"Couldn't you just wait and see what I did? How could anything I did affect you?" It was damned nice of them, I thought.

"Which brings me t' the most important point: if you'd communicated with the American family, sayin' their descent was from this man, you'd have given out a bit of misinformation that could 've raised all kinds of mischief. For they aren't!" He glared at me, almost belligerently. It did seem silly, this quibbling over such minor things.

"But I was trying to find that out! I don't give out fiction as fact, Duncan, even if it may seem so. I take pride in doing a good job—didn't even know about the Cause."

"Aye! We found out that y' didn't know when we read your letter to your friend. Do forgive me—I'm sorry t've been forced t' reading your personal letters, though I must say, Hor-rtense, there's no need for you t' apologize about your age and condition—you're still a bonnie lass!" He smiled gently.

I nodded, a slight smile acknowledging the compliment. He spoke again before I could ask my question. "We can tell you positively who was the man t' start that American line: it was Alan Bruce."

"I know. I read it in the pine closet downstairs, in the old documents." He was waiting, and I regarded him levelly. "Why do you make so much of it, Duncan? Is this the reason you put me through a three-week slimming diet, plus torment, the disappearance of my nephew, to say nothing of physical violence?" With such friends, who needs enemies?

"Nicht, but lass—the reason is impor-rtant! Because, madam, the man sittin' there in the window seat with his legs crossed so jauntily is the one livin', straight-line, first-son descendant of the Clans' Chief of Chiefs!" He seemed to think that he had made a remarkable answer, one to explain everything, and he jutted out his lower jaw and nodded toward the Scot as if he claimed the power and the glory.

It was incredible! I looked at the Scot and back at Duncan. "Malcolm Cromarty?"

"*Not* Malcolm Cromarty, madam! Stewart Bruce!"

The Scot watched without a change of expression. I looked at Sarah, who smiled and nodded. "I didn't know, really. Believe me—it was a well-kept secret until we all came here, worried about you."

"Hmfp. A lot of things seem to be well-kept secrets! Does it make any difference? I don't see how." If I sounded angry, I was.

Sarah put her hand on my arm. "Just listen, he's trying to explain. I've been kept in the dark as much as you. Honestly, I didn't know when we talked."

"And now, Hortense, if you'll stop feelin' sorry for yourself one wee moment, I shall resume—but I grant you'll have t' listen for a while until it all comes clear, and I do beg your continued forbearance." He spoke like a school principal with a child. It was clear that he expected me to listen, had practically commanded it.

"Now, t' us, the Chief o' the Clans is the Leader. The leader of all us Scots! That's the impor-rtant point I've got t' get into your head, madam—it's tr-raditional, the Scot's way! No one changes that tradition except . . . God!" Having found the word, he chuckled to himself gently, pleased.

In a lower tone, as if only to me, he went on, "Further-rmore—and please forgive this before I say it—for ye must know how it is with some Americans—they come over here and swagger around, proud o' their newly discovered line, a' wavin' their papers, trying t' establish a small empire on our old ruins, not knowin' a damn thing about it, or us, or what we stand for! And a couple o' fool Americans swaggerin' around and gettin' in th' way just now is exactly what we don't need. Not at this particular moment!"

He was unaware of how greatly he infuriated me. He had put me down, and even if I realized that it was unintentional, it smarted.

I restrained my anger when I answered because it was apparent that he had no idea of what he had said.

"I understand. Some Americans are boorish, loud, swaggering. They're not all like that. I dislike fools as much as anyone, and they're not always Americans. Now will you tell me why this is important?"

He was again unaware of my meaning, and went on in his reasonable tones, "There are many cogent reasons for particular care at the moment. The most important is that we're finally gettin' ourselves together, ready t' take a stand among the nations of the wor-rld, here in this small land. And we now have our symbolic Head, our Clan Chief of Chiefs, back from roamin' the world since the war, where he was tryin' t' make a living! The world doesn't know that we Scots are bein' bled dry! Too many o' our best have had t' roam elsewhere t' make enough money t' eat—that's the reason! We're about t' put an end t' it, and we don't want any interference! We have organized, woman!"

They surely had. I had interfered, and I had found out. There had been no gentleness and warm understanding in it. I looked at the Scot. He was listening, a look of seriousness on his pink face, but otherwise he showed no emotion. He nodded. "He speaks the truth. We Scots support a high percentage of the British population with just the whiskey industry. Did you know, madam, that scotch whiskey can't be made anywhere else in the world? Well, it cannot. Only the Scottish people are able to make it, and part of the profit goes to England. That's a great amount of money, you know. We need what is ours. It's time that money came here."

"Aye! Right on!" The kids were stamping again, moving about and showing their unity. No doubt of it—they had accepted the man and the movement without any reservations.

When we were again quiet, Duncan said, "We've been gettin' our young people ready t' take their rightful place in the world—we're through bowin' down to the English! The lads and lassies are learnin' how t' deal Scotland in!"

"I didn't know you'd been dealt out."

"*You* may not have, but you're American! The government treats

Scotland like a stepchild. We want more representation in Parliament. We've come of age! We demand it!"

Stewart Bruce nodded. "We're having a great meeting in Stirling in September. He's right. Our young people are aroused."

I sat there and heard the kids yell and stamp, and thought about scotch whiskey. Great jumping hounds of heaven! Problems everywhere, not only in America, with the blacks fighting for their identity. Women, too. Perhaps it should have made me feel better, but it did not. When would adults develop? Did it take a next life? Sometimes it seemed that it did, and often of late I had felt that only the possibility of another existence could explain this one.

I had thought the Scots gentle and perceptive, adult, mature. I had been sentimental. They were just like the rest of us.

I said, "The pamphlets at Culloden? A part of the Movement?"

"Yes, madam. We try to reach everybody that we can. We print them at our own expense and distribute them where we can. Culloden is the very center of our independence—you know about the Uprising?"

I nodded. "I do." So it hadn't been finished, once and for all! Scottish independence had been driven underground. The kids were proof that it was very much alive. Somehow the knowledge made me feel extremely tired. All those men killed . . . the places burned . . . crops damaged. Dear God—how we need the certainty of the next life! So useless, so little point to it, all the suffering!

I returned to the hut in my thoughts. "I saw the literature there, then I went in to get it, and it was gone. I've never understood that. It's puzzled me ever since."

"They were taken away. To be more precise, we were made to take them away. Didn't it occur to you that the couple with the knapsacks might have brought them, and that the men who talked in low voices were from the government? They objected to our right to put our own literature in the very center of Scottish independence."

I could see it, now. It was the typical, quiet way. Unobtrusive, controlling, the eye carried away to other, more pleasant things, the ear charmed by the gentle voice.

"It's like fightin' a marshmallow!" Duncan had been silent, but now his voice cut heavily across the gentle sounds of the kids' softer voices. "The English say, 'Oh, come now—y' know you don't want to bother folks with things o' this kind, now do you? Perhaps this isn't just the right place for this kind of thing, old chap.' D'ye know what I'm sayin'? They're damned polite about it, and persistent!" He hissed the word and it sounded like a thrust of a dirk. "We have t' take a stand! They don't move back an inch!" He smacked his glass onto the table with such force that I was surprised it didn't shatter.

I nodded. I saw the bobby, the mother with the struggling child, and the grandfather with his reasonable tones while his words implied extreme violence.

The Scot was saying, "The lads who blocked you, madam, they knew that you wanted some of our material, but under the eyes of certain people we are cautious. We take pains, until we're permitted to be free.

"We use our Gaelic, the language that's ours! Long before the Anglo-Saxons developed, madam! Are you aware that English is a bastar-rd language? That the present government has long been in the control of the Hanoverians?"

It was an epithet. He spat out the word. The kids were screaming. This went right into them. The room was a din, and kids shouted loudly to be heard above the other sounds.

"—they listed the Bruce line ended. It wasn't! We knew better!"

"—he'd gotten across the Channel—you can't read it anywhere!"

"—they even took our national flag, and made it the base for theirs—"

"—and our lion!—And the Stone of Scone!—"

"Aye! They take! They don't let us have any voice in our own affairs!"

Both the Bruce and Duncan seemed to savor this exuberance, and sat listening, smiling quietly. It was music to their ears. I wondered if they had strong feelings for others' rights, as much sympathy for the blacks in America, for the Jews in the world. Their belief in freedom was commendable, but did they mean freedom for all? America, America—only in America! I wanted to cry.

I had been denied freedom, and in the pine closet I had read names and dates and knew how to put them together. I knew why my mother's people had left the old country, why they had gone far from food and comforts and had endured privation to establish a land of the free.

But a young woman's voice was coming through. "We talk about the way they forbade us to wear our tartans, how they denied us our national music—the bagpipes—how they drove off our cattle and sheep, and butchered our women and children, and whoever they couldn't catch, they drove up into the glens."

Her voice was as sweet and as ripe as a melon. She had the ear of everyone in the room, and it was her melody that had captivated, as well as her words. "What you know, what anyone learns of it depends on the particular volume of history you're given. The point of view is important. It can be of great difference, for even when names and dates of battles are the same, the interpretation is changed . . . it's slid sideways, somehow . . . the emphasis is lopsided."

She had also the voice of reason. She seemed to understand something which the others did not. Could this kind of thinking prevail? Had they all any idea of the deprivation I had endured at their hands? Would any of them understand?

When they had settled down, I asked to have Rose's actions explained; why had I been taken to the castle? And where was Rose?

Duncan snorted and looked at Sarah, for she had caught a signal from the dining room, and had stood. "Can't we finish this while we eat? I'm sure you're all as hungry as I am—" And we followed them out.

It took a little time to get ourselves settled, but eventually the roast beef was distributed, the Yorkshire pudding red in its juices, the vegetables passed around, and everybody contented. I asked Duncan again, but it was Stewart Bruce who answered.

"Ah, madam. We didn't intend any of that—it was not our doing. This is so, believe me. Our plan was only to keep you here, quite safely, with a slight delay in your journey until we had clarified what you were about. I'm afraid that we didn't take into consideration your insatiable curiosity, and the fact that Anabel resented you quite a lot."

He did not apologize, but explained with the intention that I accept it. "She did all that without our knowledge, and she had no right to do it. This is not our way! She had been told that you would have to come to a stop near here, and her orders were to act as your hostess. She alone decided to take you to the castle." He smiled and inclined his head.

I nodded, listening. "And now you've got her locked into the castle?"

He smiled. "Well, not exactly. Let us say she is no longer in our employ. We hope that you will excuse the trouble and pain she has caused, not for any feeling for her, but because it happened here. We regret it deeply."

He cut his meat and placed vegetables on the back of his fork, then lifted the arrangement to his mouth. When he had swallowed, he said, "I must tell you that the escape you made was amazing. I have seen many things, madam, and that was a feat of daring and courage."

"It was foolhardy, but I had no other choice. I, too, believe in freedom."

He looked at me closely and resumed eating. Duncan, who had not noticed this little repartee, said, "At first when you escaped, the lads rushed about a good deal, as you must've known they would. And they finally discovered how you had got out. We owe you thanks for that, woman! We'll take that bolt hole into our plans in the future."

"Bolt hole?"

"A hole into which one bolts, usually rather abruptly," the Scot said dryly.

It made me laugh, and when I'd stopped, he continued, "As to why you weren't found and brought to safety sooner and with less cost to your strength—unfortunately, soon after you disappeared at the ammo level, Mrs. MacPherson—you call her Rose for some reason—left, also, taking the only car there. She won't return, which scarcely needs telling, does it?"

"But she's part of the Movement!"

"Madam, we thought so, but she's not coming back because she's a double agent. She's afraid to."

"A spy? She said I was!"

"Precisely what she intended us to think." He waited and then said, "It gave her time to carry out her plans, and you were most convenient."

I choked. Sarah leaned out and patted my back. When I could talk, I wanted to be told more, and as soon as I had quieted down, the Scot explained.

"She had a contact in England—an older man, quite respectable, really. He was a most unnoticeable-looking grandfatherly type. As a matter of fact, he met her in Chipping Cranford, which is where you and I first met, I believe."

"The man at the table in the Queen's Arms!"

He looked puzzled. "A man who will not be learning any more about us, thanks to you."

Duncan said, "We simply didn't know you'd gotten away—matter of fact, we had no idea where you'd gotten to. We had all come up looking for you as soon as we heard you'd disappeared from the lodge, but we didn't know it until you escaped from the castle, and then not until quite late in the day. Mrs. MacPherson drove off, leavin' no orders. There's no telephone at the castle, and the chaps thought perhaps she'd gone off to call, or after you. She'd not left any directions. So, quite late, this lad walked up t' the petrol station and called here, thus startin' a mad rush t' the lodge by all of us."

Sarah said, "Do you know you were within a mile of the petrol station? If only you'd walked the other way—"

I shook my head. Luck had been against me all the time.

The girls were bringing around huge bowls of trifle. Duncan filled his plate with a heaping portion, and when he had tasted it, licked his lips with deep satisfaction, and dipped in the second time. I asked why it had taken so long. "I was here for two weeks before the castle. Surely you must have been able to learn my bona fide qualifications before that, Duncan."

He shook his head. "Now, that's the tragic part, lass—we just weren't in the area. Th' Bruce was travelin' in the small villages, and I was in Barra—no telephones, and boats for transportation. Finally they got a letter to me, but before I could return, the weather closed in. No planes—they land on the beach, y' know. Finally found a lad with a boat and a good stomach. Came as fast as I could. In the meantime, we thought you were safe here, maybe enjoyin' yourself."

"Aye, that he did, once we found where he was. He'd said he was going up to the Highlands to buy drums. I tried all our suppliers. It's a croft industry, did you know? It took a long time to locate the man."

"I don't tell Sarah everything," Duncan said, jerking up a shoulder.

I was beginning to fit it together. But there were places where the puzzle had gaps, still. "Why the shots, that night at the castle? Did you know about that?" I asked.

"Hortense, there're other spies besides the ones you've learned about—some of 'em 're Scots, traitors t' our national cause. Some live among us here in our own country, not all 're English. It's a sad thing that some men have closed their minds and won't even listen t' what we're trying to say. They walk away shakin' their heads, they're even willin' t' let the English bleed us. They say it's all over, it's history, even the will of God!"

Veins in his throat stood out and he jabbed his fist down on the table. "They even say it's been settled for all time!"

I nodded. "I know. People are afraid to get involved. I've seen them in America, too, in the country that planned change into its basic structure. They're timid souls—they gnaw their lips, peer through squint holes in their doors, cling to people like themselves, afraid of their own shadows."

He nodded. "Aye, but some're curious! They won't do anything to help, but they can't stand not knowin' what's going on. On the night in question, one of our good neighbors near the castle had let his bump o' curiosity grow so huge that he followed the lorry and sneaked inside the castle with a shotgun, hidin' himself in the sentry box. That's the small space built just inside the portcullis gate, and you might have missed seein' it; it's not large. We've stationed one of our lads there now, to keep off intruders like him, but it's a sad day when Scot guards against Scot!" His head sagged forward and he looked at his empty plate as if it held a dismal picture. It was a measure of his acting ability that we all watched him, entranced. Evidently none of the others had known of the shooting incident and were curious now.

Finally Duncan shook his head, as if to clear the image from his eyes, and continued. "He had a small band of kin stationed up over the crest of the hill. When nothin' seemed to be happening, this lad sallied down for a look, and came quietly up behind the chap, scarin' him considerably and causin' him to explode his firearm. And that made the other one shoot. Poor lad—ye can't blame him, can ye?—he couldn't see a thing in the dark."

I laughed at him and the way he said it.

"Now, *our* chaps, bein' alerted by the noise, ran out t' see what was happening, and a few more shots went up into the sky. Luckily, none of ours was hurt. We shoot up, and when we shoot straight on, we know where the bullet'll strike!"

So target practice was a part of their training.

The Bruce said, "It's not for the sport alone that our old chiefs kept our people playing the Highland games. They were a deliberate plan to keep up spirit and morale, and muscles fit. After the thrashing at Culloden, something was needed. They wanted a nation of brawny men when the final accounting came. That's why they sponsored yearly competitions—tossing the caber, putting the shot—things like that. It wasn't just for the fun, alone. We want freedom, in peace, we hope; if not in peace—we shall have it by some other means."

"Aye! Our men'll fight if they have to! Our exiled dead are buried all over the wor-rld. They've fought for many nations, now it's time we fought for ourselves."

I said, "I stood at the window a long time, but I didn't see anything after the truck left. Was anyone hurt?"

"The one in the sentry box by his friend. The other got clipped a bit on the heel when the lorry passed him. I hear he's wearin' a bit o' white now. In the form of a plaster cast." He shook his head. "Such kind know a few facts which keep us from becomin' too comfortable, but that's a risk we take. There's a risk even if you live in America, y' know." He nodded at me.

"Touché!"

Duncan looked around the table. "Well, now, we're all finished. Come, let's go into the other room, where we'll be more comfortable." He led the way and we grouped around the fire. Someone had set out a coffee pot and cups on the low table, and Sarah poured.

Gilbert and Elizabeth had seated themselves closely on the sofa, his arm around her shoulders. The look on both faces was a special joy to see. I had seen young people smile at each other like that before, and the message was clear.

But there were things about Rose which I still could not comprehend. How had she been accepted and given such trust? I wondered if they'd made a proper investigation of her, and I asked Stewart Bruce for the answers to my questions.

"Mrs. MacPherson's an Englishwoman, madam." He said it as if that explained everything, and when he saw that I waited, he added, "Not that she didn't do her part to operate this establishment. But she's the daughter of an old family who've been traditionally antagonistic to Scotland."

Duncan heard us, and he joined in. "She married Ian MacPherson, who was killed with the Commandos, and she'd lived among us for a good number of years, so we knew who she was. A few years ago, when our work began in earnest, she approached the man she knew as Malcolm Cromarty, who happened to be on one o' his rather frequent trips to England. She was out of work, and she'd been runnin' an inn there, since Ian's death. She said she wanted t' come back t' live in Scotland, and did he know of any employment for her."

"Sounds qualified," I said.

"Aye, that's how it seemed. Well, it happened we needed someone t' keep an eye on our lads and lassies, and she fit the bill—could run a place o' this kind, 'n all. The right age to work with young folk, too. So we hired her. A good number of months passed, and everything seemed to be open and aboveboard. So we rather stopped keepin' such a sharp eye on her."

The Bruce took the story on. "In the last weeks, about the time you came to our country, Mrs. Sutherland, we've had some problems related to the receiving of munitions. And some of our messages didn't get through until too late—that kind of thing. And then she sent us word to keep an eye on you."

"I see. From this time forward I shall pay a great deal of attention to my hunches." My remark was not understood by either man, and I did not try to explain. The kids had finished with their coffee and some were clearing away the cups. Sarah and Elizabeth started up the stairs for the powder room, and I watched the way Gilbert followed the girl with his eyes. She was wonderful to look at; I could understand how he immediately was attracted, for her color was high—the cool damp air had given her a complexion that was superb. And with the brilliance of her eyes and russet hair, she was one to turn around to notice.

When Sarah and Elizabeth returned, Duncan arose. He commanded silence with an upraised palm, and when he had it, he said, "It's necessary t' say before the assembled group that Mrs. Sutherland is a bona fide researcher in genealogy. T' be sure, her questions in Inverness aroused doubts, but they're all settled. We had everything looked into, and we want you all t' know."

The kids stamped and cheered. They had all been kind to me, and this little show of warmth was appreciated. But Duncan hadn't finished. "Y' might be interested in knowin' that her own lineage is from the oldest kings o' Scotland." He bent and asked, "Did y' know that, madam?"

"Yes."

Gilbert swung his head suddenly in my direction, a look of astonishment on his face. "I learned it after I got here," I said, "from documents I found in an old chest in the basement." Gilbert, his face a study in mixed emotions, gently shushed Elizabeth's whispers and shook his head rapidly, his eyes fixed on my face.

It seemed my turn for a speech. "That was a long time ago."

I had hoped to dismiss the subject, but they waited. Much had happened since I had come here, and I had at first loved Scotland with a passion—unreasoned and sentimentalized. What I had endured in the name of her freedom was yet a source of jumbled emotions, and I hesitated to speak just yet. I needed time to sort out feelings and ideas. But the crowd wanted more, waited for a more gracious discourse. I could not be rude.

"As your guest, I want to be thoughtful about the things I may say—I do not wish to offend you." It seemed to be a good beginning, for they were still listening with pleased expressions. "And yet I have to tell you that Americans don't pay much attention to that sort of thing—to kings, to bloodlines. In America, when one speaks of having good blood it usually means that he's healthy."

The kids were laughing.

"Perhaps the thought of royalty angers Americans. I think so. I've heard Americans say that they had no use for kings, and I agree, it does sound funny."

They were laughing hard, and I joined in for a moment. When they were quiet again, I said, "It may be difficult for people who have been accustomed to monarchs to understand that in my country, if one might claim royal blood, he might not be inclined to let it be known, for several unpleasant things could happen.

"Americans respond to such a thing in peculiar ways. Either they get their backs up, or they fawn on the person, so that life for the one who claims such lineage is never quite the same. And I think the reason might be because our nation sprang from people who resisted royalty, often justly so, having been persecuted by rulers in the countries they came from." I was speaking slowly, thinking in unaccustomed channels, and the kids seemed to understand. They were quiet, and they seemed interested.

"I hadn't known about my lineage until I came here. It was a surprise to me. There was time when I was in the castle, and I thought about these things. I now believe that my mother knew, but that she preferred to make nothing of it, to say nothing about it, and to let the knowledge die a natural death. In America, all men are considered equal. And anyway, our line came through daughters, not the sons of kings."

"The blood's there!"

The Bruce was on his feet. He had been quiet, and I had almost forgotten that he was still in the room, watching the kids and Gilbert, speaking to them, really. He took a step forward. "My line, also, came through a daughter. But blood will tell!"

I smiled. He reddened and bowed in a courtly manner. "I beg forgiveness for that cliché. Nevertheless, I sincerely believe it true. I have seen people in all the countries of the world. The old adage is borne out oftener than it is disproved."

The room was very quiet. I could not argue with his conviction. He was sincere, and he compelled respect. He held his ground, erect and very quiet.

"I beg your pardon for the interruption. You said that your line came through women, madam—daughters, not the sons of kings—"

I accepted his words. "I'm glad for your good opinion of women, especially now, when so many of us have gotten militant about our sex." It wasn't meant to be funny, but the kids took it that way. They looked eager for a verbal battle, but I didn't go on.

Now it seemed as if the afternoon was at its close. The young people, their expectations fading, began to stretch and move, and Gilbert and Elizabeth came close, to talk with excitement about their discovery of royalty. Afternoon sun poured through the window glass and gleamed across the tables and the polished floor.

"Tell us what you learned," Gilbert asked, his face shining with eagerness.

I made a little gesture with my hands. "Oh, Gilbert—that was long ago—the thirteenth century. Yes, I'll tell you what I learned: a Scottish lady, a daughter of a king, lost her husband in war. He was only a lord, and he fought in a war that the king brought on—an act of fealty."

Elizabeth made a little shudder with her shoulders, a small twist of thrill. There was no hope except to go on with it, but I tried to put them off. "Look, dears, I memorized it, and I'll write it out and give it to you. I'll tell you later." Their look of disappointment was so real that I gave up.

"Well, only that after his death, she married another man, one of the Border Lords. His line's still there—very important persons."

They nodded eagerly. "The children of her first husband, the line we came from, disinherited, moved into England, and I don't wonder that they wanted to get away—the classic story of the stepchildren, I think. Anyway, they went as far as they could go—to the southern-most part of England."

Sarah had moved closer to hear, and I now noticed that the Bruce and Duncan and the kids had stopped talking, and had heard for some time. There was no hope for it now.

"In exchange for loyalty to the king, they were allowed to bear arms. In those days you were either a serf or a knight, and they were intelligent, I guess, and wanted to rank with their peers. So it seems to me. I have bare-bones facts, and fleshed them out. I don't guarantee this—it just makes sense.

"We've had a copy of the armorial bearings for years, and I recognized it in the old documents I found. Until I read them, though, I hadn't known the oldest source—the Scottish line. I find it delightful to have Scottish blood—it explains so many things about myself that have puzzled me until I knew."

Gilbert and Elizabeth were laughing. Even the Scot seemed to like it.

"Then another king ascended to the throne, and he took away their land and wouldn't let them move away. They'd been the Disinherited; now they became Dissenters. They were the first to leave for a new land, and I'm sure that they deliberately set out to make it better than the land they'd known."

I shrugged, but they waited. Finally, trying to conclude, I said, "Well, you know the classic American story—a man's land belongs to him, nobody takes it from him; he is free to carry arms—to defend himself, not his king or government; a man is judged by his acts, not by his blood—he's noble if his actions are. It's too well known to tell, really. That's the American's belief."

I hadn't counted on such a climactic response. The kids drummed their feet, Gilbert jumped, his arm around Elizabeth, and brought up a fist, and I had a strange sensation of not really having left the stage.

"What my good aunt is really saying is—you chaps have a lot of support for your cause on our side of the Atlantic. There are more of us now. Right on!"

It was pandemonium, Fourth of July, conga line, encounter group stuff—choose your era and the name for it that suits. I watched the hugs and tears, and wondered what had really happened, and when we were all quiet again, the Bruce sitting near beside the fire, I leaned toward him to ask about that signature I'd noticed on the pamphlet I'd gotten at Culloden. It had stuck in my mind, a tiny point that wouldn't fade until I settled it. This was a good time.

He bent close to hear, and a rather sweet aroma wafted toward me, not bay rum or cologne, nothing false, but a personal odor which must come from soap and, perhaps, hair pomade. "It was a way of letting our people know I was on the job, that I hadn't forgotten. You realize that I've had to live elsewhere for long periods of time, that I found employment in other countries? I couldn't be in Scotland among them?"

I nodded. "Sarah asked me if you were American."

"I have lived there, too. One makes a good living. The people—some of them—seem rather uneducated."

"About certain things. Not about others. Not all people. We are many."

He nodded, uninterested and businesslike. "About the pamphlets —I regularly put such messages into circulation, similar to the one you took. They were always couched in scriptural language—a good camouflage, a kind of code, or cipher, which our people understand. The translations were for those who don't understand Gaelic. Certain words have special meaning—something like the Book of Revelations." He shrugged and concluded, "Nobody, not even the government, could take offense at a message from a saint. Wouldn't you agree?"

"So St. B. is really Stewart Bruce. Cryptic and clever." There was a quiet hum in the room now, and Gilbert and Elizabeth had that special look. The gold from the sun poured through the windows and touched the Bruce on the head, and red lights showed up in his hair. He leaned toward me out of the sunlight and spoke so softly that I had to strain to hear.

"I hesitate to ask more of you, madam, especially as you've already suffered much at our hands, but I do want you to know that we appreciate the many things you've done for us. We'll try not to forget our duty as your hosts again."

His face had become a deeper pink, and his eyelids, rimmed by gold-colored lashes, reddened. "We'd like to make it up somehow. I thought—perhaps you might help me—stay on a bit—that is, if you don't find it an inconvenience?"

I reached for the coffee pot on the table at my knees. "Help you?" I held it out.

"You misunderstand." He chuckled. "What I wish to say is that our young people can use acting techniques. I wonder if you might stay on here and instruct them—how to seem casual while the heart beats wildly—things like that. You'd be a fine instructor, and in the process, you might enjoy yourself. We'd expect to pay you, put a car and driver at your disposal. The young people admire you. I believe they'd respond well."

But I could not answer. Duncan was moving toward us, and already his strong voice boomed loudly over the other sounds in the room.

"Hor-rtense, my lass, Sarah's been sayin' that we haven't properly explained that we had no notion of Mrs. MacPherson takin' you away —she did it without permission, so t' speak—and that when she brought you to the castle, none of our lads down there knew she did it without our direction. They were used to seein' her, takin' orders from her. She went there often for supplies, and they'd gotten into the habit of obeyin' her, so it never occurred to any of 'em t' ask and find out about it. And we assumed they'd have said, known if you were there."

Stewart Bruce said, "Incidentally, madam—this may be a comfort to you—she was picked up before she'd gone very far. As soon as the chap called, Duncan alerted the police. The car was in his name, and they got her quite soon. Mrs. MacPherson's resting quietly in jail on charges of auto theft."

"Duncan," I asked, "what would have happened if you'd caught

Gilbert with me, that night I walked into the lodge? If he hadn't gone off the other way to find help?"

"*Caught* you? A-ach, lassie! Now I ask you from the bottom of my hear-rt, what kind of way is that to think of us? We meant to detain you both, gir-rl. Your young nephew eluded us." His expression was pained.

I smiled. How like himself he was proving to be! I nodded, agreeing outwardly with his change of words. "All right. If he had been detained."

"Well, Hor-rtense, my dear—that would have made it a different kettle of fish. Ver-ry different." He gazed at the ceiling for a moment. Suddenly he smiled broadly. "I suppose it was just as well that it wor-rked out as it did. For, had he been with you, both of you would have been under lock and key here. That is, until we clarified matters, y' see. For havin' a str-rong young man roamin' about isn't quite the same as a lady who's br-roken her hip; now, is it?"

He shrugged his massive shoulders and smiled, his eyebrows up to his hairline. "And ye may be thankin' your lucky star-rs t' have had such a goodly amount of fr-reedom, my lass. 'R-rose,' as you call her, might have been a bit of a pr-roblem, but she did obey our orders t' let you move about on the moor. You've got t' admit that."

The Bruce nodded. "Perhaps it worked out as well as could be expected. Gilbert's presence here would have called for other measures. I'm sure you can understand."

I nodded. I did understand, perhaps more than they thought.

Sarah said, in the little silence, "Hortense, dear—as soon as we got that call about you escaping from the castle, Duncan got so worried! He did! He got in the car and started off, determined to find you, to move earth, itself. He said he'd not come back until he'd found you." She looked anxious.

I shook my head, smiling gently. "And all that time I spent 'up a tower to the east—'"

Duncan squinted. "Hor-rtense! That's an *English* poet you're quotin'."

"There were many strange thoughts on my journey in the rain that night, Duncan. I even quoted American poets."

"Ach! You poor lass! I drove many miles and turned around and was comin' back, and then I found you. I'd about given up your ghost, woman! Then I spied you in the middle o' the road, wavin' that damn sword!"

"I didn't intend to go down without a fight."

"A brave, bonnie Scot! Y' were practically walkin' on your knees, and yellin' a bloodcurdlin' yell—a genuine Scottish war cry."

"I didn't know that I knew one."

Duncan turned to the others. "The time's past for speeches, but you must know that this poor, abused woman is one of the gr-reatest actresses in the United States! If she were livin' here instead o' that wild country where she resided, long ago she'd have been made a Dame of the Kingdom."

He picked up his wine glass. "To Dame Hortense!"

I waited until the toast had been drunk, then picked up my glass. "To the glory of Scotland!"

We all drank to that.

Hortense—Dame at last!

Are you back? Wait until I'm alone. Who needs a ribbon and a medal? This is glorious!

"I can understand, if you'd rather not." The Bruce waited, watching me, and for a moment I couldn't recall what it was that he referred to. Then I did.

"Oh—I was considering it. I'd like a little time. I could go to Chipping Cranford later. Nobody expects me there. I could send for my mail. Even if there are new commissions, I can do them as well here. And their secrets will keep—they've been waiting for centuries."

There was a puzzled look in his eyes.

So now the Brainy Dame of Astolat's an acting teacher. Well, well. Don't say you're about to do it. You couldn't, could you?

Of course not! Three weeks out of my life seems like nothing to them—it might have been the last three weeks of my life. Stay here? I'll go home, back where I belong.

America, America, God shed His grace on thee . . . from sea to shining sea . . . and crowned thy grace with brotherho—My God! I must not cry! After what's happened . . . they've all been so apologetic, so quick with explanations. Gilbert told them they'd have lots of friends in America, cheering . . . love of liberty, love of freedom . . . they love freedom so much that they kidnapped me, using its name in vain. Freedom—theirs, not mine. In America it's freedom for all. Stay? I'll go home!

I can't go back there—no place for old people there . . . just solitary confinement, called Nursing Homes . . . If I try to live by myself there, can I endure much longer the pushing people, their insulting snarls, those long-haired militants shouting for revolution—it's my turn now, you've had yours, you Anglo-Saxon White American! Can I stand in line waiting my turn to be told that I'm taking up space, to be slapped by my "brothers"? . . . like the parking lot attendant who whispers, so that I have to ask him how much money I owe again . . . Brotherhood? I've grown old trying to make it happen! And the drivers—no one has time to wait for the old, they honk if you don't drive fast, as fast as they want to go. Adults? They're hateful children.

Edinburgh. Go there. Fade into the crowd, disappear. There must be a nice apartment somewhere there. The police are kind; you saw them; you know. There are places to walk—sidewalks. You won't need to drive. They understand old people. The Scots are genuine. They're warm, mature, kind. They care.

They do? I've just lived through an example of how they care. They care about themselves. Genuine, warmhearted blackguards! The most cold-blooded kind. They scheme, plan, plot. They schemed to bring me here, scheme now to get out of letting me go. If I went, I might go to England and report them, and they know it. If they meant me to be free, why didn't Duncan take me to Edinburgh, instead of this lodge? Serve whiskey, a lot of it, say Madam and Dame. They kidnapped me! I have a case! If I go to Edinburgh, I could be watched. I'd never fade in a crowd.

If you stay, maybe you can work up to Queen. What's the name for lady Chief of Chiefs? Clan Chieftess? Stop it, you'll burst out laughing.

I'd like the chance to rule. Certain things should be done at once —laws against plotting and kidnapping, for instance. If I were Chieftess, I'd reforest these bare bogs, plant trees for windbreaks, start a pulp industry . . . paper . . . what else? The kids like me; they do, and they feel sorry for me, too. Some small residue of guilt, probably. And it is a time for women, I believe that, but slowly, slowly . . . Have I got that long?

You've got The Blood. The Bruce said it, himself.

Yes, but he's got the name. And he's a man. Tradition! The time's not ripe for a woman . . . an older woman. I'm really American—mother was a third-century American, an old line . . . one of the First Families, if you set any store by snobbery. I'm really a mongrel—all different kinds of blood, mixed. Blood! Can a woman with Blood—an old woman—have a chance against a Man with a Name?

Gilbert and the beautiful girl had gone outside, savoring the last light, the incredible Scottish sky. They came in and were coming toward me.

"What have you been doing with yourself? You look like three weeks of Elizabeth Arden!"

"Now, that's the kind of talk I like! Yes, Elizabeth Arden—Scotland's special brand—a basic, reducing diet and lots of exercise and fresh air. I'm a new woman."

He put his head back and roared. Elizabeth took his arm in her hands and squeezed it, looking up to him as if he were a young god.

Elizabeth, her hands still around Gilbert's arm, her eyes shining, was speaking to me. She looked regal, the bold line of her cheekbones outlined by the fire. "Gil said so much about you. I had an impression of a much older woman—much stouter, too. He was wrong—the first time! He had your personality right, but not your appearance."

"Watch out for the scientific types. And he was right. I used to be much older. It has made me young to be here—keeping watch on the ramparts has slimmed me down. I lost so much weight that I can do without my cane."

He *asked* you, not ordered. You *can* leave. Go to Chipping Cranford, start up your genealogy business there. It's a nice town, close enough, not too close to a city. Places to walk, and old people even ride bicycles in England. Or motorcycles. They like eccentrics like you in England.

I'll ride a forklift. Those cold people? Their overdecorations—their concealments. If I go nosing around the wall, that polite bobby will come along and say, Pardon me, but have you seen the roses, let's just go down this pretty street, it happens to have the jail on it, also.

"I suppose you'll miss all this when you leave? Even though you had some bad moments? I know it was fairly grim, wasn't it?" Elizabeth's eyes had darkened while she waited for me to answer, as if she feared she'd touched a tender spot.

"You're a dear. I'm glad Gilbert stayed footloose so long. He waited to bring the blood back."

She flushed, and I liked that. "I don't understand."

"As a matter of fact, I won't be leaving for a little time. I've been offered a job. Here. I'll throw in my lot with the crowd of young people. I've got a Cause. I shall learn Yoga. They're going to teach me."

"Great!" She did sparkle. Her eyes danced, and blue sparks danced from them. "You'll be at Inverness for our wedding? Gil's cabled the university, and he has a couple of weeks."

"I'll come, and I'll drive there, myself. I'll have a car."

"Good deal, Aunt! We were worried that you'd miss me."

"No chance. I'm a member of a Commune. And I already have your wedding gift. How does this sound—an antique shield and sword, to hang over your fireplace? I'll have to remember to get the shield. I'm the only one who knows where it is."

I can't leave. I'm hooked. I'll show them that I'm really interested in the Cause. I am. I don't have to pretend that I love freedom—I know what freedom is, I'm experienced. Twice in their jails. They're not suspicious of me now. I'll stay for a time.

Gilbert and Elizabeth will come back, she's a native. They'll be part-time Americans. Maybe they'll have children. Someone to look forward to. By then, perhaps the world will be fit for children. I'll have a try at it. I'm supposed to teach acting, but it will be freedom.